We hope you enjoy this book. Please return or renew it by the due date.

You can renew it at www.norfolk.gov.uk/libraries or by using our free library app.

Otherwise you can phone 0344 800 8020 - please have your library card and PIN ready.

You can sign up for email reminders too.

D0774715

**NORFOLK COUNTY COUNCIL
LIBRARY AND INFORMATION SERVICE**

AWAKENED BY THE PRINCE'S PASSION

Bronwyn Scott

MILLS & BOON

First Published in Great Britain 2018
by Mills & Boon, an imprint of HarperCollins*Publishers*
1 London Bridge Street, London, SE1 9GF

© 2018 Nikki Poppen

ISBN: 978-0-263-93300-0

Printed and bound in Spain
by CPI, Barcelona

To Sveta, Zhenya and Irina,
in celebration of the twentieth anniversary
of our summer together in Pskov.
Spasibo.

Chapter One

London—late August 1823

The trouble with revolution was that it made unlikely bedfellows, in unlikely locations, and at unlikely times. One moment Prince Ruslan Pisarev had been peacefully asleep in the bedroom of his newly acquired London town house, the next he was sitting behind his desk, dressed in nothing but his banyan and green silk pyjama trousers, reading reports that were at once exciting and horrifying. Part of him hoped the man across the desk was telling the truth and part of him hoped the man was lying, because the truth was dark.

Kuban, his home, was in turmoil. The Summer Palace outside the city—a place he'd visited multiple times—had been overrun by Rebels and set alight. To prove that change had come at last and permanently two months ago, the royal family had been dragged out and executed at dawn on their front lawn. The Tsar, his wife, his sons. Peter, Vasili and Grigori, boys, now men, whom Ruslan had grown up with.

The thought of his boyhood friends murdered in such a fashion threatened to swamp him. Ruslan pushed his grief aside. There would be time to mourn them later, in private. Right now he needed his wits, yet the thought lingered. *All* the House of Tukhachevsken dead, wiped out in a single morning. Well, nearly all of them, *if* the Captain sitting before him in the pre-dawn darkness of his study was telling the truth.

Ruslan studied Captain Varvakis with shrewd eyes, assessing the steady gaze and the straight posture of his 'midnight' caller. The term was loosely applied. Midnight had come and gone hours ago. The Captain was a military man to his core and with that core came a strong, unbreakable sense of loyalty to the organisation he served, in this case, the royal family. Varvakis had no reason to lie. Still, Ruslan had not survived this long without always asking the 'if'.

Ruslan pushed a hand through his thick hair, a bad habit he indulged in too frequently since it left hairs sticking up on end. But what did it matter? He was already rumpled from sleep—a little more tousling wouldn't matter as his mind assimilated the barrage of information. 'You mean to tell me Princess Dasha escaped the fusillade and she is, right now, sleeping upstairs in my guest room?' He'd seen little of the bedraggled woman Captain Varvakis had carried in upon arrival.

Captain Varvakis didn't hesitate. 'Yes. I pulled her out of the flames myself.' Ruslan closed his eyes and let the Captain describe the scene. In his mind's eye, he walked every inch of the rescue with Varvakis. He could imagine with vivid clarity the Rebel hordes crashing through the wrought-iron and gold gates of the palace, marching up the wide drive with manicured green lawns on either side, to the huge double doors with their panels of carved bears, smashing the artistry of centuries with ramming logs, torching and looting as they went. The aesthetic in him wanted to weep over the destruction. Whether or not he agreed with the Tsar's policies, the Summer Palace had been a place of beauty.

'We fought them, but there were too few Loyalists to offer real resistance.' Varvakis shook his head sadly. 'Princess Dasha was trapped upstairs. I saw her on the landing, fighting and trying to run, but the Rebels saw her, too. They already had the others and it was clear what they intended. I fought my way to her. They'd pushed her back to the flames. She had no choice but to burn or surrender. The flames would have taken her if the mob didn't.' Ruslan could see that staircase in his mind; it was curved and elegant. He'd slid on that banister in his youth. It was good for sliding, but not so good for fighting. It would have been difficult for a man coming up it. Varvakis had had no easy task.

The news disturbed Ruslan on many levels, not only the destruction and death but the politics beneath it. 'The mob rules Kuban then?' Ruslan put his head in his hands. While he favoured change, he did not favour violence. Hadn't the French taught the world that? Now Kuban, too, was executing royals.

'Yes, for now,' Varvakis affirmed, his mouth set in a line of grim disapproval. A man like Varvakis would dislike chaos of any sort. For his part, Ruslan didn't like it either, yet chaos had come to him. It was here in his home—a home he'd just purchased as a commitment to moving into his future and moving away from Kuban. He'd gone to bed one step closer to being a Londoner in truth and woken up only to be dragged back into the fray. His country was on fire, a fugitive princess was upstairs and a captain was begging for sanctuary.

'It will not always be chaos,' Varvakis was saying. 'There will be a time when cooler heads rule, when Kuban will need their Princess again, someone who can bridge the gap between the old and new.'

Conveniently, Varvakis would be waiting with the Princess in tow. That was something to be wary of. He wouldn't be the first military man to have political aspirations. Ruslan sighed. He could see it plain. Good God, the Captain wanted more than sanctuary. Varvakis wanted to continue the revolution under his roof, wanted to make him an accomplice in whatever political plan the factions had hatched. A drink might come in handy, just now.

Ruslan rose, went to the sideboard holding his array of decanters and poured two glasses. He had questions in spades now. Ruslan passed the Captain a brandy in the hopes that Varvakis having a drink in hand made his questions feel more like a conversation and less like an interrogation. 'Here's to journeys completed.'

They'd barely raised their glasses when a scream shattered the night. Ruslan exchanged a look with the Captain and dashed into the hall as a second scream followed. Ruslan's eyes went up. At the top of the stairs, a woman staggered, her arms flailing at invisible enemies. Whatever tortured her did so from somewhere unseen.

'Your Highness!' Captain Varvakis called out. The woman's wild eyes slid towards the sound of her name. She looked like an escapee from Bedlam; her gaze was vacant, her ash-blonde hair loose and tangled at her shoulders as if it hadn't been washed or combed for some time. She came closer, nearing the stairs unsteadily, arms still waving. Ruslan saw the danger immediately and raced forward, taking the steps two at a time. If she reached the steps, she would fall.

Ruslan set aside any sense of formality in the hopes of waking her in time. He bounded upwards, racing against the inevitable as she took a step, teetering when her foot achieved nothing but air, her foot searching for purchase, finding none and coming down, the move putting her body off balance. Ruslan closed the distance, wrapping her in his arms as they fell in an inelegant sprawl atop the landing, safely pushing her back from the stairs.

Ruslan was acutely aware of the body pressed to his might-as-well-be nakedness. His banyan and pyjama trousers offered little protection against the feminine onslaught of soft curves straight from a warm bed. Beneath him, sharp eyes flashed with a spark of awareness as sleep transformed to wakefulness. For a moment there was peace when he looked into those eyes. And then she screamed again.

Where was she? Panic rocketed through Dasha. Not that the question or the panic were new. She hadn't known where she was for weeks. Now, there was a strange man on top of her. She screamed and fought him out of habit and an instinct to survive. She thrashed beneath him, forcing him to subdue her, which he did with alarmingly little effort. This man was lean and strong, and barely clothed in a dressing gown and silk sleeping trousers that left little of him to the imagination.

'Your Highness, please, be still. You're safe. We're in London. We made it.' Captain Varvakis's voice ended her resistance, his words bringing back what few new memories she had. 'You were dreaming again.'

Dasha stilled and let her mind work, processing what she knew to be true. She'd been sleepwalking. Again. She was in the middle of a hall, propelled out of bed by the nightmare. Despite the horrors of the dream, it was the one thing that was hers entirely, her one complete memory. It had existed before she'd awakened in a wagon racing out of Kuban, of that she was sure. It had existed before Captain Varvakis had told her who she was. In the dream there'd been fire and fighting and death. She had a sword. *She* was fighting. There was someone at her back, someone she was protecting, but whom? She didn't know. She always awoke before she could turn and see. Perhaps there was no one. Perhaps it was merely an invention of the dream as the Captain suggested.

'Your Highness.' Varvakis was worried. Again. She'd been nothing *but* worry to him. 'Are you all right? Let's get you back to bed. You need to rest.' But it was the man who held her who helped her to her feet and wrapped a steadying arm about her, lending her strength as he waited for *her* response. Too many other men would have followed the Captain's orders.

'Perhaps some warm milk, or something stronger?' he offered. This man might've come straight from bed. His hair was dishevelled. But his eyes were sharp, too sharp for a man newly roused. He'd been awake a while.

'Both. Warm milk with brandy would be nice.' Through the long window in the hall, she could see the fingers of sunrise flirting with the hem of the night like an eager suitor. It would be morning soon. Bed seemed pointless but the milk and brandy would calm her. She wanted to be calm and clear-headed. She was in a new place, with new people. It was inevitable there would be questions and she wanted to do the answering for once.

The gentleman in the banyan ushered her down the stairs to a study already filled with light and warmth. He pulled a bell cord and smiled. Even in total ungroomed *dishabille*, it was easy to see he was a handsome man. Thick, unruly red-gold hair framed a lean face with keen blue eyes and cheeks that rounded when he smiled, adding depth and dimension. 'We'll have milk here momentarily, and an early breakfast, too. Until then, perhaps introductions are in order. I am Prince Ruslan Pisarev.' If anyone could look regal given these circumstances, it was this man. Even in nightclothes, even in the middle of the night, even after tackling her and being attacked by her, he still managed an elegant leg.

'Princess Dasha Tukhachevskenova, or so I am told.' The wryness in her tone caught his attention. His gaze slid towards Captain Varvakis with question and censure, proof that Varvakis hadn't told him. He didn't know about her particular condition.

'Varvakis, what is that supposed to mean?' the Prince asked.

But it was Dasha who answered. She might be confused, she might have spent the last weeks wondering where she was and who she was, but she was tired of having men speak for her in her presence. She met his gaze evenly and, she hoped, without shame.

'What it means, Prince Pisarev, is that I have no memories of Kuban or who I am. I have only this good man's word.' What would Prince Pisarev make of that information? Dasha settled into one of the chairs near the fire, taking comfort in the warmth. She was so very cold. Cold and empty, as she had been for weeks. The fire could do something about the one, but not the other. It seemed nothing could. Not even the information Captain Varvakis had given her filled the void. The Prince was looking at her with his steady blue gaze and something akin to hope leapt in her. Did he know her? Had he known her family? Was there something he could tell her that would help her remember again?

She wouldn't ask him here in front of the Captain. He might feel compelled to give a certain answer. She would wait and get him alone, where he could only tell her the truth.

The tray arrived and the next few minutes

were spent pouring drinks and making little plates of toast and jam and hot sausages. The Prince's gaze never left her for long. He was gathering his thoughts just as she was gathering her resources. Her body and mind were tense in anticipation of defending themselves. He would want to question her, to prod her about her memories, and then, when she failed to recall anything, he would condemn her. But the Prince did none of that.

'I know a doctor, a specialist who can perhaps help you,' the Prince said when the servants had gone. 'After the Peninsular Wars, many of our soldiers suffered memory loss from the trauma of battle. I'll arrange for a visit today, if you'd like. I will also arrange for a lady's maid and some clothes until we can get you to a dress-maker. I already have my footmen preparing a hot bath for you in your chambers.'

Embarrassing tears stung Dasha's eyes. How silly it was to cry now over a bath and clean clothes and brandy-laced milk when there was so much loss to mourn. Her home, her country, her mind, her family. She'd not cried when Var-vakis had told her. She'd been numb with hor-ror, not only at the nature of their deaths, but at her lack of memory. She couldn't remember them, she could only mourn them as an outsider mourned the inherent wrongness of a tragedy. She'd not cried when the boat they'd journeyed in from Ekaterinodar foundered in the Black Sea. She'd been brave for weeks. She'd not broken down once, but Prince Pisarev had managed to reduce her to tears in a matter of sentences over the smallest of kindnesses. She willed the tears away with a fierce determination.

'Thank you for your hospitality, Prince Pisarev. It means more than you know.' She rose to leave, knowing they would discuss her when she left. But it was either stay and fall apart in front of the Prince, or leave and preserve her dignity.

The Prince stood with her, capturing her hand in his. She felt the warm strength of him again flowing into her. 'It is my pleasure. Please ask for anything you need. We will speak again later, when you're settled.' What a courtier he must have been. He was the sort of man who was able to arrange things for others without making them feel small or dependent. The sort of man who knew how to take charge without diminishing people. That could be dangerous. She would do well to remember how easily he wielded that power. She wanted to be under no man's thumb. But that was a problem for later. At the moment, she could afford to bask fully in his generosity. Only a foolish woman turned down the offer of a hot bath after weeks of travel and, whoever she was, Dasha was no fool.

Chapter Two

'The Princess is here. Congratulations, Captain. You've made it this far. Now we need to talk about *why*. Why me? Why London when there are places of safety far closer to Kuban?' Ruslan put the long-forgotten glass in Captain Varvakis's hand and picked up his own, taking charge of the conversation and its direction. Now, he really did need a drink. The Princess was a woman who could take a man by surprise and not let go. Even as bedraggled as she was from travel, there was beauty to her wildness: the ash-blonde hair, the sharp emerald depths of her eyes, the willowy strength of her body, slim and strong like Damascus steel when she'd fought him. But her most appealing attribute was her courage, her confidence. She'd not hesitated to speak for herself, or to challenge him with the truth—that she was a broken princess, a woman with no memories. It was a formidable circumstance for her to be in, and for him, given his family's rather recent, rather tragic relationship to the throne.

'What do you expect me to do with her?' Ruslan mused out loud. Surely, Varvakis was not entirely oblivious to his severed connection to the royal family—a relationship his family had not chosen to sever, but one that had been deliberately cut off by the Tsar himself, disgracing the House of Pisarev. It was a disgrace Ruslan would erase if given the opportunity. Ruslan had his own plans, his mind was already whirling through options, but it would be interesting to see what Varvakis's intentions were.

'We keep her safe for Kuban,' Varvakis said without hesitation, 'until it is time to return and guide the country to peace.' It was what one would expect from a man like Varvakis, a reliable officer with his country's best interests at heart, a patriot to the core.

Ruslan made a mental note to confer with Nikolay, who'd been a captain in the Kubanian cavalry. Perhaps Nikolay knew of Varvakis and his reputation for the truth. 'Well, then, it's no wonder you came looking for me.' Keeping a princess safe was no simple matter. 'Safety' could take a variety of forms.

'As to why we're here; you are the best. Your

work in the underground is legendary among those who know.' Captain Varvakis complimented deferentially, aware that he addressed his superior. 'If there is anyone who can keep a fugitive alive, it's you. Allow me to say, your reputation precedes you.' Varvakis did not refer to his reputation as a prince, a man known for his royal arrangements, although he had a reputation for that as well. If the Tsar wanted a grand entertainment, or a hunt organised, Ruslan had seen to it. Everyone knew Ruslan was an expert organiser and an expert organiser had an exquisite network of connections.

As impressive as that accomplishment was, it was not the one Varvakis alluded to, but his other reputation as part of the Union of Salvation, the liberation underground. He helped certain people, who might otherwise find it unhealthy to stay, to leave Kuban. People like Prince Dimitri Petrovich's sister, Anna-Maria, who needed to escape an unwanted marriage; people like his friends, Nikolay, who would have been tried for treason and found guilty, or Illarion, who'd committed *lèse-majesté* with a poem. He was known to those who faced danger.

And now he was to help the woman upstairs. Fugitive, future Queen, daughter of the man who'd cast his family into disgrace after generations of loyal service. Dasha Tukhachevskenova lived life in the extreme, at once both a woman with and without a country, a woman with a history and without, a woman with and without power. It was something Ruslan knew a little about. He, too, was a prince without a country. He'd chosen to vanish and, in doing so, he'd given up his claim to all he knew and, for the most part, all he had. The only difference between him and the Princess was that he remembered it.

Ruslan swirled his glass, watching a centrifuge form in the centre. 'She remembers nothing at all?' It was a question he'd not wanted to ask her. It seemed too intrusive. But he had to know if he was going to plot accordingly. It would be difficult to persuade others to follow a woman in her condition.

'Nothing of merit,' Varvakis admitted. 'She remembers snatches of what happened. She dreams of the fire. It's what gives her the nightmares, but she recalls nothing substantial.'

'Except what you've told her?' Ruslan asked pointedly. That was an interesting angle to consider. Her memories would come from Varvakis's telling. He was the keeper of what she understood to be true. A Latin phrase ran through his head from John Locke: *tabula rasa*. A blank slate in the hands of the wrong man was a dangerous and powerful weapon. The Princess would believe what she was told. She had no alternative, no base to check the knowledge against. It was more important than ever to meet with Nikolay and determine if Varvakis could be trusted. Already Ruslan sensed the Captain had his own agenda.

'As for protection,' Ruslan went on, 'I think we have two choices. First, we can assume Rebels have noticed her escape and have chosen to follow her to London for the purpose of assassinating her. That means we must keep her hidden. The other option is to assume we are beyond the Rebels' reach. We take her out in society, such as it is in the autumn, and drum up support for her cause. We protect her by building a network abroad that will help her establish her claim to the throne when she returns.' Such actions would make a Charles Stuart of her. Hopefully with better results.

'Or we do both,' Ruslan continued. Either option pointed towards Varvakis's agenda: restore a Tukhachevsken to the throne, this time, one who favoured modernisation and reform. It hardly mattered what Dasha's political beliefs were. She didn't remember them. Varvakis would have the power to reshape those beliefs into a platform the country would accept. Ruslan smiled neutrally at the Captain over the rim of his glass, giving away none of his concern over such a strategy. 'When do you intend to go back?'

'That will depend on whatever news we receive about the revolution,' Captain Varvakis said. 'A queen must always be ready to serve her country.' Or those who controlled her, Ruslan thought cynically. He pitied the woman upstairs bathing. Was she aware Varvakis viewed her as an artefact to be protected until it was time to be revealed? Did she share those views? That was what Ruslan needed to know next. He had no intention of promoting a restoration if the monarch in question was unwilling. Nor did he have any intention of promoting a monarch with a false promise simply for the expedience of putting a Tukhachevsken back in power. Kuban had risen up to claim a new life. He would not destroy that effort. It was a direction he and his family had wanted for the country, had sacrificed for.

Ruslan pushed a hand through his hair, his fingers meeting tangles. He'd done enough business in his pyjamas for one night. It was time to get dressed. If it was going to be a long day, it could at least be a productive one.

Three hours later, he was back in the drawing room, dressed and organised and waiting for the

Princess. He'd sent word that she should come down at ten. The mantel clock was just striking the hour. A rustling at the entrance drew his eye and then stole his breath. The woman framed in the doorway barely resembled the ragged girl who'd gone upstairs. Her hair was done in a knot on top of her head, exposing the slender length of her neck, and a few curls had been left down to frame her face and soften the sharp heart-shaped angles of her jaw and chin. The rose gown made her skin glow and Ruslan found his eyes riveted on the simple strand of pearls that lay against the base of her throat. In a word, Dasha Tukhachevskenova was stunning.

'Your Highness.' Ruslan inclined his head from his position at the fireplace mantel. But Captain Varvakis went to her more formally and offered his hand.

'Have the two of you decided my fate?' There was an edge to her coy tone as she swept forward, disregarding Varvakis's hand. Ruslan suppressed a smile. The Princess might have forgotten precise, physical memories, but she'd not forgotten what it was to be at court, where one had to watch every word, every association. There was hope in that. The Princess might prove to be less malleable than Varvakis believed.

'I would not be so bold as to decide anything

for you, Your Highness.' Ruslan made a small bow of respect. 'However, I have sent for a physician who is both discreet and knowledgeable about memory loss. Would you care to take the air in the rose garden while we wait?' He gestured towards the wide French doors that opened into his prized garden. Garden space was at a premium in the city; he'd been lucky to find a home with one.

'I would like that very much.' The Princess shot him a considering look that said she guessed at a larger reason behind the offer. But it was a price she was willing to pay. Ruslan wondered what she wanted in exchange. Perhaps she, too, was interested in assessing him just as he was interested in assessing her—without the screen of Varvakis's presence.

Outside, the sky was overcast as they walked the paved pathway that wound through his collection of roses. They made small talk as he introduced her to each type. 'This one I got from a Lady Burton, she breeds them in Richmond. I call it the Debutante for its unique shade of white. But this one, I have grafted myself.' Ruslan stopped at an ivory rose tinted with pink edges.

'It's beautiful. Does it have a name?' Dasha bent to smell the flower, her eyes closed, long lashes fanning her cheek. If he were a painter, he'd want to capture the image of serene beauty she presented in that moment. An artist like Illarion's wife, Dove, would appreciate the rose of her gown and the pink highlights on the flower. But he was not an artist. He was a thinker, an arranger.

'Not yet.' He held her gaze as she straightened. 'Perhaps I should call it the Dasha, or the Princess. Your beauties complement one another.'

Dasha laughed. 'Very nicely done, Prince Pisarev, but I don't think you brought me out here to flirt.' He would have, though, if circumstances had been different, if there hadn't been so much at stake or so much unknown, if she'd simply been another pretty London debutante. She was just the sort of woman he liked: pretty and fresh, but not vacuous. Such traits were rather rare in fashionable society, or anywhere, actually. As a prince close to the Tsar, Ruslan had spent his days at court escorting the jaded wives of ambassadors and visiting generals. He knew just how rare such a woman was.

Ruslan chuckled. 'I don't think *you* came out here for flirtation either, so why don't we cut line. Why *did* you come out?'

They began to stroll again, her arm tucked

through his, to create the impression to anyone who might be looking on that nothing significant was taking place. It was a tactic he had used often to woo a secret or two from those worldly wives of diplomats. At court, one could never be sure who was listening.

The Princess wasted no time getting to her point. 'Do you know me?'

The blunt sincerity of the question caught Ruslan entirely off guard. He'd expected questions about plans and plots, perhaps even an interrogation of his credentials. He slid her a considering glance. She would not want his pity, although he was tempted to give it. She'd been tugging on his somewhat less than objective heartstrings since she'd fallen into his arms, although he'd do well to resist the sentimental urge. Still, he wasn't so heartless as to not recognise how horrible it must be to not know oneself. He admired her confidence in the face of such uncertainty, a reminder that she did know herself in some way, innately and instinctively if not exactly.

'I'm sorry, I don't.' Ruslan gave her the truth, although it was not the answer she hoped for. He covered her hand with his where it lay on his arm. 'I knew your brothers: Peter, Grigori, Vasili. We grew up together.' He paused, his earlier emotions of the morning threatening to get the better of him when he thought of their deaths. 'I am genuinely sorry for your loss.'

'Forgive me, but you have me at a disadvantage.' She stopped walking and turned to face him, grief etched in her gaze, but a different grief than one might expect. This grief was twofold. 'It seems you know more about my family than I do. I do not know if they were good or bad, kind or cruel, but I do know no one deserves to die that way. Don't you see, Prince Pisarev? I can't fully mourn them, not yet, not until my memories return.' She shrugged. 'Will you think I am cowardly, if I say it's a blessing I can't remember? Perhaps I am somehow spared the pain of loss.' She looked away to a point beyond his shoulder, disappointment shadowing her green eyes. 'I was hoping you knew me.'

'I would have been too old to know you. You would have been only ten when I was at court with your brothers and younger still when I was running about the palace with them.' Even at that age, he'd been arranging entertainment for the boys, always the ringleader coming up with a new adventure to fill the days. Those had been golden years, as a child growing up in the palace, his family in high favour with the Tsar. Those years had burned brighter still when he'd come of age, home from university, filled with ambition, before his family had fallen from grace. She would have been too young, too isolated to know of it. 'Besides,' Ruslan added, 'you were raised in traditional fashion and kept out of public view.' As were all gently bred Kubanian girls of high birth. They were sequestered away to the point of oppression. It was one of the contentions that had seen his friends, Nikolay and Illarion, exiled from Kuban, seen his father imprisoned and out of favour and now it had become one of the central issues that had sparked the revolution.

'It is not surprising I don't recognise you.' He racked his mind for the least bit of memory and came up with one. 'I do recall one Christmas, though. You were perhaps seven. We were home between terms from our respective universities and it had snowed. We had a snowball fight on Christmas Eve, with you, Grigori and Vasili against me and Peter. You wore your hair in braids with blue bows.' He smiled fondly at the memory. 'Kuban gets the best snow, not the wet stuff we have here in England.'

'It sounds lovely, like something I'd want to remember.' Dasha looked away, her gaze troubled.

Ruslan was quick to offer her consolation. Consolation came easy to him. He'd offered reassurances to other people in seemingly hope-less situations over the years. 'It's only been a few weeks. These things can take time. Some-times the best remedy is to not try too hard to remember, to just let it happen.'

'You are very kind.' She offered him a faint smile and he did not bother to correct her. He was not kind. He was merely doing his job. Pretty as she was, she was just another project like all the other people he'd ferried out of Kuban over the years. The difference was that while they had wanted to get out, she wanted to get in.

'And yourself, Prince Pisarev? It's your turn. Why did *you* want to get me alone?'

'I wanted to know your opinions about Var-vakis's plans. He would see you restored to the throne. That is an ambitious, if not dangerous un-dertaking, and one I would not support without your consent. Is that a road you wish to travel?'

They had reached the edge of the garden where a fence separated his luxurious home from the alley. She paused to fiddle with the ivy grow-ing rampant against the wood. 'I should wish it, shouldn't I? A princess *should* want to go back, I *should* want to rally people to my cause, to my throne. Perhaps I should even want to avenge my family.'

'But you don't want those things?' Now they

were getting to the heart of it; not just her fear, but her doubt of her capabilities.

'No, I don't. Right now, anonymity is appealing. I would rather fade into nothingness than return to a place that might prefer to drag me out on my lawn and finish the task they started instead of negotiate with me, simply because of my father's policies.' She paused and gave him a reflective stare. 'What sort of princess doesn't want to go home or rule her people? What sort of princess chooses anonymity?'

Ruslan studied the woman beside him with careful eyes. She'd meant to shock him. The defiance in her eyes said so and she had. If she doubted her ability, others would, too. Her reservations would have to be downplayed or, better yet, changed.

'Have you said anything about your concerns to Captain Varvakis?' Ruslan asked quietly, intrigued by this new revelation. It seemed Varvakis was not only more confident in her ability to retake the throne than she was, but he was also more committed to the idea as well.

The French doors opened and Captain Varvakis hurried towards them. They hadn't much left of their privacy and Ruslan had something more to say. 'The doctor has arrived, Prince Pisarev.

You must come at once. The butler isn't sure where to put him.'

Ruslan nodded slowly, indicating he was going to be less flustered by the doctor's arrival than Varvakis. 'If you wouldn't mind, Captain, we're nearly finished here. If you would, please, go ahead and tell Thomas to put the doctor in my study.' It was a masterful dismissal, the kind of order Captain Varvakis was used to taking without question from his superiors.

Dasha smiled as the Captain hurried off again. 'Why did you do that?'

'Because I have something to say to you, Dasha, just you.' Ruslan held her gaze for the space of a few seconds, long enough to let silence fall between them, long enough for her to acknowledge these words were not to be taken lightly. When one was talking of rulers and restorations, it was deadly serious business. 'I am your ally whether you seek the throne or not. You should feel free to use the safety of this house as you desire. If your desire is to stay hidden and recover your memory, or simply to stay hidden and a build a new life, to take a new name and set all trappings of Kuban behind you, I will support that as I am able. If you wish to stage an effort to reclaim the throne on the grounds of modernising Kuban and abolishing archaic law, I will support that, too. But I will not pressure you one way or the other. No one can decide what happens next but you.' It was the same reassurance he'd given others who had nowhere to go and nowhere to turn, although on a far less grand scale. Never before had those people been members of the royal family. 'You are safe with me. I am here for *you*.' Nothing less than honour and objectivity required that be his position.

'Whoever that is?' she questioned sharply.

'Yes, whoever that is, *émigrée* or refugee princess.' He dismissed her with an encouraging smile. 'Now, go and see the doctor.' He'd brought her the best and he was confident she'd be well taken care of. As for himself, he needed time with his thoughts before he faced Varvakis again. It was entirely possible the revolution would succeed or fall without any intervention from Princess Dasha, especially if no one suspected she was alive. He certainly wasn't going to stake his life on forcing the issue unnecessarily and he definitely wasn't going to force anyone else to do so, least of all a woman who might not be interested in the plots of men.

A single word from you, a little persuasion, could change that. You could make her see the possibilities such plots presented.

The temptation whispered itself into being

and took up residence in the lodge of his conscience.

You could do it, too, you've done it before, helping men and women see things the way they needed to be seen, especially the women. You remember how to seduce...

Yes, dammit, he did remember. It had been a point of pride to know that when the Tsar needed a diplomat to change his mind on a trade agreement or an export tax, he'd sent Ruslan to 'speak' to their wives; 'pillow talk,' he'd called it. In that way, Ruslan had served Kuban and his Tsar, although it had all amounted to nothing when his father had fallen from favour. That was the way of Kuban. If one member of a family was disloyal, the entire family was blackened with the same brush.

You would be serving Kuban by persuading her. Varvakis is right, she's the one they need. She can heal the country's breach.

His conscience was relentless.

That was the larger temptation, because the ends did quite nobly justify the means. Persuading the ambivalent Dasha to return *was* in the country's best interest. Under that aegis, he could conveniently overlook the personal gain to himself. Whatever he gained could just be a beneficial happenstance. He'd told Dasha he would not make that decision for her. But he'd said nothing about attempting to influence the decision. Would she even be aware he *was* influencing her?

Such things, as crass as they might be, must be contemplated when the fate of a kingdom hung in the balance. Revolutions created all nature of opportunities for those bold enough to take them—even opportunities for him. Which was why he had to remain absolutely objective. He'd been right to tamp down the wash of sentiment that had swept him in the garden. It would be easy to be lured by Dasha's beauty, her desperate strength in the face of her personal tragedies. He could not afford to give into those emotions. Restoring the Princess was another project, not unlike the ones he'd done in the past, nothing more. The game was in motion once again. He'd do best to remember that small nuance.

But snuffing out hope was easier said than done. That tiny flicker of excited hope inside him refused to be extinguished entirely. *If* the Princess chose to take her place on throne, *if* he could see her successfully restored, perhaps he could find a way back, a way to erase the stain on the family name, to prove once and for all a Pisarev was loyal to the bone. It was the one thing he'd given up trying to do.

Ruslan looked about his newly acquired town-house garden. This house was proof of that decision. Proof that he'd given up thoughts of returning. A home implied permanence. He'd been moved in for all of two weeks. Ruslan laughed to himself. Just when he thought the door was finally shut on his past, it was starting to open again. Some would say Fate was a bitch. They were wrong. Fate just might be a princess.

Chapter Three

Prince Pisarev called it an intimate supper. Dasha called it a council of war. She surveyed the assembled guests from her vantage point at the drawing-room fireplace with a wary eye. The day had been spent in cautious meetings such as this; first with the Prince in the garden, then with the doctor and now this gathering. It consisted of one Russian diplomat in Alexei Grigoriev, the consul from St Petersburg; one Russian officer in General Vasiliev, also of St Petersburg; and three Kubanian princes. With the exception of Klara Grigorieva Baklanova, Dasha was the only woman present, further proof this was no ordinary supper party.

She sat at the foot of the table, a prince to her left, the darkly brooding Stepan Shevchenko. To her right sat another prince, Nikolay Baklanov, and his wife beyond him. Prince Pisarev sat at the head of the table with His Excellency Alexei Grigoriev. General Vasiliev and Captain Varvakis filled out the spaces between. Dinner was a tribute to Kubanian cuisine: a borscht soup with sour cream to begin, followed by beef and baby potatoes, all accompanied by wines from Ekaterinodar, one of the few areas in Russia where vineyards could be cultivated.

At the other end, Prince Pisarev raised his glass. 'A toast to our lovely guest, Princess Dasha Tukhachevskenova. To safe arrivals and happier days. *Na zdorovie!*' The Prince toasted her as if she were an honoured guest on a state visit, instead of a fugitive gone to ground.

Around Dasha, the words became a polite chorus. She smiled at the guests, graciously accepting the toast as if she had a right to the fiction the Prince created, all the time wondering how many of them, like herself, questioned her ability to make good on the claim. How many of them were sizing up the potential benefits of believing in her versus risks? No one did anything for nothing and supporting a princess with no memory of her own identity was no small thing to ask. This was the worst part of not remembering, of not knowing. Who did she trust? Who could she turn to?

When the chorus died down, she raised her

own glass. 'To our host, Prince Pisarev, whose hospitality has been unending.' The Prince gave a slight incline of his head, his eyes steady on her as he drank. Was he also calculating the situation? Of course he was. His questions today indicated as much and he'd be a fool if he wasn't—something she was certain he was not. Helping her was not without danger, should she choose to return to Kuban and embrace her heritage. It would be far easier for him if she chose anonymity. Far easier for her, too.

She wondered if, despite his vow to support her decision regardless of her choice, he would try to influence the situation towards a certain outcome? Would she ever truly be sure of his neutrality? Or truly sure that any decision she made was entirely hers alone? It occurred to her that Prince Pisarev was the man at this table she needed to be able to trust the most and the one she should probably trust the *least*, simply because he wielded the most power. She was in his house, under his protection, under his direction. Everything that had happened today was because of him—from her bath, to her clothes, to the excellent doctor and the dinner tonight. All of it was because of him. Thankfully, she didn't have to decide anything tonight. But she'd have to decide soon, judging from the tenor of the conversation.

'Are you saying the military is split on the rebellion?' General Vasiliev questioned Captain Varvakis with a sharp eye. 'If so, it is no wonder the Loyalists didn't stand a chance, no ruler does without a unified show of military force.'

Captain Varvakis nodded in agreement and explained. 'The Tsar's restrictive marriage and career policies affected noble families perhaps the most. The younger generation of nobles felt increasingly alienated by the Tsar. He cut his support out from under himself, losing the allegiance of young nobility who were officers in his army.' Along the table heads nodded. She did not know these men, Prince Nikolay Baklanov and Prince Stepan Shevchenko, but perhaps they had fled Kuban for precisely the same reason those left behind had rebelled. Her gaze rested on Prince Pisarev. Why had he left?

The consul, Alexei Grigoriev, looked contemplatively at his wine glass. 'That being understood, the people in power would not be eager to welcome back a member of the Tsar's family. The last thing they'd want would be a return to the past.' He gave her a small, apologetic nod. 'I speak frankly, Your Highness, that is all. I do not mean to slander you.'

Dasha smiled her own understanding. 'Of course, no insult taken, Your Excellency.' He'd done her a favour with his reference to her title, a subtle assumption of her authority. If he accepted her legitimacy, perhaps the others would, too.

'That's where you're wrong, Your Excellency,' Captain Varvakis broke in quickly. 'Princess Dasha represents the middle ground. She is of the royal bloodline, a natural ascendant to the throne as far as the hierarchy is concerned. But she is also young, and she has resisted her father's policies as assuredly as the other young nobles of the kingdom have. The Loyalists will like and accept her as a ruler based on her lineage. The Rebels will accept her politics.'

Dasha tensed. Were those her politics? She didn't know, quite honestly. As much as she didn't like Varvakis or anyone else speaking for her, there was much she *couldn't* speak for herself on. Who was she to say what she did or didn't believe? It was a dangerous position for a future leader to be in. She was a blind woman, entirely reliant on Varvakis as her guide. She did not like feeling so exposed.

Prince Pisarev's eyes were on her again, a small smile twitching at his lips. Perhaps he guessed her quandary, but his question was for Varvakis. 'What rebellion is this? How has the

Princess resisted?' Yes, how? It was what she was wondering, too. What had she done? She was thirsty for knowledge as much as she loathed the need for that knowledge. She should *know* what she'd done. Dasha fought back the frustration that welled whenever the emptiness threatened. She would not let herself feel helpless. She would face the emptiness and she *would* fill it.

Captain Varvakis met the question squarely. 'A year ago there was a marriage arranged for her with an important Turkish ally that would help secure trade routes along the Dardanelles. The Princess refused, vehemently. The Tsar feared the refusal would spark trouble beyond the palace walls coming so close as it did on the heels of General Ustinov's young wife's suicide, so he dropped the matter, but not before key nobles learned of it. They will remember the Princess stands with them, that she would be unlikely to continue her father's practices.'

'You remember none of this, Princess?' Prince Shevchenko fixed her with dark eyes.

'None.' She paused, gathering their attention. Honesty would be her best way forward and theirs. 'I might not ever remember any of it.' That was the reality she needed to prepare herself for. The doctor today had said as much. Memory loss was supposed to be short-term, but hers showed no sign of abating. Prince Shevchenko shot a knowing glance around the table with a dark eye brow arched at the improbability of their quest. They were supposed to return a princess with no memories to Kuban and place her in power. They were gathered together tonight to discuss the risk analysis behind such an action. One by one, each of the men assembled looked away, gathering his own thoughts about the revelation and what it meant. All except Prince Pisarev. *He* smiled, unconcerned.

'It's far too early to decide either way and far too much is unknown. Anything could happen. The Princess may not want to go back. Her memories may yet return. The doctor suggested some memory aids. We are not without tools and resources.' There was comfort in the Prince's words, reminding her of his words earlier, that she was not alone no matter what she decided.

Men shifted uneasily in their chairs, restless with her presence. It was her cue to leave. They needed to talk amongst themselves. Dasha rose. 'Princess Baklanova, if you would care to join me in the drawing room, we can let these gentlemen get on with their port.' And their gossip. She was well aware she'd be the main topic of conversation with only Varvakis and Prince Pisarev to defend her. The others were likely to be merciless.

* * *

Sleep was mercilessly elusive. Long after the guests were gone, murmuring polite goodbyes while scepticism lurked in their eyes, Dasha was wide awake. At least awake, she wouldn't dream. That was something to be thankful for. Lamp in hand, she made her way to the library. She didn't dare indulge in any more brandy-laced milk. Maybe a book would help take her mind off the events of the day, which had not gone as well as hoped.

Perhaps she'd been overly optimistic. She'd hoped Prince Pisarev would recognise her. She'd hoped the doctor would give her a magical cure. Those things had not happened.

Dasha ran her hand over the spines of books. They were new, their spines stiff. Everything in this home was new. She'd noticed that today: the carpets, their bright hues not yet dulled from generations of boots; the curtains with their rich colours. It was all tastefully understated, but it was still *new.* Everything lacked the truly aristocratic patina of age and successions.

She selected a book of Russian fairy tales and took it to the sofa by the fire. The pages had been cut, but the book still gave a crackle of newness when she opened it. She ran a finger down the table of contents: *Ivan and the Fire-*

bird, Father Winter, Ruslan and Ludmila... Her finger stopped on that one. Ruslan the Knight. She'd forgotten. It had been a long time since she'd read fairy tales. Pushkin had published a poem by that name as well a couple of years ago. She turned to the page, letting the story come back to her in pieces—the beautiful Ludmila stolen from home on her wedding day, the gallant Ruslan riding to her rescue and facing down a series of foes while Ludmila lay unconscious and unknowing. Dasha looked into the fire. She might enjoy the tale more tonight if the parallels weren't so obvious, right down to the very name of her own gallant knight.

'Ah, so you've discovered the library. Have you found anything good to read? I haven't had time to explore the offerings yet.'

Dasha jumped, casting about for a weapon. Her eyes lit on the poker. Could she reach it? How could she have been so careless to sit down defenceless?

'I don't think you'd reach the poker in time.' Prince Pisarev stepped forward, dressed only in a shirt and waistcoat. His jacket and cravat had been discarded. Without the jacket, his lean body was on full display, elegant and urbane even in moderate *dishabille*. 'If it's any consolation, I didn't mean to startle you.' He took the chair on her left, a glass in his hand. She felt silly and self-conscious. Who had she thought it would be? Who *could* it be but Prince Pisarev or Captain Varvakis?

'Old habits, I suppose.' Maybe. Who knew if she made a practice of beating people over the head with pokers, or even if she had need for such a skill? She tugged at the light blanket she'd thrown around her shoulders before coming down, reminded suddenly of how underdressed she was for meeting a man at midnight, even if that hadn't been her intention when she'd left her room.

'Nothing wrong with old habits.' Ruslan smiled and took a swallow. 'Can't sleep? Would you like something?'

'No.' Dasha played with the folds of her nightrail, pleating them between her fingers.

'I confess I'm glad you're still awake. I'd like to discuss a few things, if you're up to it.'

She nodded her permission. Did this man never sleep? It was after midnight, approaching twenty-four hours since her ignominious arrival on his doorstep, and he was still working.

'Thank you. The doctor suggested it may help prompt some memories if you surrounded yourself with reminders of your old life, if you lived and acted as if you knew yourself to be a princess. To that end, I've engaged a few individuals who can help with that: a dancing master, a dressmaker, a French tutor since everyone at the Kubanian court speaks French, an etiquette coach. At the very least, the skills will help you feel more at home among the English aristocracy.'

'And at the best?' Dasha asked sharply, not entirely liking where this proposal was headed and what it might signify.

'It may prompt your memories. You might discover you are already fluent in French, or that you can already dance. It might be all you need to break through your mental block.'

'Or perhaps it is all *you* need to convince people I am truly capable.' Did he think she was naïve enough to not see what this was? She was to be trained. If she could not remember being the Princess, she could be transformed into one effectively enough to convince anyone who needed convincing. It made the option of becoming an anonymous *émigrée* moot. London society would not let a Kubanian princess with a right to the throne fade into anonymity. Anonymity required a new name, a new history.

Dasha rose and paced before the fire, her mind racing. 'So it's already been decided, has it? I left the room and your war counsel decided I am to go back, as if I am a pawn without any say in the matter.' She speared him with a hard stare. 'I hoped for more from you, Prince Pisarev. Your promise to me was merely hours old before you broke it.'

Broke his word? How dare she imply such a thing, especially to a man who had nothing *but* his word? The Princess went too far when she impugned his honour after all he'd done for her today, without question, and there *were* plenty of far less pleasant questions he could have asked. Ruslan narrowed his eyes, letting his gaze suggest his displeasure, his tone cool. 'Nothing has been decided. I meant every word. I will not force you to go back. But should you decide to return, you will need certain skills, certain pieces of knowledge. What you can't remember can be taught, but it will take time and we don't know how much of that we have. We have to start now. We have to be prepared.'

'We?' Dasha snapped. 'The last time I checked, there was just me. Just one Princess.'

'That's where you're wrong. The moment you entered my house you made this my concern. I thought I had made that clear.' If anyone needed safeguarding, it was she. Dasha was brave, but she was entirely vulnerable even among those who meant to help her. He'd seen just how vulnerable at dinner, listening to Varvakis discuss her political views because she couldn't, and later, listening to the men take her apart in her absence, bandying about words like 'puppet princess'—a clear indication that she would be the front for those who would run the government on her behalf. Such an assumption would have led to a duel had she been a man. Despite the practical objectivity required of such analysis, something fierce and protective had risen in him in the dining room on her behalf as General Vasiliev had bluntly outlined the risks of helping her and the potential rewards of controlling the provincial kingdom in exchange for the effort. Ruslan would have gladly taken his dinner knife and gutted the man if it would have served any purpose, but despite his anger he had an aversion to killing people for telling the truth.

'If we're in it "together", as you suggest, you have the unenviable job of being my advisor of sorts.' Her tone suggested she was not satisfied with his answer. Her eyes sparked as she crossed her arms over her breasts. The fire caught her slim silhouette beneath her nightrail, illuminating long legs that disappeared up beneath the opaqueness of the blanket she wrapped around herself, but not before the sight of those legs reminded Ruslan she was naked beneath the cotton. Being her self-appointed advisor would be a far easier job if she was a tad less attractive and a tad more clothed.

Ruslan crossed his leg over a knee, trying to dispel the beginnings of arousal. Politics aside, Dasha was a beautiful woman and he was naught but a man. Circumstances being different, he might have acted on the burgeoning attraction, but politics and opportunity could *not* be put aside or compromised. She was a princess in exile with a decision to make that would decide the fate of a nation. That was complication enough.

Dasha hugged herself, some of the anger leaving her body—anger she had every right to claim, Ruslan reminded himself. She was no fool. She knew what had happened in the dining room after she'd left. 'I don't know who I am supposed to be. A princess? An exile? Someone else entirely?' The desperation in her eyes drew him.

Against his better judgement, he set aside his glass and went to her at the fire, his hands firm at her forearms, his body close, his voice husky from the lateness of the hour. 'Think of your situation as a blessing. Many people would envy you that choice. You have a chance to remake

your life, to remake *yourself*. You can be whoever you want to be, no history, no backstory, no
chains to your past. That can be a gift, Dasha.
I will help you find a new name, a new life if
you want.' Being this close to her was wreaking all kinds of sensual havoc on his body. He
was doing this for encouragement's sake, or so
he told himself. But his body had other ideas—
all of them bad.

Ruslan licked his lips, his mouth suddenly
dry, his mind aware of the details of her. She
smelled of sweet summer roses, she was warm
and naked beneath the nightclothes. All the in-
gredients for a disaster were there: the late night,
the long day, a beautiful woman in distress looking at him with emerald eyes that begged for res-
olution and relief, comfort and companionship.
She must have sensed it, too. He felt her body
move into his. It was the smallest of movements,
but it was enough to warn him, her lips parted
in slight but unmistakable invitation.

His reflexes were faster. He placed a chaste
kiss on her forehead. 'You've had a trying day,
Your Highness.' He was giving her absolution,
an excuse to fall back on when she awoke in
the morning and realised what she'd done, what
she'd asked for. Given the circumstances, it was
entirely understandable. She was confused and

alone. She would seek comfort where she could. He had no such convenient excuses. He had to resist the temptation on behalf of them both. Ruslan stepped away from her. 'Best get some sleep, Princess, lessons start tomorrow.'

Chapter Four

She'd nearly kissed him! That one thought kept running through her mind as Dasha pored over pattern books in the morning room. The dressmaker, Madame Delphine, had been there since ten o'clock, trying patiently to tempt her with fabrics and designs. But her attention was having difficulty focusing on anything except that moment last night: his hands on her arms, their heads close together in front of the fire, his voice low and private, their bodies so near. It had only been a matter of inches, the tilt of her head, such small, insignificant gestures to manoeuvre for a kiss.

Dasha understood why she'd done it. It was only because of circumstances, because she was desperate. She couldn't connect to herself so she wanted to connect to someone else, with someone else, and Ruslan had been there, full of command and control, a tangible human bulwark against the abstract form of her despair. Understanding her rather immediate attraction was theoretically simple. The Prince was empathetic, shrewd and yet kind, and he was easy on the eyes—a handsome prince in all sense of the word. He was the Ruslan of fairy tales come to life. He would fight for her, whatever she chose. Did she dare believe he meant it? The offer was too good to be true. Inherently, such conditions made the offer suspect. The monster of distrust reared its ugly head. Could she trust Prince Ruslan Pisarev? Could she trust Captain Varvakis, a man who, according to his own account, *the only account*, had saved her from certain death?

Her conclusion was that trust came with a price. She could trust these men *if* she gave them what they wanted. She *knew* what Varvakis wanted: a princess of his choosing on the throne. What did Prince Pisarev want? If she hadn't been foolish last night, she might have known. There'd been more he'd wanted to discuss, but they'd never got to it.

Dasha turned a page in the pattern book absently. Madame Delphine would be disappointed in her progress. She wondered what Captain Varvakis would do if she chose not to return? Would he be as generous as the Prince? All his plans would be in ruins without her. He would have risked himself for nothing. It was easier for the Prince; he had less to lose if she chose to stay. Perhaps he'd even prefer that. It would be less effort on his part and less risk. And yet, what did the Prince gain if she did go back? Surely there must be some benefit for him, otherwise why go to all the work to hire tutors, to house her, to dress her? How would he feel about that level of investment if he knew her real fear?

Dasha turned more pages in the pattern book, marking a few items that caught her eye to appease the dressmaker, her guilt growing. She'd not been entirely truthful with the Prince in the garden. She *did* remember nothing; she *did* doubt her capabilities to rule without those memories. That was all true. But she'd held back her third fear: that the reason she doubted her ability to rule, the reason she hadn't remembered being the Princess, was because she simply *wasn't* the Princess. Surely a real princess would not question the decision to return to her country. And yet she did.

Dasha stared at the pattern book, unseeing. Questioning her identity was not a conclusion she'd been drawn to out of mere whimsy. That damnable dream had pushed her there, night after night, leaving her awake and screaming.

In the dream, she felt someone was with her on that flame-engulfed landing, behind her as if she was protecting them. But who? She always woke up before she was even sure there was someone. She woke when the flames killed her. She'd heard it suggested people only woke up when they 'died' in their dreams.

The incompleteness of the horror left her with a final question. If she was not Dasha, who was she? In the absence of an alternative, the question was answered by default. She was Dasha Tukhachevskenova because Captain Varvakis rescued her and he said so. She was Dasha Tukhachevskenova because Captain Varvakis, and the Moderates who kept Kuban from outright civil war, needed her to be, because Dasha Tukhachevskenova was more useful to powerful men like Ruslan Pisarev than a woman with no name and no lineage.

'Your Highness, have you decided?' Madame Delphine stood at her shoulder expectantly. Dasha scanned the page and pointed at random to a gown. Madame Delphine nodded appreciatively. 'An excellent choice. The gown is simply cut but, with the right fabrics, simplicity can be its own elegance. You have a good eye.' She gestured towards the fabrics laid out across chairs and sofas. 'Let me show you some materials, perhaps the silks. Here's a nice aquamarine for that gown.' Madame Delphine passed her a swatch.

Dasha ran her hand over the dressmaker's fabric, rubbing it between her fingers. She held it to the light, checking the lustre. 'Do you have something more delicate perhaps?' This was not high-quality silk. There was nothing wrong with it. It was sturdy enough, pretty enough to fool the casual observer, but she knew instinctively this was not what a convincing princess would wear.

The dressmaker smiled knowingly and went to an unopened trunk. 'I think I have something you will like. It just arrived from India.' Inside lay bolts of fine silk in varying colours.

Yes, this was more to her taste. Dasha rubbed the first bolt. Eyes closed. Good silk sounded a certain way. It seemed ages since she'd had something fine and she relished the little luxury after weeks in coarse, often dirty clothing. But the luxury was followed by guilt. A pretty dress was a petty concern and it was charity. Her family was dead. She had no money of her own. Nothing of her own. Dasha set aside the silk to the alarm of Madame Delphine.

'Is something wrong, Your Highness?'

Dasha gave her a soft smile of reassurance. 'The silk is fine. It is too expensive, however. Perhaps there are some muslins that would do?'

'The Prince has given instructions that price is no object,' Madame Delphine scolded, sounding more imperious than a queen. 'You are to have a full wardrobe. Undergarments, nightclothes, day dresses, walking dresses, carriage ensembles, ball gowns, pelisses and all the necessary accessories: bonnets, gloves, shoes, stockings.' She tutted, taking in Dasha's outfit, another dress borrowed from Nikolay Baklanov's wife. 'No woman is herself when she's walking around in another woman's clothes.' Madame Delphine pulled out a tape measure as if all was settled. 'Now, let's get your dimensions so my girls can start on your new wardrobe.'

The wardrobe took the better part of the day. Building one from the basics up was ridiculously exhausting. Dasha had just closed the last pattern book with relief when Ruslan appeared at the door, dressed for going out in buff breeches and a jacket of dark blue superfine, his unruly waves combed into something close to submission. He looked immaculate and fresh despite the day being nearly gone, the exact opposite of how she felt and probably how she looked. Feeling self-conscious, Dasha tucked an errant curl behind her ear.

'My morning room has been overrun, I see,'

Ruslan said expansively, clearly in good humour. 'I stopped by to see how things were getting on and to see if I might persuade you, Your Highness, to come for a walk. It's a lovely day out.'

A walk sounded lovely after being cooped up. Dasha smiled at the offer. 'Let me just tidy my hair.' Then she paused, smoothing the lavender skirts of her borrowed dress. 'Is my gown smart enough?'

Madame Delphine was all brisk efficiency. 'We have a ready-made walking dress that should do from an order a woman didn't pick up.' She snapped her fingers. 'Suzette, help Her Highness change, quickly now, while *monsieur* and I step into the hallway.' No doubt, Dasha thought, to inform the Prince of the atrocious bill that awaited him and perhaps even to tell the Prince how she'd performed today. Suzette came forward to strip off her gown and Dasha sighed. A princess had no privacy. Her body, her actions, her every movement was up for public dissection, it seemed.

Suzette had her transformed in record time with a saucy hat perched on her head to match the blue walking ensemble and soft ivory-coloured half-boots and gloves. Ruslan was waiting for her in the hall, while Madame looked smugly pleased with herself. 'Definitely worth waiting for, you look lovely.' Ruslan offered her his arm and the awkward moment last night loomed large between them in her mind, although not his. Dasha wished she could be as assured as he, able to act as if her misstep last night had not happened. But she couldn't forget she'd tried to tempt him to kiss her and that he'd rejected the overture. Well, technically he'd only *averted* the overture. She wasn't sure if that was because he simply didn't want to or because he was being a gentleman.

The air outside was crisp and fresh. Autumn hung in the balance as the seasons transitioned. The trees bore hints of yellow in their leaves. 'There's a garden at the centre of the square, it should be private this time of day.' Ruslan led her across the street, helping her avoid the carriage traffic, and opened the gate with a small key from his pocket. He held up crossed fingers and gave her a friendly smile as he ushered her forward.

'London is a busy city,' Dasha said, slightly breathless after the adventure of crossing the street. The garden was quiet and empty in contrast.

'It takes some getting used to.' Ruslan shut the gate and the busyness behind them. 'It's an exciting city, though, full of modern advancements. I am eager to show it to you, as soon as you feel able. There's an international district in Soho with a Russian neighbourhood. Prince Baklanov has his riding academy there.' The hints were subtly layered as they walked and Dasha did not miss a single one. To go out into London required making a decision. How was Prince Pisarev to introduce her? How was she to see London? As the Princess Dasha, frequenting embassy balls and state events? Or as a woman who had yet to be named, an *émigrée* who would take up residence somewhere in Soho with others looking for new lives far from home? No one in the Prince's lofty circles would maintain a long acquaintance with that woman.

'How much time do you suppose I have?' Dasha asked bluntly.

The Prince did not pretend ignorance. 'I would not wait long. Word could come from Kuban at any time, although I would not expect it for another month. Still, by the time news comes, it will be too late to start preparing. We'll have to be ready to move at a moment's notice.'

He allowed her to walk in silence beside him. She appreciated the conversational reprieve. He was giving her time to ponder that news, but there must be more. He was patiently holding back, perhaps recognising either decision was daunting. To reinvent herself meant to give herself up entirely, to stop seeking answers, to stop hoping she'd wake up one morning and remember. Instead, she would have to hope she would never remember. Remembering risked discovering she was wrong. What if she woke up one day and knew with a certainty she was Princess Dasha? She'd have thrown away a chance to lead her people when they'd needed her most. That guilt would haunt her the rest of her life. 'It is an impossible decision,' Dasha said. They'd reached the far corner of the park where a bench waited under a tree.

The Prince sat, dusting leaves off the seat beside him for her. 'Not impossible, just difficult. Would you like to talk about it?'

Why not talk with him? Hadn't he, too, decided to reinvent himself? 'How did you decide?' Dasha sat, arranging her skirts. There were *some* similarities between them. He was a prince, a man of status and wealth and family in Kuban. He'd known her brothers. He'd been close to the royal family. Of the two of them sitting on the bench, he knew her life better than she did herself. He knew precisely what reinvention would cost her.

Ruslan gave her a smile. She was learning to read him. It was one of his wry smiles, the sort where only part of his mouth curved upwards. She thought far too much about his mouth. Best to look elsewhere. 'I didn't think about it, I just did it. When the moment came, I just kept going and never looked back. My friends needed me and, I suppose, I needed them more than I needed Kuban.' It posed a question, perhaps as he'd known it would. What did she need more than Kuban? What was she willing to do, willing to give up?

Dasha leaned forward, the intrigue of his statement irresistible. 'Tell me.'

Chapter Five

If reticence had a facial expression, Ruslan was sure his face was wearing it now. Tell *her*? The woman who was the daughter of the man who'd imprisoned his father and caused his friends to flee their homeland? Ruslan did not miss the irony. But, he could not bring himself to hate Dasha simply because of her relationship to the Tsar, any more than he'd been able to bring himself to despise his boyhood friends, the Tsar's sons, for the actions of their father. Neither could he overlook the importance his story would hold for Dasha. It *would* influence her decision, depending on how he told it. Told one way, it would encourage her to stay; told another, it would encourage her to go back. As a man of honour, he could cross neither line. He must tell it with all neutrality possible. 'It may be unpleasant, Your Highness,' he warned. Unpleasant for them both.

'Much in my recent life has been unpleasant,' she countered. Then she went on the offensive. 'You promised to help me, no matter what I chose to do. How can I choose wisely if I don't have information?' It was entirely unfair to use his own words against him. He saw the steel in her then, the strength that lay beneath her beauty and her youth. Being young did not make her naïve.

Ruslan held her gaze, letting her see his own resolve, his own warning. 'It began as an attempt to smuggle Princess Anna-Maria Petrova out of the country. Like you, she faced an unwanted marriage, but it became so much more.' It became the largest group of people he'd ever smuggled out of the country at one time, a group that contained everyone he cared for, everyone he loved. That alone had raised the stakes considerably. 'The four of us, the Princes you met at dinner last night, plus Illarion Kutejnikov, who is on his honeymoon, had been friends since we met at school at the age of ten. Since then, I cannot remember a time when the four of us weren't together. As we came of age and assumed our positions in the court, Nikolay and Illarion acquired a habit of speaking out against the Tsar's restrictive policies regarding the ways in which the noble families may serve Kuban.'

Dasha interrupted him with a hard look. 'You are being delicate. It is not necessary. I, apparently, know precisely what the Tsar was capable of. Even his own family was not spared the opportunity to marry well for the country. Have you forgotten Captain Varvakis's mention of my own engagement?'

Ruslan nodded. 'I had not forgotten.'

She gave him a sharp look. 'Good. Then you needn't be careful for my sake.'

Ruslan continued. 'Illarion had written a poem called "Freedom", and shortly afterwards, his friend, Katya, who had married General Ustinov, killed herself. The Tsar blamed Illarion. Nikolay protested quite vociferously and not for the first time. One night, the Tsar sent an assassin in the form of his cousin, Helena, Nikolay's current mistress, to Nikolay's bedchamber. She attacked and Nikolay killed her in self-defence, but he was severely wounded and arrested. The Tsar intended for Nikolay to stand trial for treason and he was in the process of having Illarion arrested for writing libel against the crown.'

He watched Dasha take in the news, letting her digest it before he continued. 'It was apparent Nikolay would not get a fair trial. The Tsar meant to be done with him. Stepan arranged to have Nikolay taken home to recover from his wound, but we knew we had to leave immediately. I arranged our departure. We gathered the wealth we could carry and our fastest horses, strapped Nikolay to a saddle and left in darkness.'

Even with more than a year's buffer between him and that fateful night, he could remember it with perfect clarity. Nikolay, burning with fever, barely able to stay upright as his father hugged him goodbye; Stepan on his huge black horse with Anna-Maria seated before him, a protective arm wrapped about her; her father, looking too frail to survive the journey, mounted on one of Nikolay's Cossack-bred warhorses. Ruslan had ferried his friends through backroads and discreet mountain passes to the borders of Kuban, spending long nights keeping watch and nursing Nikolay. When the moment had come to go forward or go back, Ruslan had known they needed him. Stepan and Illarion could not manage caring for Nikolay, watching the company's back *and* arranging the rest of the journey. Arranging was *his* specialty, so he'd taken that step over the border.

'Until then, had you not known you would go?' Dasha was studying him with her green eyes, lining his story up with hers, looking for parallels and guidance.

Ruslan shrugged, thinking of the substantial

wealth he'd packed for the journey. 'Maybe. I had brought supplies with me, like the others. Perhaps I knew in my heart there was a good chance I wouldn't return. I was prepared for either eventuality.' There'd been nothing to return for at that point, besides vengeance. His father was dead by his own hand in prison, his mother a few weeks later of a broken heart.

Dasha's eyes flared and he knew she understood *that* parallel. 'Then I should play the Princess a while longer, regardless of how I might choose in the end? Is that your advice?' she divined.

'Yes,' Ruslan said. 'I think that is the safest course.'

'But a short one. It does not remove my choice.' Those green eyes were piercing, alluring. They could look into a man's soul.

Ruslan nodded at her astute assessment of the situation. 'Nor does it delay it.' He gathered his words. 'There is something more I meant to tell you last night that might affect your decision. If you go public with your presence here, as the self-proclaimed Princess, a lone survivor of a royal massacre, the Rebels will know you're here with a certainty they may not currently have.' He shook his head. 'I am not so worried about that. Kuban is far away, news takes time to travel and plans take time to make. I am more concerned about that news reaching the local *émigré* cells. The Union of Salvation, do you know it?' He looked for recognition from her, but she offered no confirmation of knowledge. 'It's also known as the Society of True, Loyal Sons of the Fatherland,' Ruslan explained, 'but now it's sometimes referred to as the Union of Prosperity. Anyhow, it's a secret society, there's a northern branch in St Petersburg and a southern branch headquartered in Tulchin in the Ukraine.'

Dasha laughed. 'As secret as all that? If you know where they are, how secret can they be?' Then she sobered as realisation hit her. 'You know because you're a member.'

'No, not exactly,' Ruslan hurried to clarify. 'I've done some work for them. I'm not an official member.' Neither were his friends, but Nikolay and Illarion were indeed *closely* aligned with the group. 'I share their goals, but not their methods,' Ruslan explained. 'They want a constitutional monarchy. I don't disagree with that. But they are willing to see it done at the cost of armed revolt. Violence in the name of democratic progress is acceptable to them. It is not acceptable to me.' It was easier for Nikolay, he was a soldier. He'd been raised to violence, but Ruslan was a diplomat.

Dasha pondered the information. 'The Rebels Captain Varvakis speaks of are members, then?'

Ruslan nodded. She was quick, intelligent. 'Yes. They are most definitely behind the Rebel forces. They will want a monarch who will work with their new parliament, if they tolerate a monarch at all.' He highly suspected, drunk on their own power, they'd want a monarch they could control, a person of their own choosing, or that they'd see no need for a monarch at all. While he, as a student of John Locke's teachings, was not opposed to such models of self-government, such an arrangement did pose a danger to Dasha.

She saw that danger immediately. 'They will not want a Tukhachevsken. They will want to start fresh. But the Loyalists will cling to the old, to the Tukhachevsken name.' She paused, her fair brows knitting in thought. 'Certainly, that is a danger if I return. But you said as long as I was in London that threat was negligible due to distance.'

'It would be, if the Union was limited to Russia and Kuban. The concern is that Russian *émigrés* have a cell of the Union here, that they will learn of your presence if you declare yourself, and, not having the insights or guidance of the Moderates in Kuban who see you as a bridge to peace, they will act on their own and seek to eliminate you.' And by doing so, fuel open civil war.

'You're talking about assassination,' Dasha replied coldly, her face pale.

'Yes, I am. And civil war, too, if they are successful.' If she didn't want him to dress up the facts then he wouldn't, although he would spare her the weight of these decisions if he could. It hardly seemed fair after all she'd been through to add to her burdens.

She rose from the bench, pacing, as she thought. 'Is anonymity even a possibility any longer? After last night, so many people know. And now, Madame Delphine…' Her voice trailed off, implying the rule that secrets were hard to keep among many. At least nine people knew there were aspirations of her being the Princess.

'Those men at dinner have no desire to expose you against your will or to trigger a civil war with their carelessness. I personally assure their discretion,' Ruslan vowed.

'And Madame Delphine? Can you vouch for her, too? Dressmakers are notorious gossips. It's good for their business.'

'You have nothing to fear from Madame Delphine.' Ruslan chuckled. 'Do you think I would allow such a woman as you describe near you?' Perhaps he was bragging a bit here, wanting to impress this intriguing woman who matched him thought for thought.

Dasha looked up, recognition sparking in her eyes. She smiled. 'She is one of yours, isn't she? An *émigrée* you helped reinvent herself.' She blew out a breath. 'What happens if I don't go back? If I let you reinvent me?'

'Then the various factions will have to find a new leader. Hopefully they can do it peacefully. I think there's a better chance of that if they think there was no choice, that you died with the family, than if the Loyalists think you were deliberately gunned down in London by the opposition.' Ruslan watched her dissect his words.

'But the *very* best chance of a peaceful transition is if I go back and become the bridge between all factions,' she surmised. 'Is that what you want?'

'It doesn't matter what I want,' Ruslan challenged carefully. She was watching him closely. 'Varvakis has asked me to protect you until the situation is resolved. That is all.'

'That is not all. It does matter. Why are you doing all of this for me if not to get something for yourself in return? Why would you simply do what Varvakis asks?'

Why indeed? He had shared uncomfortable truths with her and now it was time for him to face some of his own. His dilemma was a strong one. Who did he protect? The woman who stood before him, or the country that might be born with his help? Protecting the woman would mean hiding her away along with her true identity, to let Princess Dasha fade into history. To birth the nation his father had died for, his mother had died for, Nikolay and Illarion had suffered for, might require permitting Dasha to become a sacrifice. 'Can't I simply do this for you in memory of your brothers?' He opted for an easy answer. 'I would help you, as a way to honour them.' He rose and brushed his hands against his breeches. It was time to head back before she could ask any more uncomfortable questions. But his efforts were too late.

'That's a nice sentiment,' Dasha replied sharply, her tone implying she didn't believe him. 'Is that why you wouldn't kiss me last night? Because I am the little sister of your friends? Or because I *might* become the future Tsarina instead of another anonymous *émigrée*?' A more perceptive woman Ruslan had yet to meet. Damn that perceptiveness, though. He could do with a bit less of it.

'Perhaps both.' He trod carefully here. Kissing princesses came with political entanglements. He was aware of the emptiness of the park, the light breeze. No one would know what transpired here, no one would hold them accountable. But *they* would. Kissing her was still a bad idea.

She reached for his hand with a touch that made his blood pound even through their gloves. 'If I was nothing but an *émigrée* woman like Madame Delphine, would you kiss me?'

Yes. Without hesitation. His objectivity was under siege.

She moved into him, her arms about his neck, her hands in his hair. For a young woman raised in the seclusion of the palace, Dasha was bold. 'Then, it's best you kiss me now, I think, while I am still in limbo, while I am still nothing.'

'You could never be "nothing".' Ruslan's response was a low rasp.

'Then what are you afraid of, Ruslan Pisarev?' Her hips shifted against him in subtle, perhaps accidental invitation. Lord, the woman was a temptress.

'I'm not afraid,' Ruslan growled. Her physicality flooded his body with abrupt desire, her convenient logic flooding his better judgement. He was going to regret mixing business with pleasure, but perhaps it would be worth it to prove to her a kiss was not worth the crown. Better she learn that lesson from a man she could trust, whether she knew it or not, than from a man who

would not hesitate to manipulate those desires
for his own gain, and there would be plenty of
those if she went back. He would not always be
there to protect her, but he was here now and
perhaps this kiss was a sort of protection. Feeling justified in his rationale, he bent his head
and captured her mouth, all for the purpose of
instruction…

Chapter Six

~~~~~~

Dasha gave a low moan that was part-gasp, part-murmur of surprise. She had not been prepared for this, for the heat that flared low in her stomach and bled into her veins like slow, deliberate lava, for the warm strength of his body against hers. Kissing was more than mouths on mouths, more than the brief pressing of lips. It was hands and bodies, tongues and tastes. It was an offer of comfort and communion, momentary completion. How remarkable to feel such a thing, with this man she barely knew but was irrevocably drawn to, and how *addictive*. She wanted to fall into it, wanted to give herself over, to his hands, to his mouth. Her own hands, her own mouth, joined his in this quiet, lingering exploration. In the still of the garden, there was no rush to end it, her only compulsion was to savour it. Who knew when it could happen again, or if it would happen again? Her hands tangled in his hair, those glorious, unruly waves, as if she could hold him in this moment for ever.

He made the slightest of adjustments and deepened the kiss—they were moving from tasting and testing to something more. Seduction, and what a seduction it was; not just a seduction of the body, but of the mind, a taste of what the *émigrée* could have, but the Princess could not. Was that what he meant to show her? What woman would choose a throne when it meant giving *this* up? But that was illogical. It was one kiss and that kiss *would* end. There were no promises beyond it.

Somewhere in the distance of reality, the garden gate opened. Ruslan drew back, the eternity of the kiss broken. Time had lost all meaning, but now it started to run again as she stepped away. She smoothed her skirts to give her hands, her mind, something to do. What did one say after such a kiss?

'We should return. Madame Delphine will have last-minute details to clear with you.' The words were not what she expected. They were perfunctory, as was the way he snapped back to reality without hesitation, as if the kiss hadn't overwhelmed him, as if it hadn't meant as much to him as it had to her. That's when she knew it hadn't. While she'd been losing herself to the fantasy, he'd been…leading her on and nothing more. It was not a pleasant realisation.

She straightened her shoulders and lifted her chin, gathering her dignity. She couldn't retract all the emotion she'd allowed herself to display any more than she could pretend it hadn't happened. But she could call him on it and make him accountable. She met his gaze with an even stare that she hoped was as aloof as his. 'Why did you do it? Why did you kiss me?'

Why did you make me feel as if the whole world rested on that kiss?

'You needed instruction.' Ruslan dusted at his immaculate sleeve.

'Instruction in kissing?' That was appalling. She couldn't help the flush that crept up her cheeks. How embarrassing to appear so desperate as to need charity kisses.

'No, not in kissing. In guarding your emotions. Better to learn that from someone who has your best interests at heart than from a scoundrel who would willingly seduce the crown out from under your pretty head, or for any number of royal favours.'

Dasha looked away, her cheeks burning. How naïve he must think her, how stupid. She had indeed been willing to be seduced by that kiss, been willing to believe someone cared for her. She was far more lonely, far more desperate than she'd thought. She gave a curt nod. 'Then you have my thanks, Prince Pisarev, for such a necessary and instructive lesson.'

'Ruslan. Please. We are to be together far too much in the next weeks to stand on ceremony,' he offered, giving no indication that he'd witnessed her embarrassment.

'And you must call me Dasha,' she offered in return, taking his truce. He'd kissed her to prove a point because she'd provoked him. They were square now.

Ruslan smiled and took her arm. 'Tell me all about your new wardrobe.' The walk back was mercifully taken up with discussion of her dress session. He had all sorts of questions. Had she ordered enough? Madame Delphine felt she should have more, perhaps she would reconsider adding two or three more dresses to the order and another ball gown?

Dasha laughed. 'You make it sound as if spending more of your money is a favour. I assure you, I've spent plenty.' Especially if she decided to fade away. A penniless *émigrée* would not have a finer wardrobe than she already had, if that was what she chose. Ruslan stopped them before the gate and covered her hand with his where it lay on her sleeve, his gaze serious. 'Money is no object. Think of spending it as a favour to me, to see you gowned as you ought to be.' *As a* princess *ought to be.* Was he so sure she'd choose that path even after that kiss? Although after his disclosures, that option seemed more likely than it had this morning. In fact, it hardly seemed that she had options at all.

'You've been generous.' She was hesitant to accept too much. No one did anything without getting paid and her debt to Ruslan was mounting. 'I have no money and no promise of money in the future to repay you with.' Especially if she decided to fade into anonymity. He must be very certain of her indeed.

Ruslan narrowed his gaze. 'Do not insult me, Dasha. I am not doing this for money. This is a matter of honour.'

'Do not insult *me*,' Dasha cut in. 'A man is not the only person with a sense of honour. A woman has pride, too, and there are other forms of payment besides money.'

Sexual, political, promises of power.

Ruslan's jaw tightened, his mouth set in a grim line, but he did not dismiss her concern. 'I do not think you are the sort of woman who can be bought for a few dresses and pretty baubles. I would hope you'd believe I wasn't the sort of man who would think so little of you.' He opened the gate with a curt nod and motioned for her to pass through. No, she didn't think that of him, yet how else was she to explain the grand kindnesses he'd shown to her?

He gave her a small smile. 'I know, you can't help it. It's a consequence of court, of royalty, always thinking of motives. Take it as a good sign, though. You are thinking like a princess.' It was ruefully said. 'It is how a prince thinks, too, always wondering why people have done something for you, what they might want. What do they expect you to give them?' His hand was at her back, ushering her across the street, and she was reminded once more of the commonalities between them, or at least the commonalities that *should* be between them, assuming she was who the Captain claimed she was. What would Ruslan say to her doubts? She felt a pang of guilt. He was investing in the woman he thought she was, not just with his money, but with his reputation and credibility when he represented her to others. Was it right to mislead him? To not make him privy to her doubts? Would he take her doubts seriously or pawn them off as Varvakis had done?

Once inside the house, Ruslan bid her farewell. 'I will not be home for dinner. I have instructed Cook to prepare whatever you wish, and my staff has been apprised that you should make free with my home. Please, Dasha, entertain yourself. There is a pianoforte in the conservatory, books in the library, as you know…' He paused here and smiled at the mention of the library. 'I hope you will not be bored.'

How could she possibly be bored? She had too much to think about, a kiss and a handsome prince not the least of those things. And she had a decision to make. But she would miss him. Perhaps he knew his absence was for the best. Perhaps he'd even planned it, to give her space in which to think without being unduly influenced by his presence.

Dasha dressed slowly for dinner, savouring the luxury of sliding into a clean gown, one of the ready-mades Madame Delphine had left. Even though she dined alone, it felt good to wear well-made clothes and to take time with her appearance. This particular gown was an eggplant silk. Except for the aquamarine, she'd chosen subdued colours out of respect for mourning her family, but she hadn't chosen all black with an eye towards the other reality—that if she wasn't the Princess she needn't wear it at all. Everything, it seemed, hinged on that decision, even something as trivial as her wardrobe. Did she embrace being the Princess or did she create a new identity?

Dasha studied her reflection in the mirror while the maid put up her hair. Who did this face with its serious green eyes belong to? Was it enough to assume that because she thought like a princess she was the Princess? Why was it so hard for her to accept Captain Varvakis's rescue story? Why did the idea of being the Princess sit so awkwardly on her shoulders?

The maid put in a final pin and offered her the small jewel case. 'Might I suggest the jet earrings?' Ruslan had not only thought of everything, he'd *found* everything. Where he had found these exquisite earrings was beyond her. Dasha fastened them, appreciating their subdued elegance. They were appropriate for this half-mourning she'd fashioned for herself, for a family she couldn't remember but would honour anyway. Maybe some day she'd remember them and be able truly to mourn them.

She could throw it all off and begin again if she chose. But how would she do that? Beyond the theoretical guilt she might feel, there were practical issues. How would she support herself? How would she live? Where would she live? Would she become another face in this

Soho district Ruslan talked about? Ruslan would certainly give her an allowance to start out on should she ask and she had no doubt he'd see to the arrangements, but what then?

She could not lean on him, could not live off his largesse for ever, which begged the next question. Could she choose to live in restrained circumstances? A woman with a name that had no history except that which she acquired? She would be a fraud of sorts the rest of her days. Silk dresses and maids proffering jewels would be a thing of the past. It might be worth it, though. There was a certain appeal in anonymity. In time, she could become the wife of another *émigré*, perhaps a nice man who taught music or dancing to wealthy gentlemen's daughters. They would live in shabby gentility and no one would ever importune them for favours. She would never need to worry about being used or manipulated. She might make real friends.

But she would never know the truth of her identity. Or if she did, she'd never be able to acknowledge it, not even to her husband. However, the chances of that seemed slim. Ruslan's doctor had said the more familiarity she surrounded herself with, the better her chances of recovering her memories. Her 'familiarity' was a thousand miles away. The best chance for her to know who she was lay in going back. The best chance for *peace* lay in going back; the best chance to help her country lay in going back. The reasons were mounting, tipping the scale against the one niggling 'what if' that remained.

What if she wasn't who Varvakis thought she was? Was it enough doubt to risk the fate of a nation?

It would be so much easier if she could simply believe the Captain.

'You believe the Captain. You're going to help them,' Stepan said with characteristic boldness and no small hint of accusation as they sat over early evening drinks at White's. The table between them was cluttered with bottles in varying degrees of emptiness. It was always drinks, plural, with Stepan. A little vodka, a little *samogon*, a little whisky on occasion. Stepan thought Englishmen were too boring, too predictable with their predilection for a constant brandy.

Ruslan sat back in his chair. The emptiness of the bottles was making them both bold. 'Is there a reason I shouldn't? Perhaps it's my patriotic duty. A soldier travels across a continent and an angry sea with the only surviving member of the ruling family, shows up on my doorstep and asks for help in the name of a peaceful transition, a transition you and I were exiled for, if I might remind you. That seems like a good reason to help.'

Stepan took a long swallow from his glass. 'For a man who considers all angles, you're taking a lot on face value, including the most basic question: Is Varvakis telling the truth? It's rather convenient for him and for the Moderates to be in possession of such a valuable commodity as Dasha Tukhachevskenova and have her remember nothing, not even who she is. That doesn't even begin to explore the profit in being able to produce this valuable commodity at the right time. Need I point out how this will position Varvakis and his friends for the future? Right behind the throne?'

Something clenched inside Ruslan. He didn't like Stepan discussing Dasha as a commodity, yet that's what she was, what she *had* to be if he were to keep his detachment. Objectivity was crucial to an organiser, especially one who specialised in organising escapes. Risk analysis, he liked to call it. Without it, bad decisions were made. Dasha was merely another cargo to transport from one destination to another. 'Are you suggesting she's not who she says she is?' Ruslan swirled his drink, not wanting to admit Stepan *might* have a point. He'd been so worried about next steps he hadn't really thought to look behind and what had led to all of this.

'She doesn't know *who* she is. Anything is possible. She only knows what Varvakis has told her.' Stepan slid him a strong look. 'I suppose the only way to truly know is to dig up the grave and count the bodies.'

Ruslan narrowed his eyes against the grisly image. 'You're being crass now. She's said nothing about doubting Varvakis or her own identity.'

Stepan arched his brows. 'Why would she? She stands to be a princess, a queen.'

'Not everyone wants to rule and to make such a claim is dangerous both here and in Kuban.' He'd explained that to Dasha just this afternoon, right before he'd kissed her. If she were as power-hungry as Stepan wanted to argue, she would not be hesitating in her decision.

'Is there a chance she won't go back?' Stepan cut in. He leaned forward, his voice dropping against the chance of being overheard. One never knew in a place like White's. 'Can you imagine the look on Varvakis's face if she chooses to stay?' He chuckled at the irony of it, then sobered. 'He will try to influence her. He has the most to gain from her return. He could go from loyal but somewhat lowly palace guard to a trusted advisor behind the throne. He'd be nothing short of a national hero,' Stepan posited, contemplating his glass. 'Do you think he fancies her? Do you think he styles himself as the future royal consort to the Queen?'

'He's a good soldier, a patriot to the bone. Nikolay vouches for him,' Ruslan began, not liking Stepan's idea. Wasn't this exactly what he'd warned Dasha about a few hours ago?

Stepan laughed harshly. 'He's a man, Ruslan, who has charged himself with the protection of an attractive young woman who just happens to be a royal princess—should he be telling the truth. He's spent weeks on the road with her alone in an environment of heightened sensitivity. You tell me what sort of fantasies he puts himself to sleep with every night.'

'You didn't use to be so cynical.' Ruslan poured another glass of *samogon*. He didn't like thinking of Varvakis having designs on Dasha with the taste of her lips still warm on his. That kiss might have been a mistake. Perhaps it had taught her the lesson he intended, but at a price. It had cost him a piece of his detachment. He'd been more swept up in that moment than he'd shown her; his response afterwards more perfunctory than it might otherwise have been if he'd not been so overwhelmed. He had kissed Dasha with his entire body, but Dasha had kissed him with her soul. 'London has changed you, Stepan.' Although he wasn't sure it was London alone. When men changed, there was usually a woman behind it, for better or worse.

'Kuban changed me long before London had its claws into me.' Stepan shook his head.

Ruslan took the opening tentatively, feeling his way with care. There was another issue yet to address tied up with Dasha's appearance. 'Would you ever go back?'

'Would you?' Stepan's question was incredulous.

'Possibly.' It had occupied a large part of his thoughts in the last twenty-four hours. He couldn't think of Dasha without thinking of the opportunity. He waited for the explosion. Stepan would object, naturally.

'You would go back to the place that would have executed Nikolay for treason, attempted to imprison Illarion on false charges of slander, saw your own family disgraced, your father forced to take his own life…' Stepan's voice trailed off, recognising he'd said too much. They never talked about Ruslan's father. It was implicitly understood as a taboo subject.

'Yes, dammit, I would, so that such ridiculous, meaningless crimes could not happen again.' Ruslan calmed himself and continued. 'I could

pave the way for the rest of you to return if you
chose. It will be a time of change, a time to do
good. Being part of that is not unappealing.' Ruslan laid out his argument, in the wake of Stepan's disbelief. 'It's what I've been groomed for,
schooled for. I was meant to be a leader.' Kuban
would need him in ways England never would,
in ways his friends no longer did now that they
were settled. He could do them one last service
by making it possible for them to go home if
they ever wanted. As for his own need, he was
a man who needed to be useful. He was of little
use in London and growing less useful by the
day. Until now. Dasha needed him. His country
needed him.

'Do you have a plan, then?' Stepan stroked
the stem of a glass, his nonchalance belying his
distaste of the decision.

'I need to speak with certain political figures.
Illarion's father-in-law can arrange it for me.'
The Duke of Redruth was politically active with
several connections in all branches of government including the Foreign Office. 'If the Princess goes back, she won't go back alone. The
situation in Kuban is ripe for British intervention. If Britain can be made to understand that,
British support can be used to secure a peaceful
transition out of revolution.' It was a fair trade,

Ruslan thought. British support and a peaceful transfer of power in exchange for an amicable sharing of water rights in the Crimea. It would be a tasty carrot to dangle, *if* he could pull it off. Britain and Russia were going to have to discuss the Crimea soon, it might as well be under a flag of peace.

'That's very ambitious,' Stepan commented wryly. 'Does she know you wish to erase the blot on the House of Pisarev?' He heard Stepan's censure that Varvakis wasn't the only 'good' man with an agenda. Stepan drummed his fingers on the table top. 'She might be disappointed to learn you are not so neutral as you appear. I saw her watching you at dinner. You have become her anchor, someone she seeks to rely on. Perhaps she sees you as a neutral foil against Varvakis.' Stepan paused and held his gaze. 'Maybe she sees you as something more. What have you promised her? What has she promised *you*?' Kisses. Ruslan couldn't get past the kisses, the feel of her against him, the urgent welcome of her mouth, her bold response. That kiss had followed him all evening, objectivity notwithstanding. 'Between you and Varvakis, I don't think the Princess stands a chance of staying.'

'The Princess can hold her own. She's headstrong and she knows her mind if not her memories. I am striving to be as neutral as possible.' And he'd seen the cynicism in Dasha's eyes today, her hesitance in accepting the dresses. There were things a woman especially might want more than a crown: honest friendships, a life that was not a constant balance of power, a constant negotiation of concessions and favours. He had also felt it in the press of her body, in the hunger of her mouth. She had wanted that kiss, that connection with another human being without the strings that went with it. She'd mentioned as much. How badly did she want it?

Some of Stepan's cynicism was wearing off on him. It occurred to Ruslan that perhaps she *did* know who she was and that there might be a game within a game. Was she deliberately seeking to be the fish let off the hook so that it could swim away and be lost in the stream of time? Was she seeking oblivion and using him to get it? A man besotted with the promise of kisses would deny a woman nothing and he'd already given his word. Who had taught whom a lesson in the park today? Dasha had shown herself to be canny enough for such a game if she chose. He pushed his glass forward. 'You'd better pour me another one.'

Stepan gave him a cryptic look. 'Yes, I think I'd better.'

This was the part of the game Ruslan liked least—the part where he could do nothing but wait until his opponent made their next move. Everything now hinged on Dasha's decision: to be or not to be the Princess. He needed to reconcile himself to patience.

Chapter Seven

It was difficult, Dasha discovered in the days that followed, to reconcile the man who'd kissed her in the garden with the man who spent his afternoons pacing before her, delivering relentless lectures on the House of Tukhachevsken by the hour. If she'd been looking for any softness in him, any excuse to read more into the kiss than what he claimed, she could not find it. This was a man who put duty first above all things.

'The current Tsar, Peter, your father, married Maria Alexandernova in 1795. He had three sons: Peter, his namesake, in 1797, Vasili in 1799, and Grigori in 1801 before your birth in 1804. He took the throne in December 1805, incorporating the coronation with early Christmas festivities. There was a comet that autumn, the Pons Comet, and many felt it foretold your father's reign. Your mother kept a comet pin in her jewel box to commemorate the astronomical occasion. Your grandfather became ill shortly after the comet passed, proving the predictions of your father's imminent reign true. Your grandfather died in November.'

She should be more focused on the lecture, but her attention today was captivated by the way the window light of an early September afternoon turned the thick waves of his hair auburn and then wheat by turn. It was difficult to think of comets and pins and dead ancestors when there was Ruslan to think about. The way he smelled, like cloves and patchouli; the way his voice sounded when it was low at her ear like it had been in the park, his words for her alone; the way he'd felt when his lips were on hers, his body pressed to her own. Neither could she forget the way *she* felt: safe, protected, cared for, never mind that he claimed none of those things were intended by his sensual instruction.

'Are you listening, Your Highness?' Ruslan's tone was imperious, cutting through her day-dreams.

'No, not really,' Dasha admitted, rising from the sofa she'd perched on for hours. 'It's been a long afternoon full of maps and family trees and policies.' She stood and stretched, eyeing the long, elegant pianoforte painted in an ice-blue with gold trim done in the baroque style. 'I think some music is in order.' She strode to the instrument and sat down, running her fingers experimentally over the keys before breaking into a fast-paced polka. This was more like it. She played another song after that, and another one, her fingers flying, her head thrown back. She could play for ever…

She caught sight of the Captain and Ruslan, and came to a crash of discordant keys as her hands came down hard. They were both staring. Varvakis had risen from his seat, a stunned expression on his face.

'You remembered!' Varvakis exclaimed in ensuing silence. He turned to Ruslan excitedly. 'The Princess and her lady-in-waiting used to play the most exquisite duets for the family. The Princess was an accomplished pianist.'

'Is that so?' Ruslan strode to the piano and sat beside her on the bench, his thigh pressed to hers as he rifled through the sheet music until he found what he was looking for. 'Shall we try this one?' In response, she played a few stanzas of the opening, a slow love ballad.

Ruslan picked up his part with skill, his long fingers moving easily over the keys. He was an apt musician. Of course. By now, she shouldn't be surprised. He did everything with an air of mastery. Then he began to sing, a strong, pure tenor that filled the drawing room and elevated the simple ballad to something more complex, more ethereal.

'"As I walk'd thro' the meadows, To take the fresh air, The flowers were blooming and gay; I heard a fair damsel so sweetly a-singing. Her cheeks like the blossom in May."'

The magic of the music connected them, reminding her of what could exist between them when their guards were down.

'"Then I took this fair maid by the lilywhite hand; On the green mossy bank we sat down; and I placed a kiss on her sweet rosy lips, while the small birds were singing around."'

Dasha felt a blush on her cheeks at the mention of a kiss. She stole a sideways glance at Ruslan as he sang, looking for a crack in his stoic façade. She caught sight of the faintest of grins as he managed the line. She played the final notes, letting them fade away reluctantly.

'You're very good,' Dasha complimented.

'As are you.' Ruslan held her gaze as he removed himself from the bench with a small bow. 'I think we'll call our lessons complete for the day. Nikolay and Klara have invited us for the evening, if you're willing?'

Was she willing? Dasha nearly leapt at the

chance to leave the house. Except for walks in the garden across the street, she had not been out since her arrival. As large as Ruslan's home was, the walls were starting to close in. It was her fault. As soon as she decided how to be introduced, she could go out. 'Just give me a moment to freshen up.' She smiled and nearly skipped out of the room before anyone could change their mind.

Ruslan's smile faded as the door shut behind Dasha. 'She remembered? On purpose, or does the body simply recall that which comes naturally to it?' He turned to look at Varvakis, wanting to see the man's facial expression.

Varvakis shrugged. 'Does it matter? It's further proof that she will remember again. It will all come back. We surrounded her with something familiar, just as your doctor suggested.'

'And further proof that she is indeed the Princess?' Ruslan tried out Stepan's scepticism.

Varvakis looked stunned. 'You think I would attempt to pass off an imposter? That affronts my honour greatly, Your Highness.'

Ruslan inclined his head in apology. Behind the intensity of Varvakis's response there could be no doubt the man spoke the truth. He'd been right on that account, at least, a small victory over Stepan's cynicism. 'It is a question that must be asked, under the circumstances,' Ruslan explained in his defence. 'I would be less than my reputation suggests if I did not question it.'

Varvakis let out a long sigh. 'Yes, of course, Your Highness. No insult taken.'

Ruslan settled into a chair, crossing a leg over one knee, changing directions. 'May we speak of the factions, Captain? Who leads them?' Now that Dasha's education was underway, he could focus on the task of strategising. Who would Dasha need to persuade when she returned?

Varvakis looked more at ease with this aspect of the discussion. 'Ivan Serebrov for the Loyalists, Kolya Nemtsev, an officer, for the Moderates.' Ruslan nodded. He was not surprised. Serebrov was an older man, a long-time advisor to the Tsar. Kolya Nemtsev was likely a former member of the Union of Salvation, a man perhaps like himself who had turned away at the idea of change through violence.

'And the Rebels?' Ruslan asked.

Varvakis grimaced. 'Count Anatoly Ryabkin, a man who perhaps means well, but whose hot temper will eventually lead the Rebels too far afield. He's a man to start revolutions, but not to finish them.'

Varvakis might have said more, but Ruslan did not hear him. His mind was stuck on the very name. *Ryabkin.* The man had betrayed his father. Well, not quite betrayed him. But he'd had the power to protect him and Ryabkin had not. He'd stood aside instead of speaking up.

'Do you know the Count?' Varvakis ventured into the silence.

'Yes,' Ruslan answered tightly. 'I think your assessment is quite right.' His mind was working at top speed, wondering what Ryabkin thought to gain by leading the Rebels, by putting himself at the front of an acknowledged effort to over-turn a monarchy and commit regicide. It was a dangerous stance to take, very unlike Ryabkin who always chose to hedge his bets. Was he that sure of the revolt's success? Or just that sure of himself? He could see plainly what Ryabkin wanted—power, control. Ryabkin didn't want a new day for Kuban as much as he wanted to be King himself. He would promise anyone any-thing to get it.

Varvakis exchanged a look with him that said, *This is why you must help me with her, why she must go back. We cannot leave the country in the hands of a man like Ryabkin.*

Ruslan rose and excused himself, his mind a whir of thought. There was much to think about now. Dasha Tukhachevskenova not only stood between peace and civil war, she stood between the throne and Ryabkin. He needed time to think. He needed to prompt Dasha to action. If Ryabkin were involved, she no longer had the luxury of slipping into anonymity.

Ruslan handed Dasha down from his carriage, giving her time to survey the wrought-iron arch-way leading to the well-lit alley that made up Nikolay's large mews and the path to the riding house on the right side. The mews and alley were clean and well kept, but there was nothing overly luxurious about them. The stalls were not par-ticularly large like a royal stable and the horses were rather ordinary in their stalls. No flashy Arabians or exotic breeds poked their heads over the stall doors. But all the horses were well taken care of and healthy, that much was evident from the shine of their coats and the cleanliness of their living conditions.

Dasha was content to let him lead her through the mews, her free hand reaching up to stroke the occasional nose that came out to meet her. 'They're lovely. Look! A yearling.' The dapple-grey foal drew her attention and she stopped to rub its face. 'He's adorable.'

Ruslan smiled and fished in his pocket for a piece of apple. Whenever he came to visit, he always remembered treats. He handed her the apple. 'This is Polar. He's ten months old. Nikolay rescued him from a kill pen earlier this year.' Polar butted Ruslan, looking for more treats. Ruslan scrubbed at the horse's face, ruffling his mane. 'Now, he has an adopted family.' He gestured to the next two stalls. 'This mare next door is his "mother", and the stallion on the other side of her is his "father".' Ruslan drew her down the line, telling the story. 'The stallion was defending him when Nikolay and Klara found him.'

Dasha stopped at the mare's stall, taking in the leggy thoroughbred. 'Is she a jumper?'

'A steeplechaser. Klara rides her.' Ruslan paused, remembering how Nikolay had told him the mare had chased Klara down and begged to be taken home. 'The two are devoted to each other in a special way.'

'Yes,' Dasha said softly, stroking the mare's muzzle. 'I had a horse once I was particularly devoted to.'

'Did you?' Ruslan asked casually, wanting to prompt, but not wanting to ruin the moment. If the memories were coming, he wanted them to come organically. He certainly didn't want to scare them away by pressuring her.

She looked at him, her eyes revealing how startled she was by the revelation, and then a shadow fell. 'I don't know his name.' She looked down. 'I thought for a moment…' Yes, for a moment there'd been a breakthrough.

Ruslan smiled and took her hand. 'Don't worry. It will come. Already today has provided two new pieces: you like horses and you play the piano.'

'You're putting me back together like Humpty Dumpty.'

'*Better* than Humpty Dumpty,' he encouraged, wanting to banish the disappointment in her eyes. She expected so much of herself, this strong, proud young woman. They passed by the rest of the stalls, finding Nikolay and Klara in the cosy tack room, down on their knees beside a basket, eyes only for each other.

Nikolay rose hastily, brushing at the dirt on his trouser knees. 'I'm sorry, we didn't hear you arrive.' He gestured to the basket, full of squirming black and white English springer spaniel puppies and grinned unabashedly. 'We were distracted.'

Ruslan laughed, looking from Nikolay to Klara and thinking the distraction was due to more than the puppies. They'd walked in on something or nearly so. 'I can see that. Where did these sweet angels come from?'

Nikolay's eyes twinkled. 'Well, Klara's to blame. A farmer in Richmond didn't know what to do with them.'

'Oh! They're so sweet.' Dasha interrupted the tale about the Richmond farmer, sinking to her knees beside Klara and scooping up the smallest, who was struggling to climb over his brothers and sisters. She looked up at Ruslan and he forgot about solving the mystery of Klara and Nikolay. 'I don't know this breed. What is it?' How interesting that she'd picked the one in most need when she could have chosen one of the puppies frolicking closest to her.

'Springer spaniels. They're gun dogs for hunting. A very intelligent breed,' Klara supplied when Ruslan said nothing, too lost in his own thoughts. 'My father keeps a kennel of them at his country estate, which is where most of these will go if we don't find them homes.'

'We could have left them in Richmond then at your father's, instead of dragging them all the way into town just to drag them back,' Nikolay huffed, pretending to be put upon, but anyone could see he was infatuated with his wife and with the puppies.

'They're far too adorable to leave,' Dasha protested, hugging hers close. The little pup licked at her face until she laughed, an utterly captivating sound. The sight of Dasha with the puppy was a mesmerising one. Sitting on the floor playing with the puppy, she was neither princess nor problem; she was merely Dasha. The cares she wore so often on her face and in her eyes were gone; all of her attention, all of her enjoyment, was fixed in the moment. Ruslan wanted that moment to go on, for her sake. The puppies had done what he could not—lift her burdens. Any choice he gave her came with burdens of their own.

Ruslan bent down to join them, letting one of the pups play tug with a towel scrap. 'This is a fine way to spend the evening, Nikolay,' he teased.

'Puppies are the very best way to spend any evening.' Dasha laughed. She smiled at Ruslan, utterly unselfconscious as the words spilled out. 'There were puppies in the royal stables on occasion, but we were never allowed to have animals in the palace.'

Ruslan's smile froze. He tried to keep his eyes merry, not wanting to call attention to her words but it was too late. Her eyes settled on his. He saw again the spark of astonished recognition followed by the bleakness of despair when nothing more was forthcoming. 'You should have one, then,' Ruslan offered to cover the moment. She'd told the truth. He recalled that Grigori and Vasili had complained about not being able to have pets.

'Yes!' Klara echoed. 'You should take one. There's nothing like a puppy to make one feel at home.'

Dasha hesitated and looked to him. 'I don't know, everything in the house is new, and Prince Pisarev has only just moved in.'

'Prince Pisarev?' Nikolay burst out laughing. 'Surely he's not making you call him *that*?'

'Ruslan will do just fine, as I've mentioned before, as will a puppy.' Ruslan smiled at her. 'You're welcome to bring one home.' Surely his detachment could withstand one small puppy.

Dasha rose, holding her puppy close, her face alight with the becoming colour of excitement. 'Then I will take this likely lad when we go.'

Klara stood and looped an arm through Dasha's, calling for a stable boy to take the dogs. 'We'll discuss names over supper.' Klara looked happy in that particular way women did… Hmm. Ruslan wondered. It was possible. She and Nikolay had been married nearly six months now. Plenty of time for a strapping Cossack like Nikolay to get his nursery started. Well, he'd keep his thoughts to himself until it was time to celebrate.

Supper was a lively, intimate affair. Klara and Nikolay were easy people to talk with and Ruslan was thankful for their affability. He didn't need to carry the conversation. He could sit back and watch, and think. He'd not seen Dasha like this; so relaxed and animated. Perhaps that was the very reason he'd brought her here. Maybe he'd wanted to see her out of the rarefied context of 'princess in hiding'. Maybe he'd wanted to see just the woman.

Ruslan drank from his wine glass and gestured for some more. Seeing her this way was doing nothing for his armour other than wreaking havoc on it. This woman was irresistible and, by extension, tonight was irresistible. Ruslan caught Nikolay's eye, his friend's message clear. There could be more evenings like this *if* she were not the Princess. Did Dasha see it? Did he *want* her to see it? Was this the reality he'd wanted portrayed as he gave her a taste of *émigré* life? The answer was yes and no, and it was complicated. Did he want her to stay in London even if it meant abandoning Kuban to the likes of Ryabkin?

After dinner, Nikolay and Klara walked them through the neighbourhood, a lantern in hand. The streets were still busy with a mixed crowd coming and going; some were labourers coming home or seeking evening meals. Others were the more genteel clerks and tutors and governesses who might aspire to a more elevated evening out as someone's companion or guest—a moment in the sun of their former lives. This was more in line with what Ruslan had wanted to show Dasha—the cost of her freedom, yet he might have shown her enough to make that cost worth it. Would she be tempted? Could he afford that temptation? To save her from the maw of Kuban much would be sacrificed.

At the end of the walk, Klara put the puppy into Dasha's arms. 'I hope you will come again. Bring the puppy to visit. Have we decided on name?'

'Maximus.' Dasha held the puppy to her, looking entirely far too enticing for Ruslan's tastes. He had to yet endure the carriage ride home with the enchanting Dasha in enclosed proximity.

Ruslan offered her a hand and helped her, Maximus and all, into the carriage. 'Thank you for an enjoyable evening, Nikolay.'

Nikolay nodded, his eyes serious. 'Have a safe ride home, Old Man. I don't envy you.'

'Neither do I,' Ruslan sighed and shut the door behind him.

He'd barely taken his seat when Dasha fixed him with her green gaze. 'Thank you for the puppy.' She paused, waiting until the carriage was under way, holding the puppy close. 'Does this mean I passed your latest lesson?' Damn her, for seeing too much.

Chapter Eight

'Does this have to be a lesson? Couldn't it just be an evening out to meet friends?' Ruslan sat back against the squabs, watching her with the puppy. It was easy for him to believe his own fabrication when she looked like this: hair loose, a puppy in her arms, a soft smile on her lips. As long as he didn't look at her eyes. They were sharp, reminders that this wasn't only an evening out. Reminders, too, that what had been only a test for her had now become a test for him—what had this evening truly been about? Had his detachment slipped yet another notch, another sacrifice to showing her both sides of her choices?

Could he afford for the evening to be personal? It was what she'd want if she indeed was launching a game within a game where she only pretended she didn't know who she was. After tonight, though, he was less inclined to believe that. Her surprise at her memories had been real enough as had been her disappointment when there wasn't more.

'You wanted to show me what life was like outside the protection of my title.' Dasha was not long on subtlety. Did it even cross her mind she might be wrong?

'Not everyone would enjoy being accused of the plots in your head.'

Dasha shrugged and looked down at Maximus squirming in her arms. 'That doesn't make me wrong.' Then she relented. 'In all fairness to you, the evening *was* illuminating. You planned carefully.' Then she sighed. 'Why does everything have to come with a cost?'

Oh, if she knew! She wasn't the only one paying. Ruslan smiled his commiseration, knowing she didn't expect more of an answer. He was gratified to note that the evening had achieved its purpose. She'd caught the nuances of visiting Soho, and the implications of starting over. 'I would help you, of course,' Ruslan added. 'You wouldn't be expected to do it all on your own.' Would she choose to stay despite the difficulties? Part of him cheered that. He could keep her near. But his conscience balked. Could he allow it? If she chose to stay of her own volition, should he tell her about Ryabkin in order to change her mind?

'I cannot rely on your largesse for ever.' Again came the cynicism she'd demonstrated at the park, the fear of owing.

'Some things are free, Dasha.'

'Like puppies?' Dasha laughed a little, her eyes slanting towards him, coy in their stare. If this were a ballroom, he'd take that stare as flirtation.

Maximus squirmed fiercely and Ruslan moved on to the seat beside her to assist with the puppy, but it was a bad idea no matter how helpfully it began. At the merest touch of his leg against hers the air about them crackled, an unspoken reminder of what passed as friendship between them and what could still pass as friendship once more. No decision had been made. Yet. But it soon would be. He'd forced her hand tonight, but it had not made her any less resistible. He had hoped it would.

She turned into him suddenly, the puppy between them. She wet her lips with a furtive, unconscious flick of her tongue and he felt the beginnings of a potent arousal. Well, perhaps not beginnings, he'd been fighting it all night ever since she'd picked up the puppy. 'And your... friendship? Might I hope that is something freely given as well?' There was the slightest of tremors in her voice, suggesting something beyond friendship. The allusion was irresistible.

He kissed her then, without thought to plots and plans, as if to show her all else that might be freely given. She responded, her mouth answering the invitation of his with parted lips, her tongue eager for a taste of him. Such a reaction pushed against his sense of restraint. Her need for connection fired his need to supply it, to offer her what she sought even against his better judgement. Any kiss posed a threat to his objectivity and yet, at moments like this, a kiss seemed exactly what his job called for, the best way to serve her, to let her know that whatever she chose, whatever she faced, she was not alone. The carriage hit a rut, jostling them and catching Maximus awkwardly between them until he yelped. There was no choice but to give the kiss up.

'Was that another piece of instruction, too?' Dasha's tone was cutting.

'Perhaps,' Ruslan answered cryptically for lack of a better response. He let soothing the puppy claim their attentions for the duration of the drive, a far better option than addressing the questions in Dasha's eyes. Perhaps, if he was any sort of patriot like Captain Varvakis, he would be pushing his advantage right now, using that kiss to establish his ethos and the revelations of tonight to bolster the logic that would send her back to Kuban.

Ruslan scratched Maximus behind the ears. It still amazed him how quickly life could turn. Eighteen months ago, he'd awakened on a normal day in Kuban, prepared to eat breakfast and ride out to hunt with his friends, only to receive word one of those friends had been wounded in the night and taken up on charges of treason. Within days, he'd left everything behind to take that friend to safety. Now, here he was in London, settled into a routine of sorts and a home of his own after a year of uncertainty, only to have life turn once more—this time to leave the new behind in order to return to the old.

The carriage pulled to the kerb and the door opened. Ruslan jumped out and turned back to help Dasha. He scooped up Maximus and settled him in the crook of his arm. The puppy was so very small when considered against his arm. He gave Dasha his other arm and handed the squirmy puppy back to her when her feet were on the ground. 'Why this one, Dasha? The smallest of the lot?'

Her cheeks still bore a flustered flush but her eyes were steady when they held his. 'Because he needed me the most.' She smiled at Ruslan, softly, ruefully. His stomach tightened with want and worry. He saw the world in that smile, the good *and* the bad. That was when he knew his plan for the evening had succeeded. Perhaps too well. She would go back. The *émigré* fantasy was fading even as they mounted the steps to his home.

They spoke little as they went into the house. The footman at the door leapt to attention and led them upstairs, lamp in hand, before leaving them at Dasha's door. 'Thank you for tonight,' Dasha said. 'It *did* help. I will have my decision for you in the morning.'

Ruslan was not under any illusion that she would be up all night wrestling with that decision. Indeed, she'd likely already made it in the carriage ride home. And he could guess what it was. Dasha was, after all, a woman of duty, just as he was a man of duty. How interesting that he knew her so well after so short of an acquaintance.

He would have chosen the same way had he been in her position. But that didn't mean the decision had been an easy one. Neither was it one without risk or sacrifice. Nor did it mean that he would sleep any easier knowing that the die had been cast. In his experience, settling one uncertainty merely created more.

* * *

Dasha stood with her hands clasped before her, trying to portray confidence as she faced Ruslan and Captain Varvakis in the drawing room. Lessons were about to commence for the day, but she wanted to make her announcement first. 'Captain, last night I had two brief but significant recollections.' She glanced over at Maximus sleeping in a basket near the sofa as she recounted them. When she looked at Captain Varvakis, he was beaming, thrilled with her revelations. Ruslan was more difficult to read. He sat in his chair, splendidly turned out, his hair groomed into careful waves, his face giving away nothing.

As it should be, Dasha reminded herself. He would not want to influence her decision regardless of his preferences. Or perhaps she'd misjudged him. Maybe he cared little about her decision except for how it affected him. Dasha cleared her throat. 'I have decided we should make it known to London society and those who might be of use to our cause that the Princess Dasha Tukhachevskenova is among them.'

There would be no more hiding in the house, no more staying out of sight. There would be a certain kind of freedom in being able to go about as she pleased. And yet another kind of freedom died with those words. Whoever she might have created for herself was gone, the opportunity to start entirely fresh lost for ever. From this day forward, she would be Dasha, regardless of whatever truths she might later learn. 'We must redouble our efforts to recover my memories by all means possible.'

Captain Varvakis came forward in a grand gesture of loyalty. He unsheathed his sword and knelt before her, hands gripping the hilt as he bowed his head and kissed the blade. 'My Princess. You have my sword.'

Dasha stiffened as the memory swept her. She recognised this ritual, perhaps further proof that she'd chosen wisely in her decision. It was part of the fealty ceremony officers swore to the Tsar. To her father. Really, she ought to get used to thinking of him that way instead of in the third person. Dasha placed a hand on the Captain's head. 'Rise, my loyal Captain, and stand prepared to serve.' The response came ready to her lips, although she'd never have uttered it; she'd been too young and female. This was a ritual between men, unless there was a Tsarina on the throne instead. But she'd have seen the ceremony, probably from behind a screen or from a secluded balcony in the throne room.

Varvakis stood and her gaze went to Ruslan.

A prince wasn't expected to bow as the Captain had done, but surely some response was required of him? He held her gaze for long heartbeats. For a moment, Dasha feared he would do nothing, or worse, that he would denounce her. At last, Ruslan rose and gave her a nod that might pass as a bow of sorts, his words formal and terse. 'My service is yours to command, Princess. If you would excuse me, there are things I need to look after given this development. Captain Varvakis is more than capable of handling this morning's lesson material on the royal palace.' A lesson she had to master more than ever.

Princess. Not Dasha. She closed her eyes against the words, against the reminder of what her decision had cost. He was hers to command now because of rank and situation. They would not be equals. Perhaps they never had been. When she'd arrived, she'd been the subordinate: needy, confused, requiring his support in all ways. She still needed it, but now it would be commanded instead of given. The days of what he could 'freely' give her had come and gone in the blink of an eye. This handful of days had not nearly been enough.

'Excuse me, Captain.' Without explanation to Varvakis, Dasha followed Ruslan out into the hall, shutting the drawing-room door firmly behind her. What she needed to say to him was not for the Captain's consumption. 'If I didn't know better, I'd think you were angry.' Her words caught him in mid-step. 'Is this *not* the choice you wanted me to make?'

Ruslan turned to face her, his expression expertly veiled. 'My wants have nothing to do with the decision. It is your choice alone.' The cryptic response made her wonder if last night had been designed as a temptation to begin again or as a cautionary lesson against such temptation. She'd assumed it had been meant as a nudge towards the decision to put on the mantle of her authority. Had she been wrong? Had he been subtly arguing for her to stay all along? They were too newly acquainted for her to read anything more into it, yet she felt as if she'd known Ruslan far longer than a scant few days.

'Do you wish I had chosen differently?' She put the question to him boldly, wondering: Did he mean so that she could stay in London, so that the issue of her royalty could be set aside, so that they could explore the spark that crackled between them? But such a conclusion staked far too much on a kiss.

'I wish for you to be safe.' Ruslan's stoic façade did not crack. What a formidable courtier he must have been. In truth, she found that stoicism attractive, a sign of his strength, even as she wished to crack it, perhaps because she'd seen the boyish smile he was capable of on the other side of this coin.

'I hope you have made this decision thoughtfully with an understanding of the dangers you will undoubtedly face.' In these moments, he was acting the part of her advisor, a man who must present the facts without emotional attachment. She could not allow herself to view him as the man who'd kissed her senseless, twice now. Nor could she attach any meaning to those kisses beyond the face value he'd assigned them—instructive units, only. His kisses had to remain in the vacuum of the time in which they'd occurred. A princess knew better than to do otherwise.

'You have laid out the risks admirably and honestly,' Dasha answered with as much formality as she could muster: *assassination, rejection, failure.* If she survived London, there was no guarantee Kuban would accept her. Not everyone would be glad to see a royal survivor. Ruslan had been clear on all accounts. That task she'd set before her was daunting in the extreme.

'There are those who will doubt and test you, looking for any opportunity to discredit your claim. There will be those who won't bother to test you. The kind that will shoot first and wonder later. You will need to be on your guard every time you step outside this town-house door from now on,' he reminded her. 'Are you ready for that?'

Ready not only for the assassins, should they exist, but ready for the doubters who would call her an imposter out of their own desperation. He was talking about the Rebels, the ones who were so sure she'd died that night with her family and retainers, and the ones who had more to gain through her death. They would feel threatened by her return. Was it wrong that she was more worried about them than the possibility of an assassin's bullet?

Ruslan's hand was gentle at her elbow, 'What is it, Dasha?' Her face must have given her away. He pulled her into a small anteroom off the hall. 'Something troubled you just then.'

She shook her head, covering up her hesitation, her own worry. 'The situation is intimidating, at times. It seems my chances for success are slim and yet how can I live with myself if I do any less?' That was only part of it. What she'd grappled with last night hadn't been the risks or dangers of returning. She already understood and accepted those. What she'd grappled with was the ethics of her decision when weighed against her doubts. Even if her doubts of her own identity proved true, could she afford *not* to be the Princess? Kuban needed Princess Dasha in some form. Her conclusion was that even a figurehead would go a long way in averting civil war, if a compromise could be reached between factions.

Ruslan gave her a keen stare. 'Are you sure that's all?'

She looked down, smoothing her skirts, and gave a half-laugh. 'Yes, aren't assassins hiding around every corner enough?'

He let go of her elbow, only partially believing her. She could see the lingering doubt in his eyes. 'If there's ever anything you want to tell me, or want to talk about, you can trust me, Dasha. You *can* tell me. In fact, you *should* tell me. I can best protect you if I know everything.' *Her protector.* Not even the dramatic flair of Captain Varvakis's declaration of fealty equalled the quiet force of Ruslan's words and they set her stomach fluttering. This lean, well-honed steel rapier of a man would be a formidable barrier between her and those who might wish her ill. She'd be safe in London, she had no doubt. But was if fair to ask it of him? To expect him to protect a woman who might not be who he thought she was?

Would you protect me even if I wasn't the

Princess, even if I were only playing at it for a good cause?

Standing here in the little ivory-papered anteroom, she wanted to blurt out her last great secret, wanted to lay that secret on his shoulders if only to have someone listen to her. Captain Varvakis had merely shrugged off her worries, explaining them away as imaginings of an overstressed mind.

She didn't dare take the risk. What if her admission appalled Ruslan? What if he turned away from her? Rescinded his help? She didn't want to find out. She needed him. He'd become her bulwark in a very short time. She suspected it was his gift. He was many peoples' bulwark. He inspired that sort of confidence. She also suspected she wasn't the first woman to be so 'inspired' by him. But she might be the first who *had* to resist. Besides, she would leave London at some point. There could be nothing more than what existed between them right now. He could be her advisor, her protector. That was all a queen could have.

He touched her again, a gentle brush of his fingers at her sleeve. 'All right then, I need to be off rallying your troops and you have lessons to see to. Tonight, be ready to go out. Madame Delphine will bring the first of your dinner gowns this afternoon. You will need it.'

Dasha gave a little laugh, caught off guard with the shift in conversation. They'd gone from revolutions to dinner parties. 'We have no invitations.'

'We will.' Ruslan pulled out a pocket watch and flipped open the plain gold face. 'By five o'clock tonight, we'll have three.'

Dasha smiled, playing along gamely. 'And if you're wrong?'

Ruslan gave her a boyish grin. 'Then I owe you an ice at Gunter's before it gets too cold out to appreciate one.' He snapped his watch shut with purpose. 'Now, I really must be off or you will win by default.'

Chapter Nine

She did win by default. At the stroke of five o'clock, there were not three, but four invitations to various dinner parties being given throughout the fashionable city. Ruslan sifted through the offerings on the salver, pleased with the result, even if Dasha had the good-humoured indecency to gloat over her victory.

'However did you manage?' Dasha looked over each invitation with him in the hall, Maximus in her arms squirming while she petted him. Both of them recognised the invitations were nothing short of a social coup considering it was well past the Season and anyone who was anyone had decamped from the city in mid-August for their grouse moors. Still, the running of an empire didn't stop simply because Parliament was out of session. There *were* important people about town if one knew where to look. Ruslan knew where to look.

'When Nikolay started taking an interest in Klara, I made it my business to know every notable in the Foreign Office,' Ruslan explained modestly. He'd done more than know them in a nominal sense. He knew their connections, their situations and their politics. He knew which diplomats were unashamedly ethnocentric in their outlooks on empire building and which ones had a care for the natives already in place. He knew which ones had a true thirst for the work of international relations and which ones persevered for the sake of lining their own pockets.

'Well.' Dasha set Maximus down on the floor. 'Which one shall we choose?'

'This one.' Ruslan extracted the third invitation from the pile. 'Lord Bradford-Piles. I have it on excellent authority that Canning, the Foreign Secretary, is to be on hand. He is exactly who we want to meet. He has liberal politics that should work to our advantage. I'll explain them to you in the carriage. Dinner is at eight. You'll have time to dress and go over your information one last time with the Captain.' He paused in his list of orders, catching the hesitation in Dasha's gaze as it drifted away. Ruslan forced himself to slow down. 'Tonight is important, Dasha. Canning can give us funds and support to march back to Kuban.'

Dasha's eyes flashed. 'I know.' Her tone was sharp. He saw the flash of hesitation in her eyes reminiscent of the afternoon. Something was bothering her, something besides returning to Kuban. 'That's why I'm worried. What if I'm not ready?' She reached for the stack again. 'Perhaps we should pick someone less important and start small?'

Ruslan covered her hand with his. 'You're ready.' Besides, there was no time. It was sheer luck Canning was here at all. The Great Powers were meeting in Vienna. Canning was supposed to be there but had sent Wellington at the last. Still, as good as the opportunity was, Ruslan would not have pushed it if Dasha wasn't ready. She was prepared, in many tiny ways. He'd feared they'd have to teach her everything, how to walk, how to talk, but she knew all that instinctively as if it were second nature to her. All he and the Captain had to teach her were the details; the history of her family, the layout of the palace, the politics of Kuban and key players who represented each side. Yes, there was more to learn, but she knew enough. She was ready enough. 'If we don't go now, when, Dasha? It's too easy to put it off. If it's any consolation, I doubt Canning will drill you with minutiae. He doesn't know much about Kuban. He'll be more interested in your escape and that you're here. He'll want to know what your plans are.'

'And my memory? Are we to tell him about that?' she asked the question tentatively.

'I don't think it will come up.' Ruslan would make sure it didn't. There could be no doubt that she was capable of leading. This was the one sticking point in the plan. If anyone learned of her memory loss, now that she was declaring herself publicly, there would be scandal and worse. She could end up branded as delusional and, if the Union of Salvation learned of it, she might find herself tucked away in an asylum for being crazy—a perfect solution for the problem of an inconvenient survivor. 'Hopefully, by the time anything is decided, your memories will have returned in full force. We've already made quite a bit of progress.' He would not burden her with his concerns. She had enough to worry about. He could protect her from assassins, but asylums might be trickier. She had no family to speak for her if it came to that. Well, he'd cross that bridge if they ever came to it. In the meanwhile, he would do his best to see that they didn't.

Ruslan gave her an exaggerated bow, trying

for levity as he sent her upstairs. 'My dear, tonight, I introduce you to society. You have much to do.' As did he. There were coachmen and outriders to brief for tonight's excursion across Mayfair to Lord Bradford-Piles's residence. Ruslan didn't expect trouble tonight. It was too soon. Trouble would start tomorrow once news of her presence made the rounds. But it was always best to be prepared. His eyes followed her up the gentle curve of the staircase, stopping her halfway. 'Might I suggest the gunmetal grey for tonight?' Sombre, but elegant and expensive, it would show well next to Canning's heiress wife. He, too, would take care to look his best. Tonight, he had to go looking like a king, or, in his case, like a prince.

At half past seven, Dasha stood at the top of the stairs, fingering the necklace Ruslan had sent up a half-hour earlier, a delicate silver heart on a thin chain that lay just at the base of her neck. Below her, Ruslan waited, smiling up at her expectantly as she made her descent, head up, eyes forward, her skirts discreetly in one hand. It was the way a princess walked, all confidence and delicate purpose.

If she was a princess, then he was undoubtedly a prince. The lean athleticism of his physique was ideal for the current fashions. Tonight, he wore well-tailored evening clothes in the darkest, deepest of blacks cut in the latest style: a single-breasted tailcoat worn open to show off the silk dove-grey waistcoat embroidered in turquoise swirls and the crisp white shirt beneath, topped off with a black stock. His breeches finished at the knee, giving way to white stockings and black pumps that showed off a set of well-shaped calves to muscled perfection. He would take her breath away if she could afford the luxury of such a thing. He would take more than her breath, truth be told. He was handsome, commanding, well-mannered, forceful and yet respectful of others' perspectives. He was all things a prince should be; all things a *man* should be, title or not.

She reached the bottom of the steps and he took her gloved hand in his, raising it to his lips. 'Do I pass?' she asked, her free hand going idly once more to the necklace at her throat.

'Absolutely. You look stunning. Canning will be taken with you on looks alone,' Ruslan assured her, tucking her hand through his arm. 'Our carriage awaits.' As did her instruction on Canning's politics. The Foreign Secretary was a Tory, but his beliefs led him to steer clear of conservative attempts throughout Europe to quell the more liberal movements towards nationalism. 'I think that makes him conducive to Kuban's plight,' Ruslan explained. 'The new Kuban will be a place that seeks to shake off the old ideals of the past. He will like that.'

But Dasha wasn't thinking about constitutional monarchies. She was thinking: this is what it would be like if Ruslan was hers, always. There would be countless evenings like this one where they'd discuss politics beforehand and debrief their opinions afterwards. The thought of them driving out together in Kuban, on their way to meet with other nobles, or inviting people to the palace, standing together at the grand staircase to greet guests, was sudden and forbidden. Perhaps the latter accounted for the suddenness of the former, an ambush of a thought if ever there was one. She had no business thinking of him like that simply because he was being kind to her in a time of tragedy.

Oh, but he'd been more than kind. He'd kissed her on two occasions. She did not have to possess a large amount of worldly experience to know a man did not kiss like that simply to be kind. He'd been affected, too, and now it was up to them both to put sensibility before sense. There was a nation at stake, to say nothing of her own future—a future that she'd already begun to direct. By choosing her declaration tonight, she'd cut herself off from certain paths and risks, to embrace other paths, *other* risks. Her attraction to Ruslan was one of those risks.

'I see the necklace met with approval.' Ruslan had finished his dissertation on Canning's politics.

'Yes.' She smiled, her fingers rubbing the silver heart. 'You were kind to send it to me.' He'd not come himself, a gesture that would have been far too intimate, far too like a husband visiting a wife before an evening out. Perhaps he'd been alert to that connotation as well and had avoided it on purpose.

The carriage rolled to a halt and Ruslan peered out the window. 'We are here. Allow me to assist you.' He was out of the carriage first, looking around before handing her out. It was more than the thoughtfulness of a gentleman, she realised. It was the protection of a bodyguard, a role he would quietly play in the guise of her escort as long as she remained in London.

'Surely there will be no trouble tonight,' Dasha said, as much to reassure herself as him. The idea that there *could* be trouble recast her perspective on the walk to the Bradford-Pileses' front door. The distance between the kerb and the door seemed longer. She shook her head.

She would not give in to paranoia. If she did, she'd end up hiding away, afraid to walk past the windows.

At the top of the steps, she drew a deep breath as they were shown in and announced. 'His Highness, Prince Ruslan Pisarev, and Her Royal Highness, Princess Dasha Tukhachevskenova of Kuban.' A shiver ran through her. Dasha let herself revel in the thrill, the luxury of the announcement, as the room curtsied and bowed to her, to *them*. But there was no mistaking how very real everything had just become. She'd officially put on the mantle of Kuban just as certainly as if she'd put on the crown itself. There could be no going back, no declining the identity she'd just assumed.

Ruslan's hand was warm and encouraging at her back, guiding her directly to where their host and the Foreign Secretary stood at the fireplace mantel. 'Allow me to present Princess Tukhachevskenova.'

So began her audition for acceptance. The polite scrutiny of her first dinner among the other Russians of rank in town seemed positively tame compared to the scrutiny she now received. It came in the polite form of questions, of course. No one gave the least outward appearance of being hostile or unaccepting. Why would they?

They had no cause for not believing she was who she said she was. It crossed her mind during the beef course, when she'd told the story of her escape twice, how easy it would be to lie to them, to put a well-trained imposter in their midst. It was incredibly cynical of her to think such a thing. She reached for her wine glass and sipped.

'What do you plan to do in London, Your Highness?' The question of plans came at last from Lord Bradford-Piles.

'I mean to wait until it is safe to return to Kuban and then help my country to modernise in their practices and laws. It is time for Kuban to join the nineteenth century.'

'A very noble endeavour, Your Highness.' Lord Bradford-Piles inclined his head, but Dasha detected a slightly patronising tone. She opened her mouth to address it and felt the press of Ruslan's foot beneath the table. Now was not the time to challenge their host.

Lady Bradford-Piles rose, signalling for the ladies to join her. Dasha rose with them, although reluctantly. She'd done her part, but the play was not over. The men would discuss her when she left. The rest of the evening's outcome was up to Ruslan. He caught her eye and gave her an encouraging nod, another glimmer of what life could be like with him, the two of them sharing the delicate balance of duty. She only needed to be patient. She had every confidence Ruslan would tell her what transpired over port once they were in the carriage on their way home. These were dangerous domestic imaginings, indeed, when they had her voluntarily putting her fate in the hands of another.

That did not make them untrue. With an uncanny accuracy that paralleled her fantasy, Ruslan unburdened himself in the carriage as soon as it left the kerb. 'You did well tonight. Canning was impressed, as were the others, and where Canning leads, people will follow. He's a man who will make Prime Minister one day soon, unless I miss my guess.'

Then Canning would be Prime Minister, Dasha thought. She didn't think Ruslan ever missed his mark. He'd been right about the invitations today and he'd been right about tonight. She had been ready enough and Canning had not pressed her about the issues she'd worried about most. On a darker note, if Ruslan had been right about tonight, perhaps he was also right about other things like assassins and dangers she'd rather not think about.

'Will they help us?' she asked, eager to turn her mind to brighter topics.

'They may. They'll want something in return, though,' Ruslan warned. 'It would be prudent to think about what Kuban is prepared to offer Britain.' Her thoughts exactly.

'We make a good team, you and I.' Dasha smiled in the dark of the carriage.

'*You* make a good princess,' Ruslan clarified. Dasha's smile faded. She'd been caught up in the euphoria of success and hoped for more, some acknowledgement of their togetherness, but that was not to be. She might be foolish in that regard, but Ruslan was not. Unfortunately. For better or for worse, she was the Princess now. They would both do well to remember it.

That night she had the dream, only different. The sequence started earlier than it usually did. She was in a room, there were voices, two of them, hushed and hurried in argument…

'We will not survive the window. The drop is too far. If it doesn't kill us, we'll surely break something and be unable to walk.'

'The hall is already on fire.' It was the other voice, a young woman's voice, full of fear.

'If we can make the servants' stairs unde-tected, we have a clear path out of the house. The smoke will be our shield and we have our swords.'

'We are not soldiers. We've only ever used them in play.' The room was dark, she wished she could see the other person. In the dream she gripped the other woman's wrist. 'Come, I will go first.' She gave an experimental swipe with the sword, the blade heavy in her hand. It was true, they were not soldiers. Vasili and Grigori had taught them basics for fun one summer when the boys were bored. She remembered it now, how to parry a stroke, how to block and how to strike. If the strength of her arm held, she might make an adequate defence if it came to that.

She eased open the door, then shut it quickly again against smoke and the sound of gunfire. There was the hysterical scream of a woman, another shot and then eerie silence broken by shouts. They had to go now or it would be too late.

They stepped out into the hall. Her sword was raised in readiness, careful to use her body to block the woman behind her, to protect her. They moved fast through the smoke. They were nearly to the hall door when the cry went up.

'There they are!'

She turned and stood her ground, aware that flames guarded her back. There was nowhere to go but forward, but through whoever stood in their way. She raised her blade. *Please, Lord, let me be enough*, she prayed. She would win through or die.

Chapter Ten

~~~~~~~~~

The scream woke Ruslan. Dasha! A year of
dealing with Illarion's nightmares propelled him
out of bed without thought, his hand automatically reaching for the banyan at the end of his
bed as he sprinted down the hall. He threw open
the door to her room. Dasha sat rigidly upright
in bed, her hands groping frantically for something unseen in the sheets, Maximus yipping
frantically.

'Dasha, wake up!' Ruslan raced to the bed,
grabbing her hands. They were ice-cold and her
face was chalk. He'd never seen such thorough
terror. Her eyes flew open, for a moment unseeing. Then she recognised him and collapsed
against him with a sob. He took her in, rocking
her like a small child as he murmured reassurances. 'I'm here, it's all right now.' He patted the
bed, signalling for the frantic, loyal Maximus

who wanted to comfort his mistress. The little puppy leapt up and snuggled against her.

'Was it the dream again?' he asked softly when her breathing had steadied, her arm curled around the pup.

She nodded and drew back to face him. Her colour had returned and she was calmer, but the struggle of the dream had left its mark in the tousled hair and haunted eyes that held his. 'There was more this time. It was like the dream started in an earlier place, a previous scene. I was in a room with another woman. We were debating the window or the door.'

Ruslan listened intently to her recollect the dream, holding his questions, knowing how important it was for her to recount it before the dream faded, before the dream could become confused. 'This time, I called the brothers by name and this time there was an actual fight. I raised my sword and swung,' Dasha sighed. 'Then I woke up. I wish I could have stayed in the dream longer, as awful as it was, it might have shown me more.' She looked down and paused, her hair falling forward over her face.

Instinctively, Ruslan reached out to gently push it back, tucking it over one ear. 'What is it?' he prompted. She wanted to say more. He sensed it.

'Nothing, just foolishness, old wives' tales.'

Dasha shrugged and he urged her to go on. 'Nothing is too foolish. Tell me, whatever it is.'

'Some people say that we wake up from dreams only when we die in them.' She looked up at him at last, a hint of challenge in her eyes, challenge to admit that her conjecture was indeed childish.

'That may be,' Ruslan said neutrally. 'Do you think *you* die in your dream? That you are killed by your opponent?' That would be interesting, especially since they'd all been operating under the premise that this particular dream wasn't so much a dream as it was a recollection of real events. 'Perhaps it is just that you are knocked unconscious. That battle may be where you lost your memory. Perhaps you hit your head? The Captain did say you were unconscious when he reached you and that he saw you fighting with someone. He saw you go down.'

Dasha let out a breath, nodding in agreement. Her hands clenched inside his, hopeful. 'Do you think that's because I am remembering more?'

It was hard to deny the eagerness in her eyes, but Ruslan would not lie to her, not even for her peace of mind. 'Perhaps, but it could also be because you've learned their names.' In other words, the memory addition might not be organic, but merely a product of their long hours of study and learning. He probed for a little more, something unique, something untaught. 'The other woman in the room? Do you have any idea who she might have been?' Ruslan asked.

Dasha shook her head. 'No, the room is dark in the dream. The other woman sounds young and she feels young when I grab her wrist, as though she might be my age.' Dasha pondered the thought, her gaze retreating inward for a moment. 'Her wrist, Ruslan. It felt like it had a scar on it. Feel this.' She pushed up the sleeve of her nightrail and held out her own wrist for him to touch. Did she not understand how much torture that was? To touch her?

He took her wrist, feeling the strong pulse beneath the skin, the delicate bones of her arm as his thumb skimmed the skin. His thumb paused over the slight roughness of a scar. He looked down, searching for the tiny white line. 'You've a scar here.' He smiled.

'So did the woman in the room. When I grabbed her wrist, I could feel it. I wonder if that means anything?'

'I don't know.' Ruslan started to rise from the bed. It was time to distance himself from her. She was a beautiful temptation all fresh come from sleep and he was not in a resisting mood.

He was in a taking mood, a protecting mood. He wanted to wrap her in his arms as if his embrace could hold her nightmare at bay.

She reached for his hand, pulling him back down. 'Don't go.' The terror was back in her eyes. 'Stay? Just a little longer?'

It was his cue to leave immediately, but instead he found himself sitting against the headboard of her bed, pillows behind him and Dasha tucked against his side, her head lodged in the notch of his shoulder, her body curved against him, feminine and warm. He should have locked the door. This was a damned compromising situation should anyone walk in, but it was too late now to get up. Too late to leave. Too late for a lot of things except to brazen it all out.

Ruslan smiled to himself, looking down at Dasha and the pup. Brazening it out made it sound like a hardship to endure. It was hardly that. This was right where he wanted to be, propriety be damned. He was here not only because he stood ready to serve her and to protect her, but simply because he *wanted* to be. He rather thought he'd want to be beside her no matter *who* she was and that led to some very complicated feelings indeed. Feelings, Stepan would argue, which were mixed up with the role he was cast in as bodyguard and expert advisor. How could he possibly separate the two spheres and accurately analyse those feelings with any honesty? He had to agree with that hypothesis. How could he feel such a thing, so deeply for another, in such a short period of time? He was a logical man, a calculating man, who understood every situation carried with it multiple nuances. The idea of falling in love at first sight simply didn't resonate with him. It was not a possibility, no matter how much Illarion the poet disagreed with him.

There was a science to attraction just as there was a science for nearly everything in this world, a systemic understanding of how things worked. Attraction that lasted was based on similarities of personal experience and attributes. Physical attraction was instant and immediate, but it did not always last.

This visceral reaction to her touch, the way her gaze sent a bolt of white-hot desire through him whenever she looked his way, it *would* pass. Right now, she was new and exciting, she'd brought purpose to his days and she needed him. History proved a beautiful woman in distress was a potent aphrodisiac for many a man. It had also been the downfall of many a man. Women were not as helpless as men liked to believe. History had proven that, too. Even without history, Dasha had proven that. Dasha was strong. He'd seen her master that room tonight with confidence. Perhaps it was that strength that made her so hard to resist. The support of another was the very last thing she'd ever admit to. Her very request showed just how much she'd needed it. Dasha sighed in her sleep and stirred against him, Maximus in her arms. It was going to be a long night. If he was to survive it, he needed to redirect his thoughts. There were certainly plenty of them that deserved his attention, starting with, who was the woman in the room in Dasha's dream? That was the very first thing he'd discuss with Varvakis in the morning. Ruslan yawned, struggling to keep his eyes open. He would have to go soon. Just a few minutes more…

The morning did not go as planned. What had started out as a few more minutes lying beside Dasha had turned into a night. Ruslan had awakened with alarm in her bed, the sun already up, Dasha tucked against him as assuredly as a lover. Anyone could have walked in and seen them. But no one had. Still, no need to tempt fate any further and he began the effort of artful extraction. Once he'd extricated himself carefully without waking her, it turned out sleeping in Dasha's bed was the least of his concerns. Further concern lay waiting for him at breakfast in the form of his customary morning newspapers and a positively euphoric Captain Varvakis. 'She's done it. She's claimed London's attention, soon she will be able to advocate for the right to the throne.'

Varvakis held up the first of the newspapers, crowing with pleasure. Ruslan smiled politely, finding Varvakis's excitement annoying, although he was hard pressed to say why. Varvakis was on his side, their side. Varvakis wanted what he wanted. Perhaps that's what gave Ruslan pause over coffee. Varvakis had done his duty in rescuing Dasha but he would expect to be rewarded. What would that reward be? Power and position in the new government? Or something more personal?

Ruslan scanned the headlines that had accumulated at his plate. 'Lost Princess arrives in Mayfair', 'Royal Princess escapes family massacre', 'Princess survives revolution'. He grimaced. The papers certainly hadn't hesitated, as he'd known they wouldn't. There was little eye-catching news this time of year. He just hadn't expected to feel so *exposed*. He'd been mentioned in society columns before. All four of the Kubanian Princes had been a subject of interest throughout the Season, with Illarion capturing most of the headlines, and he'd certainly been part of gossip's intrigues in the Kubanian court, but this was different. Anyone reading the stories would know where to find Dasha.

'But so will her supporters,' Varvakis offered helpfully when Ruslan voiced his concerns. Ruslan merely raised an eyebrow at that and set aside the papers. He'd comb through them in private later today.

'The Princess dreamed again last night.' Ruslan chose his words carefully, seeking detachment. 'She reported that the dream was longer and that she knew the brothers' names. The last can be credited to your lessons, I think.' He wanted Varvakis to know he understood the power of those lessons. As necessary as they were if they were to help her remember, they also risked destroying any organic memory she had left. How long would the dream remain unpolluted from what she was learning? Ruslan did not think it would be much longer. Already from her lessons, she'd acquired family names, descriptions of the palace and the grand staircase where she'd fallen. She'd adeptly used that information last night at dinner. She'd not just acquired those facts, she'd integrated them into her psyche. It was no wonder the dream seemed richer and fuller this time.

'I am glad. We need her to remember as much as possible.' Varvakis reached for a piece of toast off the rack. Ruslan had to remind himself Varvakis was not the enemy here.

Ruslan watched Varvakis carefully. 'I am hoping we can help her remember more, but it's up to you. You were the one who found her first. Those moments are critical, I think. There is a woman in her dream, perhaps a woman she was protecting? Was there anyone there on the landing with her?'

Varvakis's grey eyes were soldier-steady, his voice grim. 'None other than the man she ran through with her blade. She couldn't get her sword out of him and the man might have finished her off in his death throes. For a moment, I thought he had, but he'd merely fallen on her.'

Dasha had killed a man.

The cold import of that rippled through him. Ruslan played with the handle of his coffee mug, not betraying the layers of emotion this news evoked. 'Why have you not said anything before?' Varvakis hadn't lied, Ruslan would not accuse him of that. Lying was a serious offence to a man's honour. But Varvakis had told him quite a sanitised version of the story, which had boiled down to Varvakis fighting his way up the stairs, the Princess falling at the last. The end. There'd been no mention of Dasha killing her attacker.

'The Princess has had enough trauma. I did not want to remind her of that final tragedy and it hardly seemed necessary.' Varvakis's eyes were hard flints, the gaze of a man who'd seen many campaigns. 'I have killed men in the line of service, Your Highness. I do not remember them all, but I still remember my first: a blonde boy my own age, who had the misfortune of being less adept with a blade than myself. I ran him through and his eyes went wide—brown eyes with long black lashes—if you take my meaning?'

Ruslan nodded. He did. He knew very well the personal nature of taking a life even when it was in self-defence and there was no choice. His work in the underground was not without its risks.

'If the Princess has forgotten such an ordeal, perhaps it's best to let it remain so,' Varvakis concluded staunchly. It was difficult to argue with that logic out of personal concern for Dasha, yet the logic in him wanted to contend that knowledge of any sort was valuable in this situation.

'What of the woman she claims was there? Any idea who would have been with her?' Ruslan returned to his original question.

'I could not see anyone. Not that it matters beyond the luxury of knowing and being able to solve the Princess's mystery dream for her. The reality, however, is that the Princess is here and whoever may have been with her, *if* there was anyone at all, was not fortunate enough to escape the flames.' Varvakis answered with a tone of finality that said he did not want to be pressed further on the subject. Ruslan let it go. He and Varvakis needed to work together. Antagonising him would not help that. But Ruslan's gut told him this was a subject to revisit tactfully another time. Between Varvakis's decision to omit certain details and Dasha's dream, there was more here beneath the surface.

A rustle of skirts at the door had him and Varvakis rising from the table. Dasha swept in, a bright smile on her face that said she'd rested well. Ruslan would like to take credit for that. 'Good morning, gentlemen. Are we ready to conquer the world?'

Chapter Eleven

They were not conquering the world, but they were conquering London, one heady dinner party at a time. The days turned into weeks, those weeks passing in a whirlwind of events as dinners multiplied into invitations to political teas, and teas into shopping expeditions, and expeditions into a drawing room full of influential women who came to return Dasha's calls as September wore on. If only Ruslan could be conquered so easily.

Not that she wanted to conquer the handsome prince. By day, he was her advisor. By night he was her escort and always Kuban was between them, the one thing binding them together and the one thing keeping them apart. There was far too much for her to deal with to think about engaging in a flirtation and he'd made it clear that, as her advisor, he would not muddy the waters of their association with a less-than-neutral relationship. But that didn't stop a shiver of awareness from skittering up her spine when he touched her, his hand light at her back guiding her through drawing rooms, or from creating the fantasy that played through her head each night. It *was* intoxicating to go out with him every evening, to watch women's heads turned when he entered a room, to see men greet him with respect, all of which was passed on to her by extension. Even more intoxicating were the moments when he looked at her and she thought for the briefest of instances that he played with the fantasy, too. Then, the moment would pass and he would be Ruslan, her handsome advisor, once more.

It was a potent fantasy, to be sure; a fantasy where she stayed in London at his side and they attended parties in glittering mansions and gave parties of their own in Ruslan's new town house, perhaps lobbying aid for Kuban. They would be the most dashing couple in town. As the days went by, it was easier to lose herself in the fantasy. There'd been no news from Kuban summoning her home. The threat of a rogue assassination had not materialised.

Ruslan seemed in no hurry to see her go. Quite the opposite—he seemed glad to have her under his roof. When she didn't need to spend her afternoons learning about Kuban's politics or shopping with the ladies, Ruslan devoted himself to her with singular attention, taking her about London to see all the sights: the Tower and the Thames, driving her through Hyde Park. He even made good on his lost wager and took her to Gunter's where she had the most decadent chocolate ice. They picnicked at Greenwich to watch the boats and visited Klara's father's estate in Richmond with Maximus. When autumn hit in full force and afternoons required them to stay indoors, he took her to the museums, the opera and the theatre. She'd never lived like this, memories or not. She'd never had the singular attentions of such a man, even if he didn't mean anything beyond friendship by those attentions.

This is what you've given up, her conscience would whisper. *This could have all been yours, but you chose to go back.*

Maybe she wouldn't have to go back. Not yet, at least. Maybe she'd have the winter. If word didn't come soon, there would be no choice but to stay through March until travel became possible again. That reality didn't disappoint her. It would be more time with Ruslan, more time to learn about him.

He might aspire to a neutral friendship, but

that didn't mean she wasn't coming to know him. She knew blue was his favourite colour, that he took his tea with milk although he preferred coffee, that his favourite desserts were blinis topped with berries.

She knew important things about him, too— that he was solicitous and kind, although he'd deny the latter. One only had to watch him with Maximus to know better. He was loyal, unto a fault. Nikolay and Stepan could call upon him any time. And he was private. He listened to others, but seldom spoke of himself. Even when prompted to do so, he was reserved in what he shared. She still knew very little about his past, though, other than his escape story, that he'd been a companion of her brothers and that he'd been responsible for planning all sorts of royal outings.

For some, such facts would be enough. Not for Dasha. They only made her hungry for more. Who was his family? Did they miss him? Were they waiting for him in Kuban? Was there a special woman waiting for him, someone who had captured his affections? She didn't like to think of the last, or that it might possibly be the reason for his staunch detachment. She tried, instead, to enjoy each moment, each outing, each evening.

There were only two blots on her happiness,

the first being her lack of memories. They had still not returned beyond brief snatches like the one she'd had in Nikolay's stable and at the pianoforte. They were helpful, but not illuminating in determining who she was. The second was the guilt. As long as her memories remained unattainable, her doubt over her identity remained intact.

What if she wasn't the Princess?

She ought to tell Ruslan her doubts, if for no other reason than to seek his reassurance. But she couldn't burden him, not after all he'd done. The point of no return had been reached, at any rate. It was too late to change her decision. To do so would be to make a laughing stock of Ruslan and all who supported her. In turn, those supporters would ostracise her from society in order to save face. No, that was one burden she had to carry alone and one that would hopefully resolve itself in time. Besides, Varvakis was *sure* of who he'd rescued. Her doubts were her own. So she forged on: Dasha Tukhachevskenova, London's latest fascination, the lost Princess of Kuban.

Dasha was an overnight sensation, her transformation into one of society's ladies a marvel. She could easily be one of them, Ruslan mused at the gentlemanly distance of the drawing-room door frame, watching as she charmed the English ladies. It was an astonishing enough feat to watch a debutante 'take' in society, a girl who'd been trained from the schoolroom to master the *ton* with all of its idiosyncrasies and hypocrisies. To watch a woman succeed here, who had never trained for London, who had spent her adolescent years in the severe seclusion of the Kubanian Tsar's palace, expecting to be out of the public eye until her marriage was announced, was nothing short of miraculous. Ruslan knew first-hand that a Kubanian princess, while well-educated so as not to embarrass her husband with her lack of literacy and understanding, was not trained to rule; yet there was no denying Dasha was capable of it. Neither was there any denying how the sight of her in his drawing room affected him.

Ruslan gave his afternoon brandy a negligent swirl, allowing himself to try on the nascent fantasy of Dasha in his drawing room with its cool pale blue wallpaper and excess of white wainscoting, hosting teas and at-homes regularly, surrounded by London's finest, his Wedgwood-blue teacups balanced on their laps. He'd not yet used the china that had been selected for the house. Dasha's tea parties were their first venture out of their carefully packed boxes. In fact, a lot of things had found their way out of boxes and cupboards: fresh linens for the dining-room table, crystal goblets, decanters for the library, books he hadn't got around to removing from crates, and an assortment of knick-knacks: porcelain horse-head bookends, a gold scale of weights and measures and more. Perhaps without intending to, Dasha had made his house a home.

Today, dressed in a gown of blue lavender trimmed with delicate grey lace, her hair done up, the thin silver chain with its heart at her neck, Wedgwood teacup in hand, she looked the perfect hostess, the Queen of her domain, kind-eyed but alert, her gaze seeing to every guest's comfort, even as she applied herself to conversation with those closest to her. Outwardly, she was calm and serene. One would never guess she wasn't English until she spoke or that she spent her nights plagued by nightmares and her days relearning all that had been taken from her the night Rebels had dragged her family out and killed them. But Ruslan knew better. That knowledge puffed him up with private pride. He knew the other side of her. He saw her with tousled hair, with rumpled bedclothes, with fear in her eyes. It made her bravery so much more impressive.

She caught his eye and motioned that he

should join her. He obliged with a smile. It was time to play his part, that of the doting host and fellow countryman. In truth, he didn't mind. They made a good team as they charmed their way through London, galvanising support against the time when they'd need all their allies if they meant to go to Kuban with a show of force.

Dasha reached up to him, catching his hand. 'I was just telling Lady Bradford-Piles about Maslenitsa. She doesn't believe me that we burn Maslenitsa and make huge bonfires.'

Ruslan chuckled. 'We do indeed. We eat the most delicious blini, too. Thin *crêpe*-like pancakes topped with jams and berries,' he explained.

'We should host a Kubanian Tea and treat all the ladies to our national delicacies.' Dasha laughed up at him, inspiration lighting her green eyes.

We. Things they should do.

'Yes, if that is what you wish.' Ruslan complied easily. For a few moments the fantasy in his head had become real, filled with images of he and Dasha hosting events together, in his home, like Nikolay and Klara. Like a couple. His home would become *their* home, together. His and hers. His teacups would never linger in their boxes. All the things he'd ordered to make this house feel like a place where he could belong would get used. He'd been wrong to think having things was all he needed to master the sense of home. *People* made the home. His house was already changed because she was in it and he was already regretting the time when she left it. The place would feel empty. He was starting to fear *he* would feel empty. He'd enjoyed squiring her about town, showing her the sights, talking with her. She was intelligent and insightful. It was something he could easily get used to. And he mustn't. Damn. His hard-won detachment was slipping. Again.

'Ladies, enjoy your tea.' Ruslan bowed and relinquished Dasha's hand. 'If you would excuse me, I have appointments to keep this afternoon at the club.'

The appointment was with Stepan and Alexei Grigoriev, Klara's ambassador father. Alexei had written this morning saying it was important, he had news from Kuban that would help them move forward in rallying support for the return of the Kubanian Queen. Their plan, if successful, would take Dasha away from London so far. Away from him. He was not a man used to courting failure, but in this case, a piece of him hungered for it. What if they tried for the throne and failed? What if the news from Kuban encouraged them to stay put in London? Such thoughts shouldn't make his heart glad, but it would be a lie to say they didn't make him hope, just a little. The advisor in him was giving way to the man.

'Well, what's the news?' Ruslan took a chair at the table Stepan had commandeered in a quiet corner of White's. He was the last to join. Varvakis and Grigoriev were already there. Stepan slid a glass towards him and a decanter of *samogon*.

'Ah, the good stuff, I see. Are we celebrating?' Ruslan said with a cheer he didn't exactly feel. He poured a healthy glass. Perhaps Stepan had known he was going to need it.

'Order is being restored. The Moderates are slowly gaining the upper hand as people see reason,' Grigoriev reported with a nod towards Varvakis. 'Just as your faction hoped. Good news.'

Ruslan looked down at his glass. Good news indeed, but not the news he was hoping for. He let the conversation continue around him, his attention perking at the only question that mattered now.

'When do we go back? Surely we should set a date on the calendar and begin planning.' This was from Stepan, who slid him a sideways look.

'It will take some work to return her. She can't go slinking back into Kuban.'

No, she'd have to go looking like a queen, with a show of pride, a show of force, all the things he'd worked so tirelessly to secure for her. They would suddenly be needed. And she would be exposed in ways she was not exposed here. Here, he could always be beside her. He could see Dasha in his mind, her head held high at the front of a column as she rode into Kuban, regal and proud, and an easy target. One shot would end it all. She'd been lucky in London. She might not be so lucky in Kuban. Unless he was there to protect her, to make the subtle arrangements he'd made here to keep her safe each time she went out.

You could go with her.

It certainly wasn't the first time he'd thought about it. He'd been thinking about it since she'd first come through his door. But now, he was being forced to contemplate that choice concretely. It was no longer a hypothetical argument to have with himself in the middle of the night.

Stepan rose from the table. 'Ruslan, might I have a word in private? Gentlemen, please continue the conversation, help yourself to more *samogon*.'

'You don't seem pleased.' Stepan directed him

to an empty corner where they were well away from the table.

'Why should I be? The further this plan goes, the more danger the Princess is exposed to,' Ruslan snapped. 'We've been lucky so far, but the danger increases exponentially the closer we physically get to Kuban. Every step away from London reduces our chances of keeping her safe.' All the barriers, the mountain ranges, the rivers, the seas, would slowly be stripped away, making it easier for anyone to get to her.

Stepan scoffed. 'Then design a secure route for her. You're an expert at that. Use our route. It proved safe enough.' He paused. 'You used to be better at hiding your emotions. This is not about her safety, not entirely.' Ruslan said nothing.

Stepan swore. 'Damn it, Ruslan. Not you, too? Don't think I don't know the signs. I've been through this with Illarion and Nikolay. You are falling for her.' Stepan pushed a hand through his hair in frustration. 'I thought you'd at least show some sense. You can't have her. She's the Princess, for crying out loud. She's going home to lead her country.' What Stepan meant was that she would have to eventually make a dynastic marriage. She could hardly marry a prince who'd chosen exile.

'I'm not falling for her,' Ruslan denied. But

he was falling for something—for the fantasy of her, for the fantasy of the life they might have had in London among his friends, comfortable and safe from palace intrigue and assassins in the night, for nights spent with her in his arms, for carriage rides that ended in stolen kisses and walks in the park. For long talks and sharing ideas, debating those ideas when the need arose. They would not agree on everything.

'The plan was always to send her back once she decided to accept her responsibilities,' Stepan reminded him, making Ruslan feel like a child petitioning to keep a stray he'd taken in and was now reluctant to give up. 'She belongs in Kuban, you know. I've been watching her. She will make a magnificent queen.' Ruslan had to agree. She would. If they could get her there alive. Stepan clapped him on the shoulder, taking his silence for assent, for doing 'the right thing'. 'This doesn't mean I don't know how hard this is for you, Ruslan.' Something in his demeanour suggested he did indeed know and understand. It made Ruslan wonder what Stepan had given up.

They returned to the table and took their seats. 'We can be ready to leave in two weeks.' Ruslan cleared his throat. Whatever his fantasies, it was time to set them aside and forcefully reassert his objectivity. 'We need time to formally alert the parties that will travel with us. Canning has arranged for a small but impressive coterie of officers and cavalry to accompany us as protection, but also as fact-finders. They will want to study the geographic situation for future knowledge.' Meaning the port access and the water routes for trade. Ruslan nodded towards Grigoriev. 'Also, I think you and the Duke of Redruth will need to organise your corps of diplomats who are interested in establishing relations with Kuban.' Diplomats would bring aides, perhaps even families. Moving diplomats and soldiers would be like travelling with a small army. Ruslan's mind was already clicking with the hundreds of details involved in mobilising a large group. There would be supplies to arrange, inns to arrange, security to arrange.

This entourage would be too large to be hidden. They would be easily tracked if anyone was interested in their movements. And they'd be slow. There might be safety in numbers, but there was no speed. It would take the entourage six weeks under optimal conditions. In reality, it would probably take seven or eight. One should never count on autumn weather being optimal.

'Two weeks?' Grigoriev tactfully complained. 'That is not much time. We need a month at least to pack and assemble.'

Ruslan faced the ambassador patiently. He was used to such complaints. It was always the same. He'd managed such outings in Kuban for the Tsar—the removal of the family to the summer palace, the return to town for winter—before he'd turned his hand to more covert manoeuvrings. 'I appreciate the comment. A month would be ideal. Unfortunately, we don't have a month. It's the first of October already. If we leave by the fifteenth, I am hopeful we can make Kuban by the end of November.'

It was, in fact, necessary. If they did not, the snows in the mountain passes would prevent them from travel until spring. If they were too late, they would have to turn back, spend the winter holed up somewhere in Germany. It was not a proposition Ruslan liked. A lot could happen in the span of a winter. Palace intrigues could increase apace with the confinement of people indoors during those months. Could the Moderates hold Kuban until spring if they didn't make it through? It would be far better to have Dasha in place, to have the winter to establish her court. And in the winter, the borders would be safe, Kuban's isolation complete.

Grigoriev nodded his understanding and rose. 'Then, if that is the case, I will see to my end of things immediately.' He bowed to Ruslan. 'Your

Highness, does this mean you will be accompanying us?'

Ruslan felt Stepan's gaze on him, steely and defiant, daring him to go against his preferences. He had no time to consider Stepan's feelings now. But Stepan should not be surprised. They'd talked of this before. Stepan had been warned. 'Yes, Your Excellency, it does.' He smiled with forced cheer—something he was going to have to get used to doing in the difficult days to come. 'I can hardly make arrangements and then not see them through to the end. I will see us all safely to Kuban.' It was happening again, the same way it had happened in Kuban, when he hadn't really thought he was leaving. He was leaving again. He'd not awakened this morning with those intentions. Just a few hours ago he'd been imagining Dasha in his drawing room with his Wedgwood.

'Shall I tell the Princess?' Varvakis asked eagerly.

Ruslan shook his head. 'No. I will tell her tonight.' He was not sure how Dasha would take the news. In theory, she knew to expect it, as had he. He knew empirically from his own reaction that expecting the news didn't make a difference. These last hours had been hard on him. He could imagine how difficult the news, welcome or not, would be on Dasha.

Outside, Stepan was not willing to let the decision stand now that they were alone. 'You are going back there for her, admit it!' Stepan grabbed his arm, forcing him to stop and face his friend and all the agony Stepan's expression wore.

'You are welcome to come. I could use a good arm like yours, and a good mind,' Ruslan offered. He didn't truly think Stepan would accept and Stepan didn't.

'I will not go back there.' Whatever evil Stepan had left behind still haunted him. But Stepan never said anything on the matter. He wasn't like Nikolay or Illarion in that regard. Those two wore their opinions on their sleeves along with their hearts. Ruslan let him be, although he had suspicions Stepan's source of torture had followed him here.

They walked towards the town house in silence, one more question hanging between them unasked until they reached the steps. 'Will you come back?' Stepan enquired quietly, his hand on Ruslan's arm.

Ruslan chuckled. What could he say? 'Let me leave first, my friend.'

'I see.' The grim tic in Stepan's cheek tensed and jumped at his jaw.

Ruslan relented. 'I don't know. I think it will depend on how things go.' With the country. With Dasha. He looked up at the whitewashed heights of his new town house, imagining Dasha inside. Was she still with the ladies or had they gone? Maybe she was playing with Maximus? 'Perhaps you could tell Nikolay for me? I want him to hear it from us first.' Ruslan paused. 'Step, don't ask him to come. He will feel badly but he can't come. We can't allow it. I wouldn't want him to leave Klara just now.'

Stepan's eyebrow arched in comprehension of his meaning. 'Really? She's expecting?'

'I think so.' He was seldom wrong about these things. A sense of loss stabbed at him. He wouldn't be here to see Nikolay's child born. Even if he returned, it wouldn't be for another year at best. And if he came back, it would mean there'd been certain…failures. Yet to not return came with sacrifices, too. 'This decision tears at my heart, Stepan,' he said softly and began to climb the steps.

It was quiet inside. Good. He wanted to be alone with her when he told her and he didn't want to wait. Now that it was decided, he wanted the revelation over. Ruslan found his way to the drawing room. She was there, her back to him, and he took a moment to savour the sight of her, the peace of her before everything changed.

She turned, perhaps sensing his presence. She looked happy to see him. She came towards him, holding an empty teacup. 'The servants missed one. Someone hid it beneath the sofa.' She had a wide smile on her lips and looked fetching in her lavender-blue gown. He wanted to remember her like this with her eyes dancing. 'Everyone is excited for the Kubanian Tea. I think Lady Bradford-Piles had it all planned before she left.' Dasha laughed. 'Lady Bradford-Piles says…' She halted mid-sentence, catching his expression. 'What is it? How was your meeting with Stepan? Not bad news, I hope?' The spark banked in her eyes, her face paling.

Ruslan tried out his new, forced smile. 'The Moderates have gained control of the country. Kuban is ready for its Queen. You are going home, Dasha.'

The teacup slipped out of her hand and crashed to the floor, smashing, like his fantasy, into a thousand irreparable pieces.

Chapter Twelve

She was going home. Dasha stood there staring, inept and speechless while her mind raced in a million directions—what did she do first? Pick up the ruined china? The cup seemed inconsequential in light of his news. Should she ask the questions rocketing through her mind? There were hundreds of them. No matter what direction her thoughts went, they only circled back to one: she did not want this. It was too soon. It would always be too soon.

Doubts swamped her. How foolish she was to have chosen this path. The hopes that had fed her decision to be the Princess had not come to pass. She had not remembered who she was in time. She'd always thought she'd go home to Kuban in full possession of her memories. She'd not thought the summons would come so soon. She'd thought she'd have the winter. Spring seemed far away. Surely by spring all would be put to rights. Maybe that was still a possibility. She found her voice at last. 'When?'

'In two weeks. We cannot delay longer if we wish to make Kuban before the snow closes it off.' She was aware of Ruslan's scrutiny. He was studying her, trying to assess her reaction. 'You are not pleased?'

She *should* be pleased. A queen should be hungry for her throne, desirous for her country. Like Captain Varvakis, she should be chafing to return. At the moment, though, all she could think of was what she'd be leaving behind, including this man who chased away her nightmares. How would she be brave without him? She'd been all too aware of how much she'd relied on him these many weeks, even though he'd tried to mitigate that sense of reliance, providing for her without her asking. 'It is something of a shock. I thought there would be more time.' So much more time.

She watched a wall go up behind his eyes. Was he disappointed in her? He must be. This was what he wanted, what he'd taken her in for, what Varvakis had brought her here for—so that she would be safe when her country needed her. For him, her return would mean so much more than a journey. He'd chosen exile, perhaps waiting for a time like this when his beliefs and values were mirrored in the policies of his country. He probably felt like celebrating. And he couldn't. Because of her. How like Ruslan to set aside his personal feelings for another's emotions. Dasha managed a smile. 'It's good news, indeed.'

'And yet it leaves you pale and shaking.' Ruslan put his arm about her and guided her to the sofa. 'What is it, Dasha? Are you having second thoughts?'

That was an understatement. She was having second thoughts, third thoughts. Her feet weren't just cold, they were *freezing*. Could she really lead a country? Would that country accept her? Was she even who she claimed to be? If she wasn't, what happened then? How could she do this all alone without Ruslan?

'I was just getting used to things here.' She was complaining after all he'd done for her to make this return possible. Without his entrée, she could never have hoped to capture the support of society. She sat straighter and tried to sound queenly. 'Perhaps we should not rush. It might be worthwhile to spend the winter here so that we could go fully prepared.'

'Do not worry, we will go fully prepared.

Even now, Grigoriev and the others are gathering their retinues,' Ruslan reassured her.

'We?' Something leapt inside her. She barely dared to give voice to it. 'Are you coming, too?'

'Yes, of course.' Ruslan's voice was steady, his gaze intent. But it was her advisor who spoke the reassurances, her friend was tucked carefully away. As soon as he'd imparted the news, Ruslan had donned his mantle of neutrality and gathered it securely about himself. He was far calmer than she. But he'd had the benefit of a few hours to adjust to the news, to think about what it meant. Perhaps in a few hours she'd feel the same.

'Of course?' She didn't see any 'of course' about it. 'But you have this house, you've just moved in. Your friends are here.' His life was here.

Ruslan gestured to the space around him. 'A house is just a thing, Dasha. It can be replaced. I've done it before. My friends understand.'

'Even Stepan?' Dasha gave a wry smile. Stepan had been wary of this venture from the first, fearing this exact outcome.

'He will, eventually,' Ruslan answered with a wry smile of his own, sharing in the dry humour between them. The intimacy of a shared joke sent a private warmth through her, his neutrality was breached for a short moment. Whoever went with them—General Vasiliev, or the ambassador, Grigoriev—didn't matter. She and Ruslan were in this, together.

Although it didn't seem very 'together' five days in. He was gone before she rose in the mornings and returned in the evenings long enough to escort her to an event, his hand always at her back, his eyes always alert. He said little beyond making the general enquiries about her days. They discussed the details of the departure, but nothing more. He was, in short, a very proper advisor.

The absence of her advisor-friend brought a certain clarity. She *wanted* the fantasy. Not just to indulge in, but to somehow make it real, a barricade against the truth; that she was going home. The merest touch of his hand was a reminder of the potential that burned between them and a reminder of all that was being held in check because of their circumstances. And yet if it hadn't been for those circumstances, she would never have met him.

Dasha gave her hair a final pat. He would be waiting for her downstairs, even now, for one more event, this one a *musicale*, featuring an Italian soprano who had lingered in London at the request of a certain lord. Ruslan had warned her ahead of time the soprano was not very good, but it was another chance to see and be seen by those who supported her return to Kuban. Dasha drew a breath and straightened her shoulders. She knew what was expected of her tonight. She would smile and laugh and say things that were witty at times, serious at others.

Everything she said, everything she did, how she treated the men who supported her, was taken as proof of her ability to succeed. It was weary work, the latter especially. The men had to be handled carefully. She had to respect their opinions and yet she could not be seen as their puppet. This was perhaps another reason for Ruslan's absence in recent days. She knew the papers delighted in naming him as her consort due to his constant attendance on her and often the speculation about what that attendance entailed was not kind. There were only so many reasons a man attached himself to a high-ranking woman, all of them unimaginative: money, power, status.

Those items were intensified when one was a princess, soon-to-be queen. She was very aware that if she were successful in her claim, she could give him back all that he'd lost when he left and more. She was aware, too, that Rus-

Ian was cognisant of that as well. Indeed, he was quite sensitive to it, always careful to make sure she understood he did not make his choices based on those supposed gains. And yet, that awareness persisted beneath the surface of what passed as their relationship.

He was at the bottom of the stairs, ready and waiting. 'I am sorry I'm late,' she said as she descended, silvery-grey skirts in one hand.

'A lovely woman is always worth waiting for. We have plenty of time,' Ruslan assured her, as he always did, but his eyes were grim tonight, or should she say, even grimmer than they'd been since the announcement of her return. He was always grim these days.

She waited until they were settled in his carriage to broach the subject. 'You are bothered tonight. Does the thought of mediocre Italian talent not please you?' She tried for some levity to erase the strain on his face and failed. The last few days had been stressful. The newspapers had run stories about their imminent departure and one bold article had even outlined the goals of her departure, making it clear to the public beyond the closed doors of Mayfair drawing rooms that she aspired to the Kubanian throne. Ruslan had cursed when he'd seen it.

'If it were up to me, we would not go out tonight at all.' He offered nothing more, but he was tense, his normal air of alertness heightened, although he was trying to hide it. She saw it in the little things he did. He took longer than usual to hand her down from the coach, taking care to look around first. He walked a little faster between the kerb and the front door to the town house. He kept his body closer to hers in a crowd. She didn't mind the last. But she did mind the reason for it and she minded that he'd apparently decided not to tell her. If she was in danger, she had a right to know. Surely it would be all right, though, they'd been safe so far.

Dasha pulled him to the side after they'd been announced under the pretence of examining her hem for a tear. She skewered him with a stare. 'You think there will be an attempt tonight.' She couldn't bring herself to say the word 'assassination'. Nor could she bring herself to word the statement more strongly. Ruslan did not merely 'think' there would be an attempt. He *knew* there would be an attempt, which made not telling her even worse. Her anger started to simmer. 'Why didn't you tell me?'

He took her arm, leading her into an alcove further away from the crowd. He drew the silk privacy curtain about them. Dasha braced herself. If he told her he didn't want her to worry, she might scream out of frustration. She wasn't helpless. Surely he knew that by now. 'I wanted you to act as normally as possible. I wanted you to do nothing that would tip the assassin off that we knew.' *That we knew.* The answer was somewhat mollifying. Even if she disagreed with how he'd handled this, it was still 'we'.

'I may not remember many things,' she scolded in a low whisper, 'but that does not mean I am naïve.' Nor did it mean she wasn't scared. The thought of an unknown assailant lurking in the crowd, dressed like the rest of them, acting like the rest of them, except for the part where he carried a weapon beneath his evening clothes, was terrifying. 'How do you know? Who told you?' Perhaps information would make the prospect less terrifying.

'Grigoriev's sources.' Ruslan was succinct. She could imagine how that news had travelled; a rumour in Soho had reached Nikolay. That meant a ragtag Rebel faction made extremist by their bitterness in exile existed among the immigrant community. They wouldn't want her on the throne based on her name alone, regardless of her politics. 'I have men stationed around the room and the grounds, watching entrances, watching servants. I am glad it's not during the Season. So many of the houses hire temporary servants for an evening then. That's not necessary with these smaller gatherings.' Ruslan forced a smile. He wasn't telling her everything. A pit formed in her stomach. There was more and it was bad, as if an assassination attempt wasn't bad enough.

'What is it, Ruslan?' She searched his face. They were close enough for her to see the small signs of care: the tiredness about his eyes, the beginnings of faint lines at his mouth.

'A mob.' To which he quickly added, 'It is rumour only and "mob" may be a generous term.' Dasha shuddered. A mob had murdered her family. She didn't need to remember such an event in detail to fear it. She knew where it would come from: Soho. The Union of Salvation, or whatever they were called these days, would whip the disgruntled into a frenzy, and if they couldn't get to her…

Her gut clenched and she reached for Ruslan's hands. 'Nikolay and Klara? The stables? Will they be safe?' She could not bear to think of anyone being harmed because of her.

'Yes, Nikolay has sent Klara to her father's and he has the stable well protected if it comes to that. I don't think it will. Stepan is with him.'

His reassurance failed. She stared at Ruslan bleakly. 'This is all my fault. If I had chosen to simply fade away, your friends would not be in danger. You would not be leaving your home.' *He would not be preparing to stand between me and a bullet.* She could not bring herself to say the last.

'You chose honourably, Dasha. You saw your duty and did not shirk from it.' Ruslan kissed her forehead. 'You need to allow the rest of us to do the same. Now, we need to go out there and watch the mediocre soprano and act as if nothing is wrong.' But everything was wrong. She didn't want men sacrificing themselves for her, losing their homes for her, taking risks for her, and she certainly didn't want *this* man kissing her forehead in chaste obeisance to his Queen. She wanted far more than *forehead*-kissing from him.

The soprano was just as bad as Ruslan had warned. By the interval, Dasha was ready to leave. 'Do you think we can slip away without causing a stir?' She would beg Ruslan if she had to. 'It might throw the assassin off guard.' In desperation, the man might expose himself in haste, or he might slink on home, his plan untried, which suited her just fine. If she could get herself and Ruslan home safe and uninjured, she'd call the night a success.

Ruslan nodded in agreement. He looked about the room and gave an imperceptible gesture to a man by the door who disappeared down the stairs. 'The coach will be at the kerb shortly. We'll wait for it inside the hall and we won't go down until it's arrived.'

A footman brought their cloaks and Ruslan settled hers about her shoulders. She felt his hands linger, another imperceptible gesture. Perhaps he, too, didn't want to settle for chaste kisses. And perhaps he was merely warning her. If it was to happen tonight, it would happen between the door and the coach, if only because that was the last opportunity left for the assassin. If the assassin had hoped for a chance later in the evening, they'd effectively taken that plan away from him.

The coach rolled to a stop at the kerb. Ruslan whispered reassurance, 'The darkness will make it hard for him to have a good shot.'

'Is that supposed to be encouraging?' Dasha shot back.

'Yes, my apologies.' There was a chuckle beneath those words. Dasha smiled. Only Ruslan could make her laugh at a time like this. 'Shall we?' His hand was at her back, ready to escort her as if this was an ordinary night. 'Remember, walk normally. If the assailant isn't aware of our leaving yet, running to the carriage will certainly alert him.'

They hadn't made it out the door when their host stopped them, huffing up in agitation over their departure. 'You're leaving so soon, Your Highness? Signora has not yet sung her famous aria,' he coaxed.

'Her Highness has a headache,' Ruslan lied smoothly. 'She needs her rest.' Something, *some-one*, moved on Dasha's periphery. She was being paranoid now, making up ghosts. Other guests were coming and going as their schedules dictated. The hall was a busy place. A perfect place.

Their host bowed. 'Of course, my apologies. Perhaps another time?' Dasha wanted to leave, she felt distinctly uncomfortable, but their host would not stop talking. He was asking Ruslan for advice about the purchase of an estate outside the city.

'Perhaps we could meet at White's and discuss it further over drinks?' Ruslan said with polite briskness as if he had time to spend an afternoon talking of estates while he was mobilising the Kubanian departure. The movement came again, closer now. She'd not imagined it the first time.

'Prince Pisarev.' Dasha hazarded an interruption, trying to look miserable with a feigned headache. 'If we might go?' A few moments ago, she'd feared the dark walk to the coach. Now, she welcomed it, a chance to get out of the light.

The darkness will make it hard for him to have a good shot.

The assassin knew it, too. In the hall he wouldn't have a good shot at all—a gun would be too conspicuous, too loud. He'd switch to blades.

Dasha's heart began to race. Her attacker was behind her now, she could feel him. 'Ruslan,' she whispered in terror, all sense of preserving propriety in her address gone. Why didn't he do something? Was he oblivious?

In the next instant, Ruslan was on the move. With lightning reflexes, he disarmed the man behind her even as his body put himself between her and the assailant. He had her assailant in his grip, the assailant's body locked against his. A slim blade flashed in Ruslan's hand before she could process what was happening. The man sagged in Ruslan's arms, hitting the floor before the guests screamed, before Dasha realised he was dead, his throat cut with a swift, lethal blade. She'd not even seen Ruslan do it. Ruslan grabbed for her hand, drawing her near, his body protecting hers as he hustled her out the door and into the night. 'There might be more than one.' He gave a harsh whisper at her ear.

'We can run now. The game is afoot, there's no sense walking.'

She was breathless from fear and exertion when Ruslan bundled her inside the carriage and followed her in, slamming the door behind them and dragging her off the seat. 'I want you on the floor!' He shoved her down, his body over hers and just in time, it seemed. The first shots hit the windows, shattered glass spraying the seats. In the clatter of hooves and mayhem no one heard her scream.

Chapter Thirteen

Oh, God, bullets! Someone was shooting at them! At *her*! Dasha muffled her screams against the floorboards of the coach, Ruslan's weight pressing down on her, his arms holding her tight, his head tucked over hers. Above them another window shattered even as she felt the coach lurch forward and the crack of the coachman's whip. Lord willing, they'd outpace anyone on foot. London streets weren't made for speed. Oh, no, what if their assailant grabbed on to the coach? She could imagine myriad scenarios where the door was flung open and the assailant fired inside. At close range, he wouldn't miss.

The coach lurched around a corner, gaining speed. Dasha strained her ears to catch the telltale sound of a body outside. Above her, Ruslan's body was tensed in readiness. He, too, was anticipating the worst. The coach took another fast turn and she felt a back wheel leave the ground. Her stomach heaved. She fought back the nausea and the fear, focusing only on Ruslan. If he was with her, she was safe. It was a flawed mantra, but it was the one security she could hold on to.

'We've made it,' Ruslan spoke at last, levering himself off her. 'We're in the alley behind the town house. You have five minutes to gather anything you need.'

A rhythmic knock sounded on the coach door followed by a low, gruff voice. 'Ruslan, are you in there?'

'Stepan, we're both here.' Ruslan pushed the door open and hands reached for her. Stepan and Thomas the butler were there. 'Get her in the house.' Ruslan issued orders behind her. 'Why aren't you with Nikolay? I thought I told you to stay with him.'

'Nikolay's fine. You needed me more. The mob is headed this way.' Stepan's words reached her ears as she ran for the kitchen door. 'Tell your coachman I'll drive. I'm a better driver.'

Ruslan was arguing, but Dasha was up the stairs, fear driving her. She didn't have five minutes, not if the mob was coming. She didn't need it. She knew exactly what she wanted. Maximus. In her room, she grabbed a satchel and, with one arm, swept the contents of her vanity into the bag: a hair brush and the few pieces of jewellery Ruslan had given her. Maximus was already snapping at her heels for attention. She scooped the puppy up in one arm and headed downstairs.

'Let them have the house, if it comes to that,' Ruslan was saying. 'The longer they think we're inside, the longer we have to get away.'

'I am coming with you,' Stepan growled.

Ruslan saw her and reached out a hand, gripping her tightly, and ushering her towards the coach. 'My coachman is fine. The others need you here. I'll send him back once we're clear.' He helped her in and she saw that he'd been busy in the time she'd dashed upstairs. Blankets and a large hamper sat on the seat along with hardy travelling cloaks and a pair of his boots.

He climbed in behind her, Stepan shutting the door firmly. 'Do you have the pistols? Do you have money?' Stepan was anxious. 'Are you sure you wouldn't rather brazen this out and leave with the delegation? There's safety in numbers and all that.'

Ruslan shook his head. 'There's safety in speed. We endanger the delegation and they'd endanger us. We'd be sitting ducks.' He drew a deep breath. 'Tell Grigoriev and Varvakis I'll see them in Kuban. I'm counting on them to get the others there.'

In the dim light, she saw Stepan grip Ruslan's hand, a hurried, fleeting gesture as the coachman cracked the whip. 'Godspeed, my friend.'

Dasha reached up a hand and grabbed the leather strap for balance. 'What is going on? Where are we going?' The exchange between Ruslan and Stepan had not yet sunk in. She was still running on fear as she held Maximus close. It helped to comfort the puppy. There was strength in giving comfort to another during a crisis.

'We are going to Kuban,' Ruslan said grimly. 'As planned, but earlier than expected.'

The import of that nearly overwhelmed her. She was glad she was hanging on to the strap and the puppy. She was fleeing London in an evening gown and diamonds, a puppy in her arms and set of pistols under the seat. The journey to Kuban would be long and arduous. It was a journey that required resources, not a puppy and a princess with no memories. She met Ruslan's eyes. It would be the two of them against the world, quite literally, with only their wits.

'What are you thinking, Dasha?' Ruslan asked, tucking the hamper under the seat.

'I'm thinking that if I could only take one person with me, I'm glad it's you,' she said softly. 'But I am sorry for the cost. I will repay you some day for all you've done for me, for all you've given up…' She didn't know how, but she'd find a way.

'Shh, Dasha.' He pressed his finger against her lips. 'There will be no talk of owing and repaying between us.'

'But your home,' she protested, already imagining the long glass-paned windows smashed with rocks, the immaculate interior looted, the ice-blue piano ruined, the Wedgwood shattered.

'It's just brick and mortar.' Ruslan shook his head. 'You are not to think about it.' But there were other things to think about, like Stepan's grim face when they'd pulled out. At a moment's notice, Ruslan had given up everything and everyone he knew in London. For her. If not for her, for what?

'Will you see him again?' Dasha asked.

'I don't know,' Ruslan answered honestly. 'He will not come to Kuban. I think what he wants is in London.' He drew a breath and changed the subject. 'We'll drive straight through to Dover and catch a packet boat to Calais. We'll go overland through France if we can't trust the seas.' Dasha let him redirect the conversation. If it eased his heartache and his conscience over what had happened tonight, he could talk about details all he liked. Immediate tasks kept fear at bay, she knew. She'd found a hundred ways to stay busy when she and Varvakis had fled Kuban just months earlier. Had it only been months? It seemed as if she'd been away much longer. She seemed different. Perhaps she was. She wasn't the scared, confused, bedraggled ragamuffin who'd been half-carried into Ruslan's town house in the middle of the night. But some things were the same. She still didn't remember who she was and the nightmares still came.

The lights of London streets faded behind them and the road became rougher as the city gave way to country. Ruslan shook out one of the blankets and passed it to her. 'Sleep, Dasha. Things will look better in the morning.' He made a nest for Maximus out of a lap robe and took the puppy from her. 'Why am I not surprised, that given five minutes to get anything you want, you grab him?' He settled Maximus in the nest with a smile. He turned his gaze back to her and made a welcoming gesture. 'Come lay your head, Dasha. You'll rest better with a shoulder for a pillow.'

She slid on to the seat next to him, snuggling into the crook of his arm as she had once before. 'Thank you, Ruslan.' The words seemed inadequate.

He chuckled, his breath warm against her hair. 'For what, Dasha?'

'For saving my life tonight. I saw what you did to the man in the hall. Thank you.'

'Any time, Princess.' He dropped a light kiss into her hair. She hated those kisses. She didn't want him kissing her hair or her forehead any more. She didn't want him calling her Princess, didn't want the whole of their relationship and their choices summed up in words like prince and princess and duty for the crown.

She looked up at him, wanting to see his face such as it was in the darkness. 'Would you have done it anyway? Even if it wasn't for the Princess?'

'Yes.' He smiled in the darkness. 'Now, go to sleep. I'm here.' And all would be well because he was.

Ruslan lay his head back against the leather squabs of his battered coach. A few pieces of glass still crunched beneath his feet despite his hasty efforts to sweep it out. He closed his eyes and listened to the rhythm of Dasha's breathing change from wakefulness to sleep, her body soft against him. He was thankful for the feel of her, warm and alive. He'd nearly lost her tonight. His mind wasn't ready to let go of the image of her in the hall, the assassin approaching from behind. Ruslan had seen his mistake immediately.

It was too dark for a reliable shot. Leaving early or leaving when the *musicale* was over wouldn't change that. The first layer of attack had always been meant to be knives in the hall.

Just the thought of Dasha stabbed and bleeding made his blood heat with rage. There were better ways to solve problems and disagreements than through violence. But the world never seemed to learn, which was why he was fleeing in the night with a princess beside him. No, not just a princess. For the first time since Dasha had landed on his doorstep, Ruslan let the enormity of the situation sweep over him. Tonight, it had become so much more than a chess game about strategies and politics, Rebels and Loyalists with Moderates in between, a princess and a throne. This had become about a real woman who was in danger because of others' political agendas, perhaps even his. Ruslan let the guilt take him. He had to bear some responsibility. Had he somehow let his own needs—the need to vindicate his family, his need to return and prove himself—shadow her decision? Had he led her down that path on purpose for his own gain?

He drew a deep breath to quell the churning of his stomach. *Dasha* had nearly died tonight. Not a figurehead, not an object, but a flesh-and-blood woman whom he cared for, regardless of title and status. He'd killed for her tonight. He'd kill for her again if it came to it.

And it probably would.

Dasha, too, had killed, if Varvakis was to be believed. Dasha had struck down a soldier. To protect herself? To protect someone else? Dasha claimed someone had been upstairs with her the night of the attack in Kuban. Had she indeed found the power to strike down a soldier to protect someone else? Ruslan let his mind follow that train of thought. Protecting a loved one enabled a man or a woman to do the impossible. Who did Dasha love in that way? Had this woman been an aunt? A cousin? A member of the royal family? Obviously, she was someone close to Dasha. It was far better for his mind to contemplate that particular mystery than it was to think about the evening: of Dasha in danger, of his knife slicing through the assassin, the bullets that had come close to making his efforts in the hall null, of saying goodbye to Stepan and of all the people he *hadn't* said goodbye to. Perhaps he would be back some day. But tonight, he doubted it. He already knew he'd stay in Kuban as long as Dasha needed him.

Ruslan dozed through the night, waking to assist the driver with changing the horses and to check their progress when he took Maximus out. It was nine hours to Dover in the daylight with good roads and fast horses. He ticked the villages off in his head: Dartford, Chalk, Rochester. They made Rochester before dawn. He had hopes of breakfast in Canterbury before the final push. With luck, they'd make Dover by mid-morning, in time to catch the packet.

That did make him edgy. The sailing to Calais only left once a day. Unless there was a private yacht or sailboat he could commandeer, they would be stranded in Dover until tomorrow with very little he could do about it. If anyone was chasing them down, he'd rather not be in Dover. If they could make Calais, they could disappear among the myriad country roads that wound through France. But until then, they were rather conspicuous.

The sun began to edge the sky, filtering through the broken windows of the coach, its rays bathing Dasha's face in morning light. Even after a night of terror and uncertainty, she looked like an angel as she slept, her face against his shoulder, her hair coming down in sleep-tousled ringlets. She would look delightful mussed from sleep, from love, waking beside him in bed. At last, after an evening of pursuing other thoughts, he allowed himself to think about that one fantasy. Was that what he wanted? If the situation were different? If he were able to be more than her advisor? To bed Dasha? Would bedding her be enough? Or did he want something more? He wasn't like Illarion or Nikolay for whom women were temporary fixtures to be traded in with the season—well, that was until they'd met their wives. Ruslan had always been more circumspect, his liaisons having a more permanent quality to them. His mistresses often lasted a year or two. She shifted against him, starting to stir.

He'd want more than bedding from her, he suspected. Dasha was unlike any woman he'd ever met. She was entirely selfless, thinking of others first. It was that selflessness that had factored in so heavily to her decision to go back. A woman like that was to be admired and protected. He would not want to see her innate goodness taken advantage of. He knew, too, that Dasha would argue with him. She felt she was able to protect herself and in some ways she was. She was astute and intuitive as she'd shown time and again, but she had a soft heart.

'Where are we?' Dasha lifted her sleepy head, blinking against the sun.

'We're coming into Canterbury. We can get some breakfast and stretch.'

Her hands went to her hair. 'I must look a fright.'

Ruslan laughed. If she thought she looked a fright, she didn't know the first thing about men in the morning. 'You look fine.' But he rummaged in his pocket for a small comb anyway and handed it to her, knowing full well she wouldn't believe him.

They refreshed themselves quickly, taking a breakfast of fresh baked buns and cheese in a basket for the coach as soon as the horses were ready, and his driver assured him he could go a few hours more. In the coach once more, Dasha insisted they devote the remainder of the trip to her training. She peppered him with questions about Kuban, about its government and her father. 'And my brothers?' she asked hesitantly once they'd exhausted the earlier topics. 'Tell me stories about them. What did the four of you do as boys?'

Ruslan smiled, remembering his summers with her brothers fondly. 'What didn't we do? We loved to swim.' He laughed. 'One day, we convinced one of the more, ah, friendly maids to flirt with our tutor so we could sneak out to go swimming instead of studying our Latin.'

'You were educated with them?' Dasha seemed genuinely interested.

'For a while.' Ruslan paused. 'The truth is, your brothers and I were closer when we were young. My family was close to your mother's, so I was brought to the palace often. When we were old enough to go to school, around the age of ten, we lost some of our connection. I went away and met Illarion, Nikolay and Stepan while your brothers followed their path.' He'd gone on to attend the school appropriate for noble families where he could be trained to serve the country as his father had served. The Tsar's sons were educated in the palace as the Tsar preferred by tutors from all over Europe. Later, they'd been sent out of the country to universities in Europe. 'But I still mourn the loss of them.' Ruslan put a hand over hers and squeezed.

'I wish I could truly mourn them. I wish I had a memory of them.' Dasha's voice wavered. 'It's silly, but I'm jealous of you, that you have those memories.'

'You will. I think going back will help you remember,' Ruslan encouraged, as much for her as for him. She *had* to remember. Kuban would be dangerous, politically. There would be those who would want to see her fail and, if they knew she didn't remember anything, they would exploit that weakness to bring her down.

Dasha nodded, but she was not placated. 'What if they don't want me to be Queen?'

Ruslan did not look away, although such a question made his heart race. Such knowledge was something he welcomed as a man, but worried over as an advisor. What if Dasha were free? 'Then we face that decision when it comes.' He smiled reassuringly. 'However, I do feel the odds of you being accepted are good. Varvakis and Grigoriev feel the same. We would not have let you return otherwise.'

She gave him a coy smile that had him thinking of other things besides kings and succession as she reached for Maximus. 'The odds? Hmmm. I didn't take you for a gambler, Ruslan.'

Ruslan's eyes were steady on her, a smile hiding in them that sent a pleasant tremor through her. 'I'm not, Dasha, that's just how sure of you I am.'

Chapter Fourteen

Dasha envied Ruslan his certainty. She wished she could borrow his confidence, all of it: his confidence in her, his confidence that they would not be followed once they crossed the Channel, his confidence that they would make the mid-day packet. Confidence, it seemed, bred success. They had indeed made the packet, with ten minutes to spare and under assumed names, her silk dinner gown hidden beneath the voluminous folds of a serviceable wool cloak.

Dasha stood on the deck of the daily steamer, watching England fade. It had been her country for a short while and London her city with its private gardens and soaring town houses. To her knowledge, she'd never been anywhere like it before. The place bustled with modernity, the largest city in the world, Ruslan had told her proudly. Larger than even Paris. 'Will we go to Paris?'

Ruslan joined her at the rail, having completed the business of their passage with the steamer Captain. 'I suppose we could manage it…' He hesitated. 'I had not thought to go that way. Paris can be…conspicuous.' The kind of place a princess would go. The kind of place that would have eyes and ears so that even in a city of hundreds of thousands, a princess would not go unnoticed.

Dasha nodded. 'I understand. No unnecessary risks.' The wind blew at her hood, pushing it back. She reached up a hand to hold it in place.

'Still,' Ruslan persisted. 'Paris has a certain greatness to it.'

'No,' Dasha answered firmly. 'We are fleeing danger. We are not on a Grand Tour. There will be time another day, perhaps, to savour the delights of Paris.' A day when there wasn't the possibility of being hunted, or the possibility of putting Ruslan in danger again. She did not want to relive those moments in the hall of the *musicale* ever again. Not just for her sake, but for Ruslan's. She never wanted to see him make a shield of himself for her, never wanted to see him take a life again for her. If Paris created such a possibility, she wouldn't go there.

Ruslan nodded his assent. He lowered his voice, his gaze never leaving the water. 'I told the Captain we are a husband and wife travelling home from London after conducting some business there regarding my wines. We have vineyards in Burgundy, outside of Dijon.' The alias was nicely done. Burgundy was in the east central part of France, the very same direction they'd head in order to reach Marseilles. They could pretend they were from Burgundy for quite some time on this journey.

'And our names?' Dasha asked, trying to ignore the little thrill of excitement that had gone through her at the mention of husband and wife. It was a silly, girlish thrill. She understood the practical reasons for designing the ruse thus. A husband gave a woman protection, his presence removed her from the speculation of other men, made her, perhaps, less noticeable. It also gave him reason to stay close.

'Monsieur and Madame Archambeault.'

'Do I have a first name or is it just Madame?' Dasha laughed.

'You are Camille and I am Arnaud,' Ruslan answered and she saw how easy it was for him, all this reinvention. He'd made them merchants so that their clothes might not inspire too much curiosity. A merchant's wife might have a silk gown if he were successful. A merchant's wife might as easily wear solid wool. A merchant's wife might lean back against her husband and take the sea air with his arms about her, so she did, and Ruslan's arms slipped about her as naturally as if they'd stood like this countless times. It was a wonderful sort of intimacy.

Dasha sighed, content for the moment. To be a merchant's wife allowed all manner of freedom, even the freedom to cultivate the path their relationship could follow for these next weeks if she was brave enough. 'It seems you've thought of everything.'

Almost everything. Or maybe he *had* thought of everything and *she* was the one who was a step behind. It didn't occur to her when they disembarked in Calais, or even as they made their way south-east to Arras, that nights might be interesting in their current disguise. It didn't fully sink in until Ruslan had the room key in one hand and his other at her back, respectfully ushering her up the stairs of the nondescript inn at the heart of the city, that there was only the one room between them and, more importantly, there was only the one bed. It was a very nice bed, draped in a clean forest-green and cream counterpane, but there was still just the one.

Ruslan's gaze followed her eyes. 'We're safer together. I will sleep in the chair, Dasha, if the floor does not suffice. I dare say these accommodations are far better than the ones we had when Stepan and I and the rest of us came over.' He helped her with her cloak and she wished for his confidence once more. How wonderful to be so comfortable with oneself, that he could talk of intimate situations with such ease. Of course, he'd done this more often than she had. How many men and women had he spirited away under false aliases? A little green monster reared its head. How many women had told him sleeping in a chair was not necessary? How many women had he obliged? Should she oblige him? That was assuming he'd ask, which of course he wouldn't. If there was any obliging to be done, she would have to do the asking.

It was a bold thought but these were bold times. She'd been shot at, nearly stabbed and forced to flee London and that was just yesterday. Such things had a way of rearranging one's priorities. Happiness was fleeting, it lived in the moment. Perhaps she should, too. There was no denying she was drawn to Ruslan and no denying that his kisses, no matter what guise they'd been offered under, had left her curious for more. She faced a daunting task in Kuban. If she was successful, her life would be even less her own than it was now. She slid a surreptitious look at Ruslan, busy striding about the room, inspecting. Yes. If the opportunity presented itself, she would take it.

'There's a bit of a fair in town tonight, if you feel like strolling the booths. It's to celebrate the wine harvest,' Ruslan said, peering out the window to take in the view. 'We should go. It would seem odd if a wine merchant didn't attend and we might find something for you to wear that's more suitable for travelling. We'll certainly find something good for dinner.' He ruffled Maximus's fur as the pup gnawed on a bone the innkeeper had found. 'This fellow should be fine here for a few hours.'

The sight of him with the puppy made it hard to keep her heart in check. What was it the old wives said about a man and his dog? How a man treated his dog said volumes about how he treated people? It was an interesting litmus test of a man's character. Ruslan passed effortlessly although by London standards he was less than perfect tonight, rumpled from travel, tired from lack of sleep, his hair unruly from endless hours in a carriage compounded by Channel winds and more road travel. To Dasha, he'd never looked more handsome, more carefree, more boyish. And yet, she did not forget that the man who stood before her was strong as steel and just as deadly. He could go from playful to lethal in an instant should she be threatened.

If she couldn't have Paris, she'd have Arras, Dasha told herself as they wandered the stalls. Ruslan was an apt guide, leading her through the market set up in the Grand Place, the centre square. Arras was known for its tapestries and textiles and it wasn't hard to find a decent collection of second-hand clothes: a pair of trousers, a shirt, waistcoat and jacket for him, and a wool skirt and bodice for her in a dark blue. Clothes found, they could turn their attention to entertainment, wandering the booths, looking at trinkets and tasting the wines. Ruslan made an admirable wine merchant, talking with each vendor about the wines' complexities until Dasha wasn't sure he *wasn't* a wine merchant after all.

The wines were rich, the meat—turning over an open-fire spit at one end of the Grand Place— even richer, so tender it nearly fell off the bone. Dasha licked her fingers and laughed as juice dribbled down Ruslan's chin while his tongue frantically tried to catch it. Ruslan gave up and wiped at his mouth. 'It's too good to waste.' Ruslan shrugged unapologetically.

After food, they returned to shopping, stopping at a booth selling milled soaps scented with lavender. 'Pick out a few bars,' Ruslan encouraged, handing the vendor coins in advance. 'They'll make travel less tedious.' It was the first purchase of many he'd make for her as they wandered. There were hair ribbons; the soft wool shawl of deep burgundy; the woollen stockings; the embroidered fichu, a small triangular shawl; and the fichu of Flanders lace, an elegantly done piece. 'For special occasions,' he whispered and she thought he might be teasing. There would be no special occasions on the road, not for them. They wanted to reach Kuban as fast as possible. Still, with a harvest moon overhead and lanterns lighting the fair, it was hard to remember exactly what was the fantasy and what was the reality; that Ruslan was not her husband, that he was making these purchases because she'd left London with nothing but her dog.

They passed a booth selling linens from Ireland and her eye fell on an exquisite nightgown. She looked away. Such a purchase was foolish, a luxury. They walked on a few booths more, stopping at one that sold knives. Ruslan pressed a leather bag of coins into her hand. 'I'll be a while here, why don't you go do some shopping on your own, just don't wander too far.' It was what any husband might say to his wife. They were playing this game far too well. Or perhaps it was just an excuse. Perhaps he'd seen her looking at the nightgown and knew he couldn't possibly purchase it for her. Not because the ruse wouldn't tolerate it, it certainly would. A husband could buy his wife any nature of gift he chose. But because their *relationship* couldn't tolerate it. If he purchased such a present for her, it only implied one thing: that sex with her could be bought, that what transpired between them could indeed be limited to a price. He was too much a man of honour to risk such an implication.

And herself? Where was her honour in all of this? Because she wanted him. If she couldn't have his confidence, she could at least have him only if for a short while. Dasha knew her answer as she handed over the coins for the beautiful nightdress. If he asked, she'd be his. And if he didn't ask? Would she be bold enough to brave the chasm of propriety he'd erected between them? Had she ever had a lover? She doubted it. The Kuban she'd been raised in would not have allowed it. According to Varvakis she'd been meant for a dynastic marriage. She might still be. As Queen, she would need to consider who or what was best for the country when she took a consort. Dasha clutched the paper-wrapped package to her chest. This might be the only time she could choose for herself alone.

At the knife stand, Ruslan had finished his business when she returned. Fiddles were tuning at the stage, signalling that dancing would begin shortly, country dancing, fast polkas, round dances and reels, dances that left you breathless and exhilarated. She gave Ruslan's hand a playful tug. 'Come on, when was the last time you attended a country dance?'

He followed her with a laugh. 'When was the last time you did?'

'I don't know.' She tossed him a smile over her shoulder, laughing at her own joke, a joke only the two of them would understand. He smiled, a warm gesture that lit his eyes. His guard was down momentarily. This was her chance, *their* chance—to be something more than a fugitive princess and a professional rescuer of damsels in distress. Dasha grabbed him by the hand and led him out on to the dance floor, such as it was. It was the last thing he let her do before he took over, as she'd hoped it would be. Ruslan was a man who couldn't go long without being in charge. He was also an excellent dancer, not just on society's ballroom floors, but here, too, on the makeshift boards of a small town.

Dasha happily let him guide them through the reels and polkas that populated a country dance card. They danced fast, turning recklessly at the top of the floor and cutting through the other couples, all of whom seemed to dance equally as fast, equally as reckless. There was laughter all around them and it was intoxicating, nearly as much as the wine.

Ruslan pulled Dasha close and swung her into another polka. There was no need to worry about proper distances between partners or a two-dance limit. There were no chaperones here. Or assassins. They were safe. She wasn't the only one who felt the euphoria of that knowledge. She could see her own exhilaration mirrored in Ruslan's eyes, hear it in his laughter, feel it in the rising heat of his body. Freedom was as intoxicating as any drink. When the musicians took a break, there was ale and wine for the thirsty and the two of them drank. There was more dancing, and more wine, more laughter. Banished were thoughts of danger lurking in shadows, banished were doubts of identity, banished were worries about what came next. There was no next, there was only now, only she and Ruslan. No titles, no troubles between them and it was heady indeed.

They were the last ones on the dance floor. When the musicians stopped playing, she looked about for the first time in hours, surprised to see the once gaily lit stalls boarded up, the Grand Place deserted except for a few couples lingering in the shadows. A little bubble of regret welled up inside her. 'I would have danced all night.'

'I would have, too,' Ruslan said softly, his voice low at her ear as he laced his fingers through hers. They exchanged a brief smile that left her feeling breathless and suddenly shy as their feet turned reluctantly towards the inn. The magic would slowly slip away if she let it.

She lay a sleepy head on his shoulder as they walked. 'Dancing keeps the ghosts at bay, I think.'

A nearly full bottle stood lonely on a trestle table as they passed. Ruslan swept it up and took a hearty swallow. Dasha laughed with mock dismay. 'Prince Pisarev, are you drinking *straight* from the bottle?'

Ruslan wiped the bottle rim on his sleeve and passed it to her. 'Yes, I am. Are you?' There was still a little magic left.

She took the bottle, her green eyes flashing. 'I most certainly am. I have it on good authority it's how they do it in Arras.' She took a long swallow, her neck arched back in blatant enjoyment. She felt Ruslan's eyes on her as the liquid slid down her throat. Was he, too, thinking decadent thoughts about his mouth on her neck, how he could trail kisses down its length, to her breasts, how her breasts would taste with wine on them, a nice full-bodied burgundy like the one in his bottle? Red wine paired well with sex.

At the inn, the taproom was still busy, the fair-like atmosphere having progressed inside. Ruslan hurried her up the stairs, wanting her away from a rowdy crowd and a little bit of reality intruded. He was becoming her protector again. She wasn't ready. She wanted Ruslan her dancing partner, Ruslan who watched her drink with a gaze so intense it nearly burned, a while longer. She let herself trip on the steps, lightly staggering against him, forcing him to touch her. Ruslan got an arm about her, steadying her, and she smiled quietly to herself.

In the room, Ruslan busied himself stirring up the fire as she sat on the bed struggling with a knot in her half-boots. He was nervous, she realised. He was pottering about the room, trying to keep busy, to be efficient, to not think about what came next: bed. It was an awkward thought indeed after an exhilarating night, *if* no one meant for anything to happen. She gave a secret smile as he shut the curtains. She did not mean for this magical night to go to waste. This might be her only chance.

Her hands reached ineffectually for her laces and she made a show of giving up. 'I've managed to make knots everywhere. I think you're going to have to help me undress.' She laughed at her hopelessness, but Ruslan stiffened, as rigid as the poker he held. Good. She was sorely testing his detachment. It was what she wanted. She wanted his damned objective wall down.

'Of course I'll help you.' He came to the bed, but Dasha thought he approached much like a martyr before the lions. 'Stand up, Dasha, it will go faster.'

Dasha looked up at him, eyes dreamy. 'Can we just do it sitting down? I'm so sleepy.' She patted the bed. 'Sit just there, right behind me, and you can get to the laces.' She scooted forward, giving him her back. She heard him let out long breath and she grinned privately. Ruslan had run out of arguments. He took a deep breath and began. She felt his hands brush the bare skin of her back. He was trying to rush. She could imagine his thoughts: the faster he went, the sooner he'd be done and away from the temptation of undressing her. It was an argument she hoped his body didn't quite believe. She hoped his body would want to linger and see what came of things. Goodness knew, it was what her own body wanted. He was doing a fine job of seducing her without even trying.

'You're good at this. Have you done it a lot?'

Dasha murmured, her own voice husky with anticipation.

His fingers faltered. 'That's hardly a fair question. How should a man answer that, Dasha, without looking like a rake or an innocent? Enough experience, I suppose, to be competent.' He finished the last of the laces and rose from the bed. 'There, you should be able to take it from here.'

Ruslan was doing his best to play the gentleman and keep his gaze averted but the hitch in his breath said he was not unaffected. 'I'll just step behind the screen and change, myself.' He stood up and dropped a kiss on top of her head, a safe, chaste show of affection. 'You can tell me when it's clear to come out.'

'No.' Her voice was firm and far less sleepy than it had been a few minutes ago. She had him cornered.

'I beg your pardon. *No?*'

Dasha gave a throaty laugh. 'Hasn't anyone ever disagreed with you, Ruslan?' She rose to meet him, to stand with him toe to toe, her eyes flashing, aware that his body was on full alert, his gaze acutely conscious that her dress was held up only by her hands. 'That's right. No. There will be no more kissing my hair, kissing my cheek or kissing my forehead, as if what lies between us is purely platonic.'

'Where would you prefer I kiss you?' His voice was a low growl. She could see his eyes begin to burn, two cobalt coals, the leash of his control was singed away at last.

'Here.' With one hand she touched her lips. Her other hand let go and her gown fell to the floor, leaving her entirely naked. Ruslan swallowed hard, the cords in his neck working as he did. She pressed her advantage. 'Here, and here.' Her hands lifted her breasts. One hand moved lower covering the shadowy thatch between her legs and bringing his eyes with it, her voice like midnight whisky and just as intoxicating. 'But most of all, here.'

Chapter Fifteen

If there'd been a thirteenth labour of Hercules, it would have been resisting this. But there wasn't, because even heroes had limits and Ruslan had just found his. Dasha stood before him, gloriously nude, her hair falling over her shoulders in tantalising waves that both hid and highlighted her breasts, like a Venus rising from the sea. The slim curve of her hip gave way to long legs and bare feet. Shyness mixed with the boldness in her eyes as her gaze held his, looking for approval, perhaps acceptance.

Yes! his body cried out. Acceptance, of course. There was no question of it. No man would refuse what she offered, certainly not this one who had hungered for her for weeks, longed for her, lived with the agony and ecstasy of each touch. A small part of him knew he should resist. If there was any honourable bone in his body left, he should pick up her gown, gently put her to bed and pull the covers over her, telling her she was merely overcome with the emotions of the past twenty-four hours.

Those words would not be lies. The last twenty-four hours would have taken a toll on anyone's sensibilities. But it was perhaps *because* of those last twenty-four hours that he couldn't refuse her. Life was short, preternaturally so under their recent circumstances. He'd come within inches of losing her in Lord Hampton's hall. The knowledge of that near loss had made her compellingly real to him and, with that reality, his detachment had slipped dangerously. There was no potency to the argument that he should wait for a better time to pursue his attraction to her once business in Kuban was settled. There would be *no* better time. In fact, this might be the best time, and the only time to act on their attraction. Life on the road was often a time out of time. His body liked that argument and, tonight, his mind did, too.

He stepped towards her, the debate won. He reached for her, taking her into his arms, his mouth sealing hers with a long kiss. He felt her arms twine about his neck, her body warm and pliant against his as she gave herself over to it. There was no rush tonight, no worry about discovery, no concern about where this would lead. This was no longer an experiment. Tonight they knew. This kiss and the one after that and the one after that would all lead to the bed, with its forest-green counterpane. Tonight, they had all the time in the world.

A little moan escaped her, her hands were in his hair as he deepened the kiss. He tasted the evening wine on her tongue, full-bodied and sweet. He moved a hand to cup a breast, to lift it and stroke its pink nipple with his thumb until another moan escaped her and he could not resist putting his mouth on it. He bent his head to her breast, her body arching as he took her, his tongue laving the soft peak of her. And then he sucked. Hard.

Dasha gasped and sat down abruptly on the edge of the bed. He was half over her, half-kneeling before her, driving her body wild with his touch, with his tongue.

He kissed her other breast, showing it the same attentions as she arched and dug her hands into the folds of the quilt for anchorage. Had anything ever felt this exquisite? Had her body ever known such pleasure? And this was only the beginning. His mouth began a slow trail of kisses down the length of her, torso and navel, soft inner thigh and…there…the place between her thighs where her body pulsed for him, where her curls were damp with wanting. He blew against her curls, whispering her name, 'Dasha', his own hoarse rasp a testimony to his need. She was not alone in this mad hunger.

'Ruslan.' She put a hand on his head, burying her fingers once more in his thick waves in affirmation that this was her fantasy, that she wanted him there.

Ruslan licked her then, running his tongue along the intimate seam of her in a slow caress that had her melting. She gave over entirely and lay back on the bed, no longer able, no longer willing, to devote energy to supporting herself. Any energy she possessed, she wanted to concentrate on this: on her legs draped over Ruslan's shoulders, on the work of his tongue, on the fire he was stoking in her belly as his head bent to her pleasure.

He'd found the core of that pleasure, his tongue concentrating now on the surface of her hidden nub, his own breathing becoming laboured, his hands clenching her legs. She gasped and shivered as her body started to gather, aware that something was coming, something magnificent and perhaps dangerous, something that would sweep her away, deeper into pleasure. Then it was upon her, brought on by his tongue, shattering her control into fractured cries that left her breathless. That left *him* breathless. Ruslan was not unaffected. His head rested on her stomach, his breathing hard and fast in the aftermath. Good Lord, what had he done to her, to them? And he hadn't even taken his clothes off. Dasha stared at the beamed ceiling and smiled to herself. She'd do something about those clothes just as soon as she could move again.

'Are you all right?' Ruslan lifted his head, looking up at her. His eyes were glittering sapphires, glowing with dark fire as if what had passed between them had not depleted him but sparked him.

'Mmm-hmm,' she answered drowsily. 'Except for one thing.' She laughed at the surprise flickering in his eyes. He'd not expected that. 'I see, it was meant to be a rhetorical question.'

Ruslan arched a playful eyebrow. 'The one thing, Madame, if you please?'

Dasha sat up on her elbows. 'Your clothes. We must do away with them, entirely. There are too many.'

Ruslan rocked back on his knees with a mocking nod of his head. 'As you wish, my lady.' He stood, fingers lingering at his stock. 'Shall I begin here, or do you have another preference?'

He was making her play and a naughty wicked

game it was. Dasha moved to the pillows and bent one leg up. 'I think starting there is fine… for now.'

He might be pretending he was hers to command, but she knew who was really in charge and it wasn't her. He directed all her attention, his every gesture ordering her eyes to take him in from the sculpted muscles of his arms to the lean torso revealed *sans* shirt and waistcoat, and downwards to V-shaped musculature that framed his abdomen before disappearing into the waistband of his trousers. She stared too long at those strong narrowing hips, her mind afire with imaginings of what lay behind his trousers. He made her pay for it with a wicked chuckle as he bent to his boots. 'Boots first, milady, if you don't mind.'

She did mind, but she gave him a coy smile and stretched on the bed. 'Don't take too long, I'm getting cold.'

He tossed away his boots. 'I'll come warm you soon.' His hands worked the falls of his trousers, drawing her eyes back to the core of him, hard, evident and rising behind the fabric. The game was nearly at an end for both of them, their bodies eager to return to one another. And he'd not had physical pleasure, Dasha reminded herself. Whatever mental pleasure he'd received from her pleasure, his body remained hungry.

Ruslan slid the trousers down past his hips, pushing underclothes along with them. Haste indeed, Dasha thought. But she welcomed it. Her body was hungry, too. She let her eyes feast first, taking in the whole of him, naked before her as she'd been before him. He was like a *bogatyr* of old, a knight errant of folk tales, all muscled strength, his body a weapon unto itself—taut as a bow, deadly as a bullet, sharp as a blade. Her eyes fell to the manly core of him where his phallus rose iron-hard and proud from its red-gold nest. There was strength even here. The thought that she would give herself over to that strength, that it would possess her, sent a shiver of desire through her, strong and swift. She reached for him, feeling his heat even at a distance. 'Come to bed, come warm me.' She drew him down to her as she spoke, the words a foregone conclusion. They were ready, there was no need to delay. This was what she wanted, her strong warrior in her bed. Tonight, they could be honest with each other, with their bodies.

She took him between her thighs, her legs parted in welcome, and yet Ruslan lingered over the act, kissing her mouth, her neck, his hand skimming the length of her, his fingers warm on her skin. His phallus nuzzled her stomach. He could not wait long, she thought. He was too ready, his own release too far overdue. His mouth hovered over hers, his eyes glowing coals. 'Dasha, are you sure?'

She knew what he was asking. Was she sure she wanted to give her virginity to a man she'd not be able to marry? She pushed the arguments away. Those thoughts had no place here.

'I've been sure for a long time, Ruslan.' Probably since that first night when he'd put his arm about her in the hall, dressed in his pyjamas, and allowed her to speak for herself. She kissed him hard, wrapping her legs about him so that there could be no mistake, no retreat. In response, he gave her no quarter, easing his length into the tight wetness of her channel, filling her slowly until she took him full. He rested then, the muscles of his arms taut where he rose above her, letting her adjust, letting her savour the sensation of the man within her. It was a wondrous feeling indeed to have him inside, a sensation made more wondrous once he began to move.

She gasped as a tiny flicker of pleasure sprang to life inside her, fading and returning with each thrust—return, retreat. The movement took up a rhythm of its own. She arched her hips to meet it, the rhythm making room for her, picking up speed as it went. Ruslan's head was tucked against her shoulder as he drove them towards a cliff, the rhythm careening towards a precipice. All she could do was hang on. Her body was beyond thought, although it had been warned, although it knew this could happen. As earth-shattering as her earlier reaction had been, this was something more, far more. Perhaps because it was shared, because this time she was not alone. Ruslan was with her entirely. The cliff came and the cliff went, and they were flying in the dark, breaking apart. Together. The fantasy complete.

The fantasy was so much more than he'd imagined, so much more than he'd anticipated. Ruslan ran an idle hand down Dasha's arm as she slept, tucked against him. Ruslan smiled in the dark. But the smile quickly faded. How many more times would he assume this position with her? Would this be the last? Now that the fantasy was fulfilled, would there be no more need for this? Would the allure of sleeping in his arms lose its appeal when it was no longer a rare treat? Surely there would be a few more times. They had a few weeks of travel ahead of them, a few more weeks of time out of time before they reached Kuban.

Ruslan shifted his position. Kuban was fast becoming a destination he both desired and dreaded. Kuban would hold answers for Dasha, it would hold her future, all that he wanted for her. But in turn for that prize, it would exact a price. If she were to succeed, it would change everything between them. If she failed...well, that outcome did not bear thinking about. If she failed, Ruslan doubted even he could protect her. She would not fail. He would make sure of it. Captain Varvakis, when he arrived, and Alexei Grigoriev and the myriad of supporters that would arrive with him would make sure of it.

Ruslan pushed the thoughts away. Those scenarios and those decisions were weeks away yet. He had time. They had time. If they were smart, they would find a way to enjoy it and turn these weeks into a rare gift. Ruslan looked down at the sleeping Dasha, beautiful and content. Even knowing what he wanted to do with these weeks, he couldn't forget the future entirely. It was in his nature to look ahead, to think of strategies and alliances. Who should they go to first? The Rebel leaders or the Loyalists? Who would be their greatest allies? Likely the Loyalists, but the Rebels might take it as a sign that Dasha meant to change nothing, that her politics would be old-fashioned like her father's. All right. So not the

Loyalists. The Rebels? And hope they weren't shot on sight or imprisoned?

Ruslan grimaced as he analysed the option. He'd rather not take chances with the Rebels, knowing that Ryabkin was in charge. If they couldn't go to either the Loyalists or the Rebels without stirring up animosity with the other side, that left the Moderates. It would help immensely if Varvakis were with them. He would know who to see, but they couldn't wait for the Captain. He would be weeks behind them. Ruslan would have to trust his own gut on this. The Moderates it would be.

He played out the following steps, assuming Dasha was accepted. He would see Dasha settled on the throne, his family name restored to honour and then he'd, what? Leave her there? Stay and serve her? Live in the shadow of her temptation for the rest of his life? Watch her marry? Watch her bear another man's children? Have a separate life he knew nothing about? Those were raw thoughts for a man to contemplate after bedding, especially for a man who was possessively protective of the people he loved.

Ruslan's hand stopped stroking, struck by the depth of that insight. Was he indeed in love with Dasha? Was the intensity of tonight due to more than a fantasy fulfilled? He knew how Stepan

would explain it—the natural outcome of stress
and close proximity. Tonight had been a culmi-
nation of emotional, dangerous, events. It was a
natural physical act, much like a soldier's need
to couple after battle. Such an explanation did
not do tonight justice. Ruslan knew how Illarion,
the poet, would explain it: beautiful, momentary
and fleeting. Perfection existed, but it didn't last.
By its very nature it simply couldn't.

Would this too fade? Would the sharp edge
he felt every time he was with her dull? Would
the excitement of her touch diminish over time?
Would her beauty, the intensity of her gaze,
knowing that it was fixed on him, become com-
monplace? Did he dare wish that it wouldn't?

Dasha stirred, coming awake. She murmured
something sleepy and seductive, her hand sliding down the length of him until she found his
core. Her fingers closed around him and he felt
himself rouse. Not that he'd had far to go, mind.
Having Dasha beside him, skin-to-skin in sleep,
had left him in a constant state of 'readiness' as
it were, a state of semi-arousal where his body
was alert should it be needed. Apparently, such
alertness was not in vain. He was going to be
needed.

Dasha kissed him on the mouth, levering herself up over him. 'It's my turn to be on top, I

think.' She cocked her head to one side in a moment of consideration. 'It does work this way, too, doesn't it? I don't see why it wouldn't. Not much different than riding a horse, I suspect.'

'Yes,' Ruslan managed to say, his erection readied now by the image she posed atop him, breasts high and firm, hair falling over one shoulder, a wicked smile playing across her mouth. 'It works this way, too.' He positioned his hands at her hips. 'Just lift a bit.'

'Ah, like a posting trot. One-two, one-two.' Dasha was teasing him now and he was rockhard as she allowed him to just touch the slick folds of her entrance.

'You're going to kill me, Dasha,' Ruslan groaned.

Dasha laughed and slid down, sheathing his length. 'Not yet. You seem pretty healthy to me.'

What would it be like to feel this way for ever? It was a dangerous thought for an exiled prince of Kuban to entertain as a renegade queen-in-waiting made love to him in the still of the night.

Chapter Sixteen

The fantasy survived the night and into the morning. Dasha woke at dawn to warm kisses and gentle lovemaking only to fall asleep and wake to breakfast in bed, tea and toast with jam delivered by Ruslan, her wine-merchant husband. 'The innkeeper thought toast would be appropriate after all the wine last night.' Ruslan laughed and perched on the bed beside her. 'How *is* your head?'

'Fine. It's my tongue that's a bit fuzzy.' Dasha made a funny face and sat up, giving him a wry, scolding look. He was trying to make excuses and she would not have it. 'I'm not hungover, if that's what you're asking. Which means—' she gave him a pointed stare '—that we can't blame the wine on anything that happened last night.' She smiled. 'Nor do I want to.' Not at all. If anything, she wanted more of last night. Was more possible? It provoked the question, how long could the fantasy last? Beyond breakfast in bed? Beyond the nights? Beyond the trials that waited for them in Kuban?

Ruslan squeezed her hand and rose from the bed. 'Neither do I.' It was an answer, but not a complete one. What did wanting resolve? What did wanting change? 'I need to see about getting the coach ready. Take your time.'

She did not let go of his hand as a little piece of reality slid between them. She met his eyes evenly. 'Are we in danger? Do you think we've been noticed or followed?'

Ruslan sat back down, careful not to slosh her tea. 'I don't know. I don't sense we've been followed. No one followed us on to the steam packet, which means we'd only have been followed if someone was waiting for us in Calais.' His thumb drew circles on the back of her hand. 'I don't know if the Union of Salvation came after you because we made your presence known in London, or because they had orders from Kuban.' The last seemed unlikely, but it could not be ruled out.

She saw a moment's regret in his eyes. He was second-guessing himself; if they hadn't left so precipitously, if he hadn't killed the assassin in Hampton's hall, they might have known. Stepan and Captain Varvakis would find out, of course, but little good it would do them on the road. 'You made the best choices you could,' Dasha offered. 'If we had stayed, there's no knowing how safe I would have been, no matter *what* the Union's motivation. Dead is dead.'

Ruslan nodded. 'Still, it doesn't change the fact that we're travelling blind. I wish I knew if anyone was behind us. I wish I knew if Kuban knows you survived. Will your arrival be expected? If so, will we be waylaid?' That was a polite wording for ambushed. He was taking care not to scare her.

'It's nothing I haven't thought of.' She wanted him to know she was no shrinking violet when it came to the realities of her life.

'I think we'll likely be safe until Marseilles. If anyone was waiting for us in Calais, we've given them the slip. At least in Marseilles, I have connections. We'll have help there.'

Dasha smiled. 'Then we have a reprieve.' She leaned forward and kissed him softly. 'We should make the most of it.' She smoothed back the hair from his forehead. 'I wish I could erase all your cares. You take too much upon yourself. Promise me you'll try to relax.'

'Is that an order?' Ruslan grinned.

'Yes. Now let me eat and dress so we can be

under way. We don't want to keep our vineyards waiting.'

'That reminds me, I want to have the inn-keeper arrange to send a few casks of the new red to Stepan.' Ruslan laughed. 'For verisimilitude's sake, of course.' And proof that they were safe, Dasha thought. The wine would serve in place of a letter and be far less incriminating. A letter could be intercepted. Intercepted wine from Monsieur Archambeault meant nothing.

Dasha ate quickly and dressed in the blue wool they'd acquired for her last night. She tucked the white fichu into the neckline of her dress, her fingers lingering on the fabric as she checked her appearance in the room's tiny mirror. She'd tucked her hair into a hasty bun low on her neck in a good facsimile of a merchant's wife, a few loose curls framing her face. But that was not what drew her eye.

Her lips were puffy still from last night, her eyes bright. Ruslan had marked her well in places seen and unseen. Beneath her blue-wool skirts she was sore and delightfully so. Just recalling the reasons for her soreness coloured her cheeks. She watched the blush creep up her reflection, her body heating at the memory of Ruslan's mouth on her, *everywhere*. He'd marked her in other ways, too, with his gifts. Her skin smelled of the soap, she wore the fichu at her neck, a white hair ribbon held her bun in place. The new cloak waited for her on the chair, ready to be thrown about her shoulders against the morning chill. All of them, reminders of his presence, of his protection. Just as he had in England, he was seeing to her needs again, keeping her comfortable even in times of distress.

Dasha picked up the cloak and smiled to herself. This time, she would see to his needs, too. He wasn't the only one who could take care of another. Dasha folded up her dinner gown and carefully put it in the satchel, with her as yet unworn nightgown from the fair.

She scooped up Maximus from his makeshift bed and took a final look about the room. It looked quite ordinary in the light of day, at odds with the momentous occurrences that had marked the night. It wasn't every night a girl fell in love with a prince. Because of that, she would make the most of every opportunity remaining to her. Nothing was certain—not who was on the road with them, ahead of them or behind them, or what waited for them in Kuban. She would be grateful for every day between here and Marseilles. And every night.

There were twelve of them. Twelve days spent in the coach studying about Kuban, talking about Kubanian policies past and present. Dasha applied herself diligently to those discussions. What impressed her most, though, was Ruslan's mind, the way he thought about situations and the people involved in them. He was fair and insightful, neutral and objective as he offered differing perspectives on Kubanian government. Even if he had not been her lover, she would have wanted him as her advisor. 'Do you think the time for a monarch has passed in Kuban?' she asked on their last day. They were scheduled to arrive in Marseilles that afternoon. 'Perhaps this rebellion is not so much about disagreement with policies, but with how those policies are made. They are imposed by one on many.'

Ruslan gave the thought his attention. 'It's possible. I had not thought of that before. I've been so close to the situation for so long that I haven't stepped back and considered underlying motives.'

Dasha leaned forward in earnest, pieces of various thoughts coming together after weeks of contemplation. 'Consider the rebellions occurring throughout Europe: the Greek independence movement, Sicily, Naples, Spain, Portugal, Brazil.' She listed off the countries. 'Sicily, Naples and Spain are ruled by monarchs. The people there have demanded liberal constitutions, Ruslan. In Brazil, colonists protest the need for representation not unlike the American quarrel with Britain last century. The world is changing. It's not just about an unfair law, it's about a way of living and governing.'

Ruslan chuckled. 'Those are dangerous thoughts, Dasha. Next, you'll have Kuban seeking to break away from Mother Russia.' But he didn't disagree. He didn't say they were silly thoughts. He said they were dangerous.

'How dangerous?' Dasha queried, leaning back against the cushions, arms folded.

'Those ideas would turn a country against the throne,' Ruslan warned.

'What if the throne was with them? What if the monarch espoused those ideas?' Dasha pressed.

'A constitutional monarchy? Like England?' Ruslan's eyes glinted. He was intrigued. 'It bears thinking about. It's what the Moderates want, although it might be a hard sell with the Loyalists.' Lord, he was sexy when he was thinking, one booted leg crossed over another, his brows V-shaped in concentration.

'Do you know what else bears thinking about?' Dasha was in the mood for a different sort of politics at the moment, having said her piece.

Ruslan grinned, very good at reading her

mind. 'How many ways I can pleasure you on the seat of the coach?'

'Hmm.' She twisted a curl around one finger. 'That is a fun game. But we played that yesterday. I was thinking today we could try a new game.' She licked her lips. 'How many ways can *I* pleasure *you*?' She slid to her knees in front of him with a wicked grin, her hands running up the insides of his thighs. 'Shall we play?'

His blood started to heat at the sight of his temptress on her knees. 'Do you need to ask?' His voice was already tinged with want. Just the prospect of Dasha's hands on him had him hard in seconds. 'You had me at "constitutional monarchy",' Ruslan growled appreciatively, as her hand shaped him through the fabric of his breeches. She'd probably had him even before that. Talking politics with her, listening to her mind work, was as erotic as watching her fall apart beneath him. They'd done quite a bit of both in the last two weeks, giving layers to the intimacy that surrounded them now, an intimacy that had become physical and emotional as well.

Ruslan shifted his hips as she worked his breeches loose, her eyes and hands intent on their task. Any argument that his attraction to her was based on circumstance and his need to protect was moot now. There was no mistaking the emotions Dasha raised in him for the emotions a caretaker, a bodyguard, might feel for his charge. These emotions went far beyond that and were summed up in a single word: *mine*.

Her hand closed over him, her thumb rubbing the tender tip of him, tempting, experimenting, rousing. She slid her hand along his freed length and his cock pulsed. Had it ever felt so good to be touched? He could not recall. He had done this before, a novelty game with his mistresses, but never with such naked intensity. Perhaps it was poorly done of him to think of such a thing at such a moment, but the comparison only served to heighten his unique need for Dasha. This, what was happening right now, was a passion nonpareil. Never had anyone given themselves to him so thoroughly, so completely.

Dasha gave him one last coy look from between his legs, her eyes sparking, before she bent her head and took him with her mouth, her tongue, murmuring her enjoyment as she went, tasting the length of him. She worked him with her mouth, squeezing and urging until he was in danger of sliding out of his seat altogether, so far gone was he. In a desperate attempt to stay upright, he reached for the leather balance strap. He should have reached for it a while ago and held on for dear, wonderful life. Life. He was *alive*. That was exactly the right word. He felt acutely *alive* with Dasha's touch on him, each nerve riveted to the sensations she called forth.

He groaned, his body gathering itself for a final surge, desperate to find relief, desperate to linger in the powerful gathering. But lingering or surging was not his choice, not within his mental control. His body was a wild thing now, with a mind of its own. It would decide for him. He could no more hold himself back than he could hold back the tides. He came hard and fast into Dasha's hand as the outliers of Marseilles came into view.

They were solemn as they approached town. Sugar refineries and oil-pressing factories replaced the fields they'd been passing for hours, a reminder that they were entering 'civilisation'. They were leaving the land of small, inconspicuous villages behind them and all that implied.

Ruslan passed Dasha a handkerchief, his eyes taking her in: her smile, her hair loose about her face, her eyes alight with the satisfaction of having brought pleasure to her man. *Her man.* For twelve days he'd been that and only that. Nothing else had pulled at him, demanding his attentions. 'I want to remember you just like this.' He wanted to remember them just like this, too, open and free to pursue their passion without restraint.

Dasha rose up on to her knees and placed her hands on his shoulders. 'I want to remember you like this, too,' she whispered before she took a deep breath and closed her eyes as if she could seal in the memory. The gesture shook Ruslan at his core. Over the past months, the past weeks, he'd seen how Dasha selected her memories, the way a diamond merchant might separate out the rarest of gems from a tray of hundreds; each one selected and set aside because of its significance, its ability to stand out from the rest. For a woman who hadn't a plethora of memories, the gesture spoke volumes. It wasn't the quantity of memories that mattered, but the quality of them. Ruslan bent his forehead to hers. He breathed in the scent of her soap, the lavender he'd bought her from the fair. He would never smell lavender again without thinking of her, without thinking of that night in Arras. He closed his eyes and joined her in the silent communion of remembering.

When Ruslan opened his eyes, they were closer to their destination in the harbour. In his makeshift bed on the seat, Maximus began to stretch; he, too, sensing that arrival was imminent. Buildings were closer together now, the streets narrow but organised as the coach wound its way to the docks. When he'd come through with Stepan and the others, Marseilles had been a godsend. Ruslan had operatives in Marseilles who knew how to hide a man or a woman, who knew how to help one acquire a new life if they wished, or sew a wound if needed. The city did not fill him with that sense of relief now. He would have preferred the small rustic villages of Provence, places where they could lose themselves, where no one would ever find them.

'Are you not pleased to be here?' Dasha rose from her knees, reading his face as she took her seat next to Maximus.

'I was just recalling how different the circumstances were when I was here last.' Ruslan busied himself with his clothing. But Dasha nodded as if he'd said more.

'I will miss the villages, too,' she said softly. Tonight, they would spend their last night as man and wife. They would go to Ekaterinodar not as the Archambeaults but as Prince Pisarev and Princess Dasha Tukhachevskenova.

The carriage turned down a final street. His friend, Guillaume, lived two streets down. They were nearly there. Ruslan felt something in his stomach clench. Time for new beginnings. Time to re-establish his objectivity. Time to avenge his family. As important as those reasons had seemed in London, when all of this had begun, they were markedly paler now when compared to the woman seated beside him.

'A penny for your thoughts?' Dasha ventured. 'Are you worried about your friend?'

Ruslan shook his head. 'No. I was just thinking how much I wanted to be a wine merchant.' He had, in fact, never wanted a vineyard as much as he wanted one right this moment. His kingdom for a grape. At the moment it seemed like a good trade.

Chapter Seventeen

Guillaume was the innkeeper of the Salty
Sailor, a weathered tavern on the docks, and he
looked the part—older, heavyset with deep-set
eyes that had seen much of the world. He might
always have been an innkeeper if it hadn't been
for the eyes. Dasha thought he might have been
something else, *someone* else, before he'd been
an innkeeper. Before he'd become French. Such
were the people Ruslan knew—intriguing, walking stories.

Guillaume welcomed Ruslan with a hearty
hug that would have cracked the ribs of a lesser
man. He showed them into a back room through
a secret door in the inn's brick wall, although
the taproom wasn't busy. 'One can never be too
cautious.' Guillaume winked at her, shutting
the door behind them. He wiped his hands on
a wide, white apron, his eyes sharp, giving her

a speculative look while he spoke with Ruslan. 'Now, tell me what is this business about needing safe passage into Kuban? Isn't it usually the other way around?'

'I need safe passage and news,' Ruslan clarified. 'What do you hear about the revolt, Guillaume?'

Guillaume raised a bushy eyebrow, no doubt wanting to know if he could speak freely in front of her. Ruslan nodded. 'You may speak openly. She's the reason we're here. Guillaume, this is Princess Dasha Tukhachevskenova, heir to the throne of Kuban.'

Guillaume's brows knit. Was that disapproval she saw on his face? For her? Or for Ruslan? The big man shifted on his feet. 'I didn't take you for a royalist, Ruslan. I thought you were against the Tsar's policies.'

'He is,' Dasha spoke up, unwilling to be talked about as if she weren't in the room. 'As am I. I mean to reform Kuban's governing practices, if given the chance.'

'If given the chance? That's the real question these days, isn't it?' Guillaume's initial hostility relented. 'I'll get some wine and ale, and we'll talk, yes?'

'He doesn't like me,' Dasha said as Guillaume left to get refreshment.

Ruslan held out a chair for her. 'Guillaume has reason. The Tsar took his land. He was nothing but a farmer who happened to have land the Tsar wanted for hunting.'

Dasha released a breath. Ruslan was watching her with steady eyes. She needed to be strong. He didn't need to cushion her from anything. 'I suppose I'll have to get used to it, to people not liking my...family. It still seems odd to say that.' She tried for a smile.

'They will like *you*, once they get to know you. They'll see that you're different,' Ruslan offered.

Guillaume came back with a tray and settled them with food and drink before launching into his news. Dasha listened intently, too intently. It was hard to eat after a while. Her stomach became a pit. No one suspected the Princess was at large. The attack in London was likely not linked to any orders from Kuban. This was all good news on the surface. She smiled, trying for confidence. 'We should have safe travel then to Ekaterinodar.'

But then the real work would begin. She would have to prove herself, not just her worthiness for the throne, as Ruslan thought, but her very identity. The latter created real fear the closer they came to Kuban. What if someone recognised her? What if they had known Dasha, by some impossible stretch of the imagination and knew she wasn't the Princess? What if she was denounced as soon as she stepped foot into Kuban? Guilt rose once more.

She should have told Ruslan before. Even when they'd first fled London didn't seem too late now in retrospect, although it had at the time. But now, her confession would be much too tardy to make a difference. Still, she owed him the truth, didn't she? She should tell him, but when? How? Or would ignorance save him? He could plead honestly that he'd known nothing if it came to that. No, that argument only provided a coward's shelter. She set aside her napkin. Her appetite was entirely gone. She had to tell him. Soon. Today. Before they went a step closer to Kuban.

Ruslan rose after they'd eaten. 'We'll need to gather supplies, Guillaume. Do you know somewhere we might find more appropriate clothes and passage to Ekaterinodar?'

Guillaume nodded. 'Passage is easy. You're in luck and that's saying something this time of year. There's a ship that sails tomorrow. As for the clothes, I know a few places to look.'

'I have enough clothes for travel. The two dresses are plenty,' Dasha protested. She didn't want to seem frivolous in front of this farmer the Tsar had dispossessed. Fancy gowns would not convince Guillaume she was different.

'Dasha,' Ruslan interrupted firmly. 'It will be hard to persuade people you're a princess when you only have two dresses. Guillaume knows what to do. In the meanwhile, allow me to show you around Marseilles.'

She understood. They would play the Archambeaults one last time. Under the alias of a wine merchant, Ruslan would send casks of the local Mourvèdre red to Stepan to tell him all was well and that they had made it this far—Marseilles, the last sanctuary.

Confession was good for the soul. The thought poked at Dasha, hard, as they walked the aisle of Église de Saint-Nicolas-de-Myre. The church was new, Ruslan shared, completed only last year. It was a testament to the cultural melting pot that was Marseilles, a port that was home not just to the French but to the Mediterranean world: Christians seeking refuge from Ottoman persecution, Kubanians seeking refuge from their provincial Tsar with his provincial policies, Greeks and Italians and Algerians coming to trade. The new church recognised that diversity. France was Catholic, but l'église de Saint

Nicolas was eastern in its flavour and ortho-
dox, too. Dasha saw evidence of it in the gold-
leaf icons, the abstract geometric mosaic and the
mid-eastern architecture. Dasha stopped before
the stand of votive candles arranged in front of
a Christ icon along the side aisle. She reached
to light one and froze. She stared into the candlelight, letting the images race fast and swift
through her mind. Words fell from her lips in
a rush in case the images slipped away, forgotten again. 'There is a cathedral in Kuban, Saint
Catherine the Martyr. On her feast day in November, we would go and light candles.'

'Yes, the royal family worships there,' Ruslan
encouraged softly, but she felt him tense in expectation and hope that a memory was coming.

She went on, clinging to the images in her
mind before they could slip away. 'I lit one for
Katya Ustinova, the general's wife. Her death
was so very tragic. I lit a candle for...' She
stopped there, cutting off the last words: *my
parents*. Why would she have lit candles for her
parents? They'd been alive. Unless... Her knees
buckled. She felt Ruslan's arms take her weight,
felt him guide her to a bench.

'You've remembered something else? Someone you lit a candle for?' Ruslan pressed quietly. She could feel the excitement building in

him over her remembrance. However, his excitement carried none of the anxiety of hers. She wanted to remember, yet she feared what those memories would show her, what she'd discover about herself.

Dasha bowed her head. She needed to tell him, *now*. What better place to confess her dirty secret than in a church? 'Ruslan, I have to tell you something and it will change everything.' Possibly even how he felt about her.

He risked his life for you, you owe him.

Her conscience stabbed at her. She hoped he didn't say meaningless words like 'nothing could change the way I feel about you'. They wouldn't be true. He couldn't love her, couldn't care for her, once he knew what she'd withheld. After weeks of travel, weeks of loving him on the road, she knew him well enough to know he would be angry over the omission, but more than that, he'd be angry she hadn't told him before, that she hadn't *trusted* him with this most vital fact.

She drew a breath and took one last look at his handsome profile. She wanted to remember him this way, the way he looked before he hated her. Then, she let her words out in a rush of hope and fear. 'What if I am not the Princess? What if there were two women on the landing like in my dream and Captain Varvakis rescued the wrong one?'

To his credit, Ruslan did not move away, did not look at her with anger. But his jaw tightened, his mouth set grim and his mind was working hard as he digested the words. She'd had months to process the idea. He had only a few moments. She was patient. She waited.

He fixed her with a stare, full comprehension dawning that she was not looking for reassurance. She was *telling* him something. 'This is not the first time you've doubted, is it?' He ran a hand over his mouth and this time he did rise from the bench as the other piece of her disclosure took him. It was the piece she feared most, the piece that would take him from her. 'You've doubted all along, haven't you, Dasha? You don't believe you're the Princess. All this time, I thought the doubts were only about your ability to rule, but they're about your very identity.'

He began to pace. She could see the full horror and complexity of the situation dawning on him. She could imagine what was running through his versatile mind, all he'd risked in bringing her this far, in putting his name to this mad scheme. To him, it hadn't been mad, merely a restoration of a rightful princess. Until now. Her confession changed all that. It was no longer a simple matter of facing down the Rebels, of persuading people knowing he was armed with the truth. He had only to make others see that truth. He would condemn her now.

Ruslan pushed a hand through his hair, making it stand boyishly on end, and her heart ached for him, for what she was putting him through. He'd been nothing but kind and she'd paid him with half-truths. Any moment, he would realise she hadn't been worth it. He turned to face her and she braced herself for the verbal blow.

'You *are* the Princess, Dasha.' This was not the condemnation she'd expected.

'Ruslan, listen, I might not be. In my dream, the other woman—' She began her argument, but Ruslan interrupted.

'We have empirical proof, Dasha. You embody the physical description right down to the scar on your wrist. You play the piano expertly, you remember not being allowed to have pets in the palace, you remember the cathedral where the family worshipped.'

'You want to justify my identity, it's only natural,' Dasha refuted calmly. 'After everything you've invested, you don't want to be wrong, not at this point.'

'No, I want to be *honest*.' Ruslan's words stung. Dasha swallowed against the implications of that simple sentence. *She* had not been honest in keeping her doubts from him. But the implications were more far reaching than even that. The issue of honesty called into question Varvakis's own story. If her doubts were true, it would mean Varvakis had lied. The very thought of that conjured up a host of other horrors—that Varvakis had lied deliberately to further the Moderate agenda or simply his own ambitions. If so, he'd made an imposter of her. She'd become a fraud with no name. She had no idea who she was but a man's pawn.

Dasha felt the world spin. Men had left their homes, risked their lives for her, for a lie. She gripped the bench. No, it couldn't be true. Her very sanity clung to Ruslan's arguments. Surely Ruslan was right.

Ruslan came to her, kneeling and taking her cold hands in his, his touch lending her strength. He was not repudiating her, but accepting her. 'It is natural for you to doubt. You have no memory of who you are. You are relying on whatever facts you can create, or whatever has been told to you, but your identity is there in other ways, too, implicit ways. You carry yourself like royalty. At dinner that first night, you knew which fork to eat with, how to handle difficult men and situations. Even the way you *think* stamps you as a member of the royal house.' He smiled here, catching her off guard. She knew he was remembering their many discussions about strategy, about decisions. His case was compelling. Even she was starting to be convinced. Perhaps her doubts *were* natural and perhaps he was right. 'Your cynicism should convince you if nothing else. You are always questioning motives, looking for angles, never accepting anything at face value. You passed the silk test.'

'What?' What did silk have to do with any of this?

Ruslan chuckled. 'Madame Delphine told me how you questioned the quality of the silk she showed you. How many people do you think would know the difference, let alone how to test it? Only a woman of exquisite calibre would know.'

Dasha froze, withdrawing her hands from his warm grasp. She missed his strength, his comfort immediately. Dismay swamped her. The dinner, the dresses and who knew what else? Maybe even the puppies at the stable had been a test of her character, or a test designed to prompt that specific memory. Oh, God, if that were true, then even bringing her here to the church had been a test. 'You were testing me.' This whole time he'd been testing her. For what purpose? But she knew to what purpose. It had been an issue of trust with him, too. He had not trusted she was who Varvakis claimed.

It was one thing for her to hold doubts, but for *him* to have had those doubts was somehow worse. A chasm began to open between them. They had not trusted one another. The unspoken accusations hung in the air between them. They'd given their bodies to one another, but in the end they hadn't given their confidences. She had not trusted him with her worries and he had devised secret tests of her worthiness, tests she had obviously passed to find herself here in Marseilles. But that only made it worse. Whatever they had between them was starting to unravel and it was her fault. She'd pulled the first thread with her confession.

'Ruslan, what happens now?' She managed to meet his gaze. Something in his eyes gave her wild, irrational hope. Perhaps they could stop the game here. They could turn back, go home to London and start again.

There could be no starting over. He could see that was the answer she craved. In truth, it was the answer he *wanted* to give her. The answer he *had* to give her was far more difficult. 'We go forward, Dasha.' He was resolute even as he was resigned to this less than satisfactory path. 'It is too late to do anything else.' Too late for Kuban, too late for *them*. What was done could not be undone as much as he wished it could be otherwise. If her doubts were founded…if she wasn't the Princess…the consequences didn't bear contemplating.

'Even if I am a fraud?' Dasha seemed suddenly fragile, ethereal, with the candlelight turning her hair, her face angelic in the shadows.

'You don't know that. Doubt is not a negation of the truth, merely a questioning of it,' Ruslan replied. 'You are a better option for the country than civil war.'

It was killing him not to touch her, but he knew if he went to her, he could whisper temptation in her ear, the very temptation she wanted to hear: that they could run. 'What do you want me to say, Dasha? That I will take you anywhere you want to go?' That he would be anything she wanted him to be, the exiled prince, the wine maker, the merchant? He would set aside restoring his family's honour for her. But that wasn't an option any longer.

She looked away from him. 'Maybe I am.' She shook her head against the impossibility of her request, and yet, what she had set out to do was no less improbable than what she asked of him—to find a way out. The only difference was honour. There was no honour in running away. Her country needed her, or at least they needed who they thought she was.

'To go forward will change everything, Ruslan.' She looked at him again, her eyes pleading silently for what she could not ask. Part of his heart broke at her remarkable strength. Even in desperation, Dasha would not beg. But she would try to protect him. He heard it in her arguments. She was warning him off.

'I don't know who I am, Ruslan. I might be a princess, but I might be someone else. I might in truth be the imposter that people may shortly accuse me of being. I don't imagine the Rebels will accept me without a fight. They will try to discredit me. If they are successful?' Her voice faltered over the words 'Well, there are consequences for that.'

Yes. Rather irrevocable ones: the block, the axe. He would spare her those images if he could. He had visions of Dasha, accused of treason, being put on trial for claiming to be the Princess. It would not be a fair trial if things made it that far and the end would be a foregone conclusion; Dasha executed through no fault of her own but through the mistake of one man. Varvakis could not be wrong. The stakes were too high. 'I won't allow it, Dasha. The Rebels will accept you. I will see to it,' Ruslan vowed.

'You will do nothing of the sort, Ruslan!' Dasha trembled, overcome at last, her bravery cracking. 'I will not drag you down with me. You can't save me from my fate.'

'No, but I can join you.' By God, he would go to that block with her and they would lie down together if need be. He did touch her then. Taking her hand, he raised her knuckles to his lips and kissed them.

'Absolutely not,' Dasha cried. 'Your death on my hands is the last thing I want. You need to keep yourself safe. Be my advisor, if you must. But give yourself some distance. Ruslan, promise me, no one can ever guess…' Her voice trailed off leaving the forbidden words unspoken. No one could ever guess they'd been lovers, that he carried her heart, that he would champion her still, after all she'd done. 'Give me your word, Ruslan.'

To give her his word meant giving her up for the greater good. He was reluctant to do that, but he was also reluctant to begrudge her anything she desired. 'Do you understand what this means?' he asked solemnly.

'Yes,' she answered quietly and he knew from the tears glistening in her eyes that it was not a choice she made easily. Going forward meant the end of *them* as they were on the road. Ruslan stifled a wave of emotion. He'd not thought today would end this way. He should have known better. Stepan had warned him not to fall for her. For all his detachment he'd fallen anyway. He just hadn't realised until now how far that would be.

He opened her hand and took a ring from his pocket, pressing it into her palm: the signet of the House of Pisarev, the one sign of his royalty. A pledge of fealty.

'You can't give me this.' Dasha tried to give it back, but he curled her fingers about it.

'Keep it as a reminder of my loyalty against times that come when you might question all those around you and feel beset by enemies on all sides.' He paused, searching for the right words. Those times would come to her soon. 'Keep it against tomorrow.'

Dasha nodded. 'But not tonight. Tonight, we are still us.'

'Yes, as much as we can be,' Ruslan promised. Tomorrow everything would change. But for now, they would be the Archambeaults one last time.

Chapter Eighteen

It would have been their last night together whether she'd confessed her horrible secret or not. To have the taint of an *affaire* about them would weaken them both in the eyes of those they'd need to impress. But there was no denying that a certain sense of foreboding and darkness had fallen over them. The evening carried with it a bittersweet edge.

Ruslan was honest enough to admit to himself they were both still clinging to the shreds of the fantasy they'd conjured between them on the road. That fantasy had suffered damage today, between their unspoken accusations and her revelation. But to what end? Mending that rift could change nothing. Tonight was about capturing one final time who they'd been on the road and a consummation of who they might have been if circumstances had been different. Tomorrow, all of this was to be forgotten.

Tonight, Ruslan came to her chamber as a bridegroom might, dressed only in a borrowed banyan, and found her waiting like a bride, her hair brushed out and loose, clad in a nightgown of Irish linen. She sat by the fire, the flame outlining the shadowy curves of her body beneath. He smiled when he saw the gown. He'd suspected she'd bought it. She'd had it all this time and had not worn it. She'd waited for a night like tonight—a *last* night? Or had Dasha, too, hoped for a different sort of night when they might celebrate in truth?

He stopped at the small table and poured two glasses of wine. He offered her one and sat beside her on the rug. *'Radost'moya.'*

To my joy. She was that. No matter what happened. No matter who she was. She had returned him to a life of purpose, not because he was going home to Kuban, but because he'd found meaning in loving her. He twined his arm around hers and they drank from one another's cup.

'A most loving cup indeed.' Ruslan kissed her and took the glasses, setting them aside. He stood briefly, capturing her gaze as he removed his banyan, letting her drink her fill of him and know his intentions. He meant to take her, here on the rug before the fire. He knelt on the rug, reaching for her. He felt her tremble in anticipation, as if they had never done this before and this were the first time. He gently tugged the ribbon loose at the neck of her gown, his hand slipped between the loose folds of fabric, tracing her breast. He watched the shadow of her nipple harden against the fabric in the firelight. He pushed the nightrail off her shoulders, revealing his bride inch by firelit inch, loving her slowly with his eyes, his hands, his mouth. He pulled her beneath him, his body positioned between her thighs, his phallus straining. She was ready for him, this bride of his. The scent of her arousal mixed with the lavender soap, heady and evocative.

He took her then in a steady thrust. She cried out, a sob of joy, of desire, and clung to him as if this were the last night of the world. Ruslan could not ignore reality any longer as he relentlessly pushed them towards completion, their bodies craving one final union. In the morning, the Dasha who'd slept beside him for weeks, who had discussed politics with him, argued policies with him, who sparked to his touch, who knew how to give unabashed pleasure, would be gone. In her place would be a queen, strong and beautiful, but restrained, unable to fully indulge herself for fear of consequences.

* * *

In the morning they dressed carefully in the impressive fruits of Guillaume's labours. Ruslan donned a long Cossack tunic of bright blue fabric with a heavily embroidered placket at the collar, the loose dark trousers of the Kuban and tall, sturdy boots. Dasha solemnly tied a wide black sash about his waist, knotting it on the side with care.

Ruslan shoved his not-so-ceremonial dagger into the folds of his sash at the last and slipped another knife into his boot. He felt as if he were going to war rather than to board a ship. But one never knew and word would begin to spread ahead of them. Perhaps the Captain who had so graciously agreed to give Prince Pisarev passage to Ekaterinodar had already sent a message on to a relative in port about his important but mysterious cargo and speculation was running in advance up the Kuban River to the capital. If so, he needed to be prepared for whatever reception awaited them. A good diplomat always carried a dagger or two.

Dasha finished the knot and stepped back to survey her handiwork. 'You look like a real Cossack prince.'

'I *am* a real Cossack Prince.' Ruslan laughed, trying to ease the strain of reality. They'd awakened tired, shortly after dawn. Neither had wanted to waste the night in sleep, but sleep had claimed them none the less towards morning. But now, Dasha's fatigue only seemed to heighten the hopelessness between them. They'd made love one last time, a rather desperate coupling, Ruslan thought, a futile attempt to hold back the inevitable. Even as he'd taken her, she'd started to pull back behind the mask of her green eyes. There was no spark in them, they existed solely as protection now, a barrier between her and the world. He missed the green fire already.

'You look quite fine as well,' Ruslan complimented. Guillaume had outdone himself in finding garments suitable for royalty. Dasha wore the results: a bright blue-wool travelling gown that matched his tunic with embroidered cuffs and an expensive cloak to match, lined in the white fur of the Arctic fox, a most queenly garment indeed. But Ruslan had been happy to pay for the clothes, just as he'd been happy to invest funds in the right sort of Captain. He'd got what he'd paid for on both accounts. This was no time to be frugal. After Dasha's disclosure, she had to go looking like a princess and that required all the trappings of royalty. Men could be dazzled by trappings. It might be that if he could dazzle them enough, they wouldn't look too closely at her claim, or at their doubts.

'Do I look fine, truly?' Dasha plucked at her skirts and straightened the clean, white fichu of Flanders lace, the one he'd bought her in Arras, he noted. 'Perhaps it is too bright? Perhaps I should have worn black?' Nervously, her hand went to a place between her breasts where it played with something on a ribbon hidden in her bodice. His ring, tied about her neck with a ribbon from Arras, yet another lover's trinkets.

'No,' Ruslan answered firmly, fetching his own travelling cloak from the peg. 'Blue is the state colour of Kuban and it is a show of strength. There will be time for mourning once this business of government is settled.'

He made no reference to the other items she wore. It was best to keep their thoughts on the business that lay ahead of them, to keep their minds occupied with moving forward instead of contemplating all the 'might-have-beens' they would leave behind in this room. Ruslan swung his cloak about his shoulders, a signal it was time to go. The Captain wanted to leave early. It would be a five-day journey by sea from Marseilles to Ekaterinodar and the mouth of the Kuban River. He opened the door for her. He dared not take her hand, not even one last time, the gesture far too intimate for a princess and her advisor.

Left behind, too, in this room would be all the

familiarity, all the intimacy of the past weeks.
There could be no more soft glances, no more
quick touches, no more familiar possession of
her body. His touches now must be relegated
to only the most appropriate—a brief, guiding
hand at her back or at her elbow to direct her attention or to navigate her through a crowd. Perhaps a stately kiss to her knuckles as he bowed
to her on the throne.

He would make the most of those moments.
He was her bodyguard now, and her advisor.
They would have the secret intimacy of words
left to them. Whenever they spoke of government policy, they would both remember other
times and other places where those conversations had occurred, and that would have to suffice, as would the small gifts she wore, each one
containing a memory.

'Your Highness, it's time to go.' Ruslan met
her eyes, a silent reminder that this had been her
choice, although he'd given her others. If he'd
been in her place, it would have been his choice,
too. They had that in common. Duty first, even
when it hurt.

Your Highness, it's time to go.
With those words, Ruslan had 'left' her, becoming Prince Pisarev to her once more, as he

had been in the beginning, a most able court-ier doing his duty. Dasha stood at the rail of the ship, her gaze riveted on the fading shores of Marseilles, while her mind relived that awful moment at the door. She had seen the wall come down in his beautiful blue eyes at the very end when she'd passed by him.

How brave he'd been to wear his feelings on his sleeve until the very last minute. She had not been that brave. She'd thought it would hurt less to 'leave' him first. She'd pulled her emotions away from their lovemaking, trying to create detachment, trying to protect herself. She knew Ruslan had noted it, although he'd said nothing.

In the end, it hadn't mattered. It had physi-cally hurt to lose him. She'd stumbled in the hallway, putting out a hand to the wall to catch herself. But Ruslan was faster, he'd been there, with a hand at her elbow to steady her. Their eyes had met and for a moment she'd thought he would break, thought he'd say the familiar words, 'Dasha, are you all right?' But the mo-ment passed, his touch effective but remote. It didn't seem to stop her body from reacting, though. Her arm was hot where he'd steadied her, her mind a riot of sensations and memories of other touches, better touches.

Ruslan came to join her at the rail, a careful

space between them, his shoulders straight, his hands clasped behind his back, his entire body alert. Alert to what? There was no need at sea. The Captain had been vetted, a Loyalist to his core, Guillaume had said with a hint of distaste. If the Captain questioned her own identity, he didn't show it. His acceptance was a relief, but a small one at that. A man like the Captain would never have seen such a high-born woman as the Princess. He had nothing to test her authenticity against except Ruslan's word. However, he had not questioned her right to the claim. Surely that was a good sign?

Of course he hadn't, Dasha chided herself over her desperation to claim any sort of victory. Ruslan had paid the Captain handsomely for his acceptance of the facts. Ruslan was her capable knight, like the Ruslan of fairy tales. He managed everything beautifully, including farewell. His lovers at court must have appreciated how skilled he was in separation—all manners and politeness, making it easy for their relationship to re-establish more neutral ground. He'd given away no emotion, no sense of hurt this morning, unlike yesterday in the church when there'd been emotion aplenty. That scene in the church remained poignantly etched in her mind, not only because of the raw power behind it, but because it could very well be the last time she saw Ruslan, the real Ruslan, exposed and naked to her, every emotion etched in his eyes. That man had been neatly put away and replaced with the courtier.

Tears stung her face. She didn't bother to wipe them away. The wind off the waves would do it for her. She fingered the ring beneath her dress. That was another image she'd carry with her always, of Ruslan pledging to be hers, curling her fingers around his ring. His ring was tangible proof of his true feelings, a talisman against the times that would come when she would doubt.

Did the Kubanian court ever see that side of him? The deep emotion, the deep loyalty that drove him, or was that only reserved for his close friends? She was not looking forward to court. She would be faced with her father's accusers, others like Guillaume whom her father had wronged, people who would hold her accountable for the crimes of a family she couldn't remember, or those who would want her to honour her father's favours in exchange for their continued loyalty—favours she knew nothing about. She expected there would be some who would push that advantage if they could, if she proved vulnerable. There would be Ruslan's lovers, too. She wanted to meet them even less.

Dasha cast a sidelong glance at his profile, the beautiful sweep of his jaw, the apples of his cheeks, the long, straight patrician nose, the wind wreaking havoc with those thick red-gold waves. The women would be glad to have him back. She had no right to expect Ruslan would be celibate. A lifetime of celibacy was not for him, nor did she wish it for him. He was not made to be a monk. And herself? She would inevitably marry and that, by its nature, would require a man in her bed. A man not Ruslan.

A lump formed in her throat and she looked away, directing her gaze out over the water. This had been her choice and she'd chosen poorly. She'd wrought this unhappiness for both of them and she would pay for it the rest of her life. Doubt flooded her. She'd had so many chances to walk away. She could have stayed in London as an *émigrée*, she could have disappeared into France with Ruslan as her husband and become wine makers in truth. She wondered if they would have been very good at it? But she'd doggedly chosen the responsible route—to be the Queen everyone saw in her, the Princess everyone told her she was, even when she didn't quite believe it herself. A country needed her, justice needed her. There were wrongs to right, many of them done by her own family. In five days, that decision which had already been tested privately would be tested publicly. Once they made port at Ekaterinodar, she would officially be home. She had five days left to learn all that needed learning, to acquire enough memories to prove she was the Princess, five days left to remember again.

'Your Highness, would you like to bring Maximus up on deck for a walk while I have cards set up in the saloon?' Ruslan directed her away from the railing. He knew too well that if she stood there, she'd be wallowing in regrets the rest of the day. 'Cards can be a nice distraction to the tedium of sea travel. The Captain has a chess set we might use, too,' he offered, sending a delighted cabin boy scurrying for the puppy.

Maximus did lift her spirits. He was a rambunctious puppy who was eager to play.

They spent the greater part of their five days on deck playing tug with Max with a piece of old rope. The puppy made them laugh and, when he settled down to nap, they spent long afternoons in the saloon playing cards and chess, which she never won. When they were together like this, the activities and the puppy between them, she could almost pretend the old days were back, that they had not deserted one another. Deserted was too strong of a word. He had not deserted her. She was by no means abandoned. He'd planned every hour of her days, been with her every hour of those days, so that she needn't be alone, or be afraid, a reminder that they were in this together.

But it simply wasn't the same and she wanted it to be. The days were tolerable, but the nights were not. Her bed was empty and she feared sleep even as she courted it. To sleep meant a chance, perhaps, to remember, but she was afraid to dream, afraid to cry out. Would Ruslan come to her if she did? She had not been afraid to sleep when he'd slept beside her. She had not dreamed most of the trip through France, her evening thoughts occupied by far more pleasant things than fire and swords, blood and mysterious women she couldn't name. She had a strategy for waking herself: Maximus. The puppy slept beside her now, curled up in a ball as if he understood she needed him. He'd taught himself to lick her face when her sleep became agitated, which woke her. But the closer they drew to journey's end, the harder it was to stave off the dream…

'Dasha! Come!'

Her sword was out and they were close to the stairs; a few more steps and escape would be in her grasp. They were going to make it despite the flames and the smoke!

Then a man loomed before her, large and heavy, intent on evil, sword drawn. Instinctively, she backed up, but there was nowhere to retreat. Flames were behind her. She couldn't go back.

She raised her weapon, parrying the first blow, but it nearly numbed her arm. This man was so much stronger. It was different than parrying for fun with Vasili and Grigori. She would have to act fast. Her strength wouldn't last. That was what the boys had taught them; when outmatched, strike fast and hard because you won't have second chances.

She took another blow, blocking it, noting how he left his left side unprotected. He wasn't expecting a woman to attack. She took her blade and struck hard with everything she possessed, the blade burying itself into the man's unprotected side, the impact sending a jolt up her arm.

She let go the hilt, staggering back in shock, the world reeling, blackness hemming the edges of her vision. No, she couldn't faint. She still had to get them out. It was hard to breathe. She stumbled. The smoke was too much.

She reached out to grab something stable

and solid in her reeling world. There was blood on her hands. The man was dead. She fell, she screamed...

'Dasha!' She was surrounded by something warm and solid at last, but she clawed at it, her mind not fully transitioned from dream state to waking. Her voice was a litany of sobs and panicked gasps. 'Dasha!' The voice came again, this time firm and commanding. The hands that held her gave her a little shake. 'Dasha, wake up, you're safe.'

Ruslan. He'd come. The *real* Ruslan had come. He was dressed in his borrowed banyan. He'd come straight from his bed next door and he'd called her by name. She held up her shaking hands, her throat working hard to get the important words out while Maximus scrambled on to her bunk. 'I killed a man. With my sword. A man on the landing.' She could only manage phrases. There was something else about the dream that had seemed odd, different, this time, but she couldn't recall it. Perhaps it was too insignificant compared to the enormity of this knowledge.

Ruslan covered her trembling hands with his. 'I know. Varvakis told me he expected that was what happened before he arrived.'

Dasha stared at him, uncomprehending at first. 'You knew? Varvakis knew? Everyone knew? Except me?'

'Captain Varvakis felt it was unnecessary to tell you. You had suffered so much trauma already, it seemed cruel to subject you to more.' Ruslan held her eyes with his, perhaps wanting to calm her with his gaze. 'Do not blame him alone. I questioned the decision, but I followed it. It is my fault, too. I could have told you. I didn't because I didn't want your dreams influenced by any more manufactured memories than it already was. You'd already inserted your brothers' names into the dream whether through real memory recovery or through our lessons. We had no way of knowing.'

Dasha was not sure she wanted to be calm, but she did want to be clear and logical. She drew a deep breath. 'No, I don't blame you. You were protecting me, protecting the dream, the only link we have to what really happened that night.' But when she saw Varvakis again, she would discuss this with him at length. More important at the moment was the implication of his omission. She let Ruslan's touch steady her, let his strength buoy her own flagging resources before she spoke. 'If Varvakis omitted this, what else did he leave out?'

'Don't, Dasha. *Nothing* can come of doubting now,' Ruslan warned, gathering her to him. 'Even if Varvakis left something more out, it's too late to change course. We are already committed.' Something in his tone caused her to look at him, noting for the first time he wore trousers beneath the banyan. He'd not risen from sleep at her cry. He'd already been awake.

'The Captain has received word that a delegation will meet us in Ekaterinodar and have arranged for us to take a barge upriver to the capital. The messenger was rowed out in a dinghy just an hour ago when we set down anchor. I have responded. I told them Her Royal Highness appreciates the courtesy and will gladly join them at nine o'clock after she has broken her fast.'

'What time is it now?'

'Nearly six.' Ruslan disengaged her hands and rose from the bunk, all serious advisor now. 'We have three hours to review.'

Chapter Nineteen

So this was where the first test would take place, at the harbour of Ekaterinodar, the contested sea entrance to Kuban. Ruslan stepped down from the gangplank and offered his gloved hand to Dasha, his eyes surveying the port, taking in the busy docks, the imposing fortifications with their cannons. An unwanted fleet would struggle to make berth here in one piece. The port had been a gift to the Kubanian Cossacks from Catherine the Great, a gift that needed defending from the Ottomans. In the past fifty years the Cossacks had successfully defended the port for Mother Russia. How fitting that this was where the delegates had chosen to meet them. Ruslan understood their message perfectly by selecting this spot, the very first point of contact with Kuban. No one got into Kuban without permission.

Ruslan offered Dasha his arm. She laid hers

atop it with ceremonial precision. The gesture hardly qualified as a touch and yet he could feel her fingers tremble in their fur-lined gloves. But her eyes were steady, her face calm, her posture regal as if not a bone in her body doubted her right to claim her identity. Good. They would need that confidence.

The delegation of two waited at the end of the pier. They would not be easy to convince, but they would not be the most difficult Dasha would face. They were the men Varvakis had mentioned. The Captain had told the truth in that regard. Now, he studied each man in turn as he and Dasha made the walk. He'd briefed Dasha over breakfast and now he ran through the few facts he had to focus his mind and review his strategy.

Ivan Serebrov, the bulky bear of a man on the right, was the father of a schoolmate, a very conservative family who had served the Tsar for long years. Serebrov was definitely a Loyalist. Ruslan would be quick to remind Serebrov of his friendship with the man's son. Ruslan was more worried about *his* reception with Serebrov than he was about Dasha's. They would be sympathetic to her even if they weren't sympathetic to him. His gaze drifted to Count Anatoly Ryabkin, the Rebel leader. That was an unfortunate development. There was bad blood between him and the Count, who had done nothing to use his influence when Ruslan had asked him to intervene on his father's behalf.

Anatoly Ryabkin was a nobleman with radical ideas. Ruslan was not surprised to see him coming to the fore in the new order, but Ruslan did not trust his motives. He would be difficult to manage, a man loyal to no one but himself. Ryabkin would benefit more from being a sceptic over Dasha's return than in accepting it. Ruslan would need to neutralise him quickly.

At the end of the pier, Ruslan made a formal bow. 'Allow me to present Princess Dasha Tukhachevskenova.'

Serebrov came forward first, bending over Dasha's gloved hand with a kiss to her knuckles. 'Your Highness, my condolences on your family. What a miracle it is to find you alive. Your father's leadership is missed.'

'It is not.' A look of disgust crossed Anatoly Ryabkin's handsome face. 'Are we going to stand out here in the cold, kowtowing to a woman just because she claims to be a resurrected princess? The family, the whole, entire damn family was taken out and shot for exactly this reason, in front of witnesses, so there would be no question of hereditary leadership.'

Ruslan felt Dasha freeze, stunned by the level of Ryabkin's vituperative invective. She had known, of course, that she would face dislike. Ruslan's hand went to the dagger beneath his cloak. 'Count, you go too far. The Princess has survived and has journeyed far to restore order to her country, and to forgive those who have wronged her family, even as she seeks to redress wrongs done *by* her family.' Ruslan eyed Serebrov, watching the man's response. Would the idea of redressing past wrongs resonate with him? Ruslan needed an ally. That ally would not be Ryabkin.

Ryabkin snorted in disbelief, making no attempt to hide his distaste. 'Are you her stooge, then, Pisarev? She sends you to beg on her behalf? You've become the official royal groveller? How did you manage that? Did you seduce her, too, like all the other women at court? Or are you simply that desperate to reclaim position at court?'

Ruslan stiffened. He felt Dasha's eyes on him, wondering at the remark. If not for her, he'd have no hesitation calling Ryabkin out. But if not for her, he wouldn't be here to face the Count's slander.

Serebrov had the good sense to look scandalised by Ryabkin's outburst. Serebrov made a gesture with his hand towards a warehouse. 'There is a samovar with hot tea and a room ready for us. If you would follow me?'

He led them to a hastily converted room. A scarred work table sat in the centre surrounded by mismatched chairs. The setting was at odds with the finely dressed lords and Dasha's rich cape. Ruslan pulled out a chair for her at the head of the table and took up a spot at her right shoulder, forcing one of the other men to serve the tea. He'd be damned if Dasha was going to play the subordinate and wait on them.

'I must apologise for the Count,' Serebrov began, once everyone had tea. 'I hope you recognise not all of us are so inclined to poor manners.' Serebrov shot the Count a censorious look. 'However, I will not ignore his sentiment as irrelevant. If I may put it more delicately, the family *was* killed. There were no survivors and then two days ago we received word that the Princess was arriving from Marseilles on a ship. You can imagine our surprise. The counsel that now sits in Kuban met hastily and called for volunteers to ascertain the possibility the Princess was still alive.'

The room was cold. Ruslan could see Serebrov's breath as he spoke. He was wary, too, careful with his loyalties as he waited to see how power would be determined in this new world. The man was a reactionary, not a revolutionary. He might call himself a Loyalist, but there was some irony in that title. When it came to decision time, Serebrov, like Ryabkin, would look out for himself. All eyes were on Ruslan, waiting for the official response. But Ruslan remained silent, letting Dasha speak. The sooner they accepted her authority, the better.

Dasha nodded her head. 'I understand your dispositions entirely, gentlemen. This is a most unusual situation.' She was calm, confident. 'I would be happy to recount the events of that night for you as proof that I did indeed escape. I would also be glad to answer any questions you might have.'

Ruslan's heart soared with pride at her command of the situation. They'd rehearsed the telling of the tale, keeping the tale succinct but truthful. There was no need to lie. Neither was there any need to say anything that would give the impression of loose ends. This would be a tale she'd have to tell over and over again. It was important all audiences had the same version. 'Captain Varvakis can verify my story. He was the man who caught me on the stairs and carried me to safety,' Dasha concluded. She gave no sign of the emotional toll it took to tell the story.

It was not an easy one to share, knowing how it ended: with a man dead by her own hand, her family destroyed and the reality that she would have been destroyed, too, on Ryabkin's orders that night, if Varvakis had not been there.

The mention of Varvakis got a reaction from Serebrov. 'Where is the Captain now? Did he not accompany you from London?'

Ruslan answered. 'He is en route with a British delegation who support the Princess. The Princess and I chose to come ahead and prepare the way for their arrival. I expect them in a few weeks.'

Serebrov sneered at the mention of the British. 'What do we want with the English? I hope you haven't sent us a Trojan horse,' he accused Ruslan, 'invading us at our most vulnerable.' He pointed a finger. 'Don't think I've forgotten you favour more liberal policies like your father.'

'I favour what is good for the country and that is the avoidance of civil war,' Ruslan replied sharply.

'And I suppose you think putting a Tukhachevsken back on the throne is in our best interests?' Ryabkin sneered. 'Perhaps that's what is good for *you*.' His eyes drifted over Dasha in an insulting leer. 'I grow ever more curious as to what she has promised you, Prince Pisarev, to put her on the throne. A place in her bed? A place in her council? Both? Perhaps she promises you the position of consort.' He looked at Dasha, his eyes lethal. 'You do know a lie of this magnitude is tantamount to treason.'

'What are you suggesting?' Dasha answered evenly, forcing him to name his accusation.

Ryabkin was not shy. 'That you are not the Princess, but an imposter set up by the Loyalists to restore their power.' A murmur circulated about the table.

'It is no lie.' Dasha was cool, her voice raised slightly, but from his vantage point, Ruslan could see the tight clench of her hands in her lap, hidden beneath the table.

Ryabkin was not impressed. He overrode her, ignoring her response. 'How convenient the Princess Dasha has not been seen for years in public. Anyone might claim to be her. Anyone might tell a story of rescue. Perhaps she's promised Captain Varvakis something, too, for his collusion.'

Ruslan did not care for the insinuation that Dasha would play the whore not only for one man but for two. But he could not react without looking jealous or without looking like the sort of man Ryabkin accused him of being. He fixed Ryabkin with a stare of steel and waited for his opportunity. 'She has told her story. Varvakis tells the same tale.' He nodded towards Ryabkin. 'You make good points, so good in fact that one wonders why she would risk faking such a thing. Why indeed would anyone seek the throne of a volatile little principality where they risk death simply by making a claim? It seems there's little to gain and much to lose.'

'Perhaps another test then, Your Highness.' Ryabkin made a lightning-quick move for Dasha's arm, but Ruslan was faster. His not-so-ceremonial dagger pinned the man's coat sleeve to the table.

'Keep your hands to yourself, Count,' Ruslan said coolly. 'The Princess has shown you every courtesy from meeting with you in this dingy room, which is entirely beneath her station, to tolerating your slurs upon her character.' Ruslan pulled his knife out of the fabric. 'If you continue, I will be more than pleased to oblige you on the field of honour.' Sometimes there was only one way to handle men like the Count and it wasn't always the most diplomatic. Still, it established a certain tone. It was best they all knew where he stood on the issue of Dasha from the start.

Ryabkin rubbed the rent left in his sleeve, his gaze malevolent. 'Does the Princess have something to hide like the lack of a scar on her wrist?'

Dasha pulled back her sleeve and turned her arm over to reveal the soft side of her wrist and the half-moon scar. 'That should satisfy, Count. I acquired this scar the summer I turned sixteen.'

Serebrov gloated his approval. 'Cool under fire, that's Tsar Peter's daughter, all right.' He stood. 'I think she has admirably passed any test we might give her at present. I suggest we escort her upriver to the capital and see what the council makes of her. There's not much more we can do here.'

Ryabkin rose begrudgingly, momentarily defeated. 'This is not approval, Princess. The Council might decide they don't want a monarch on the throne, or they might decide they don't want a Tukhachevsken on the throne, no matter how pretty.'

Despite the Count's words, however, it was still a victory and Ruslan would take it. They'd been granted entrance and escort to the capital. He didn't fool himself. This was where the real testing would begin, where Dasha would have to know more than the names of her brothers and how she got a scar on her wrist. It wouldn't simply be enough to prove she was the Princess. She would have to persuade them her ideas for Kuban were in both parties' interests. After today, Ruslan saw just how difficult that would be. Men like Serebrov would want her for her father's sake, but not her ideas. Men like the Count would want her ideas, but not her.

He could smooth the way for her, but Ruslan would have his work cut out for him. Perhaps the work would help fill the emptiness inside of him. It had been a special sort of torture to watch her endure Ryabkin's insults today and do nothing near what the bastard deserved. Ryabkin had tried to break her and she'd resisted. She'd been ready for him, intellectually, emotionally. Ruslan had been proud of her, even if he ached for her. He would have to get used to the hurting. Today, she had moved out of reach for good. The Count's insinuations made any non-political association Ruslan might pursue with Dasha beyond the pale of possibility. It made Ruslan wonder what Ryabkin hoped to gain for himself with such a show of force. Ryabkin would bear watching.

Dasha shut the door to the library behind her. It was small but well furnished, as was most of Ryabkin's town house where everyone was staying. She would have preferred to stay anywhere else, but there had been no refusing without looking rude and suspicious. She leaned her forehead against the frame and closed her eyes, breathing in and breathing out. It was only for one night. Tomorrow, they would all sail up the Kuban River on a barge to the capital. And at least she was alone for the moment.

It was a condition she welcomed and hated. She'd spent the day surrounded by men for whom she had to perform, for whom she had to be the Princess. Every movement, every word scrutinised. It was exhausting to always be on her guard. But being alone also meant she was without Ruslan. He'd stood by her side all day, stoic and watchful. He'd nearly skewered more than the Count's sleeve when Ryabkin had grabbed for her. But in other ways, he'd left her, as he'd promised, and she felt the distance keenly. He'd not met her eyes. He'd not touched her beyond what was required. He'd not made conversation with her.

She would have liked nothing more than to be in bed with him, to feel the reassuring strength of his body against hers, to talk the day over with him. Instead, he was housed in a chamber far from hers—a deliberate move, she thought, on Count Ryabkin's part. There was bad history there, although Ruslan had never said anything about it. Watching them today, she'd felt like someone who'd come late to a play, the second act already underway.

Dasha moved to the fireplace and drew a chair close to it, letting the heat of the flames warm her. She'd best get used to being alone. Ruslan was beyond her now by her own choice. She'd been prepared to let him go. She'd not been prepared for the hollowness the decision left inside, as if nothing else mattered but finding her way back to him. She closed her eyes, reaching into her mind for memories of him, of his touch…

The opening of the door jolted her awake. She must have drifted off. She turned towards the sound, startled to have her sanctuary invaded. She was even more startled to see who it was. Count Ryabkin stood at the door, still fully dressed for evening. There was the faint smell of cold weather and cigar smoke about him. He'd been out sampling the delights of Ekaterinodar.

'My apologies for frightening you.' He inclined his head and smiled. 'Are you comfortable? My town house is not large, but I like to think it is well appointed.' He gave a smile meant to convey humility and modesty, but it was self-deprecating at best. Dasha didn't think there was anything humble or modest about the Count.

'You did not frighten me,' she clarified with a cool smile. She wanted him to be clear on that point. It would be a cold day in hell before the likes of him would scare her. 'You merely startled me. I must have fallen asleep.' She made to rise. After his rather unsavoury comments about her virtue today, his dislike of her was unquestionable. She had no desire to be alone with him. 'If you'll excuse me, I must find my bed. We have a long journey tomorrow.' Serebrov had arranged for them to go upriver on a barge to the capital. He'd meant it to be her triumphal entry.

The Count moved towards her, making it impossible for her to gain the door. 'Perhaps a drink first? Have a seat, Your Highness. You and I have things to discuss, starting with your choice of advisors. How well do you know Prince Pisarev? Because I know him very well and his family, too.'

'I do not wish to be a party to gossip.' Dasha did not retake her seat. She would leave the room even if she had to force her way past him.

The Count settled himself in the chair opposite the one she'd vacated, unbothered by her effort to exit or else confident he could stop her with words alone. He let her make it as far as the door. 'It's always a shame to see an ambitious family overreach themselves and fall from grace. Of course, it's no wonder, given Pisarev's circumstances, that the Prince is so eager to see you on the throne, with his assistance of course.'

She made the mistake of looking at him. Ryabkin laced his hands over the flat of his stomach, a smug smile on his face. 'You can walk away from me, but you can't walk away from the truth. Why don't you ask him how his father died?'

Dasha slammed the door behind her. She would not give Ryabkin the satisfaction of seeing her upset. But inside she was roiling. She wanted to run to Ruslan, to beg the truth from him, to be told Ryabkin lied. She could do neither. It was what Ryabkin wanted. It would give the Count proof Ruslan was not a neutral party.

She gained her room and locked the door behind her, breathing hard as her mind worked, determined to dispel Ryabkin's ignoble insinuations. Ruslan was *not* using her for advancement. If he was, he wouldn't have broken off their affair, he would have needed that leverage. Or would he have broken it off anyway because the road to success required it? She groped for his ring beneath her clothing. No. It wasn't true. Because if it was, it called into question the motives behind all his actions, most notably, had he seduced her to get what he wanted?

Dasha sank on to the bed, feeling more alone than she ever had. An intuitive memory came to her.

This was life at court, all the guessing and second-guessing, and the game was just beginning.

Chapter Twenty

She was home! Her blood sang with the knowledge of it the moment the barge turned the final bend in the river and the city came into view with its gold domes, and whitewashed limestone buildings. She *knew* this place. Dasha closed her eyes and willed the memories to come. Snatches of remembrances made their way to the surface: boating parties, summers spent on the river, Vasili teaching her to fish. She opened her eyes to find Ruslan watching her, a private smile flickering across his lips. He was well turned out today, in a long, warm, wool coat with a thick fur collar. The wind had already had its way with his hair.

She smiled before she could think better of it, before she could remember Ryabkin's accusations. Ruslan looked away quickly, careful not to drawn anyone's attention, but not before she'd seen the emotion in his eyes. He understood. He was feeling it, too—the country welcoming him home. She ached at not being able to go to him, to stand at the rail with her hand in his and celebrate this homecoming. But it was Serebrov who was beside her, sharing the moment. 'It's a beautiful day to come home, Your Highness.' Serebrov beamed as if he'd ordered the weather on purpose for her.

Dasha made the appropriate responses because she should, she owed him that in exchange for his arrangements. But her heart wasn't in it. This was yet another level of loneliness: to be alone in a crowd. To be isolated because of who she was. If she was lonely, if she was aching, if she could not go to Ruslan when she wanted and confront him about Ryabkin's suppositions, well, that was her fault. *She'd* chosen this course, a course that meant all she could have with Ruslan were stolen moments, brief as they might be, a private smile, a look across the room. Perhaps with time, they might contrive something more. Until then, this was her choice.

She'd chosen honour and duty, and even the satisfying of her own curiosity over remaining in London, over fading to anonymity and recreating herself. *She had chosen.* It was a mantra she repeated to herself daily as she settled into the business of negotiating for the throne, the business of remembering. Her days were long, filled with meetings, and thankfully, with memories. Ruslan's doctor in London had been right. Surrounding herself with familiar things would help the memories. Every day, she remembered more: more people, more places.

She was aware Ruslan worked tirelessly on her behalf. If her days were long, his were longer. He met with people, travelled the countryside and brought back news. She knew within a moment of his arrival that he was in a room. Her body craved even the slightest touch or acknowledgement from him. The road to Marseilles seemed like another lifetime but late at night, her body didn't forget what it was like to burn even as it realised it might never burn again.

There was no opportunity to see Ruslan alone until she'd been in Kuban for two weeks and even then the opportunity was quite unplanned. She'd gone to the river to walk beneath the trees with their scarlet leaves and clear her head from a meeting gone on too long. She'd asked for privacy, but a few short minutes later, hooves pounded on the trail behind her. Dasha turned, ready with an imperious scold. Sweet heavens, could they not manage without her for five minutes? The scold died on her lips when she saw the rider. It was Ruslan, his hair a characteristic mess, as he pulled the horse to a walk and dismounted.

'Dasha! What a surprise.' He grinned, letting the smile take his face.

She laughed. 'Why don't I quite believe it? Who told you I was here?' She would forgive their lapse in following orders if it garnered her a few precious moments alone with Ruslan.

'I winkled it out of an unsuspecting page boy.' Ruslan's grin was infectious. She felt the cares of the day evaporate as he strode towards her, reins looped about his arm.

'Winkle? Is that an entirely English word?' Euphoria bubbled up inside her.

'It is.' Ruslan's gaze searched her face, his grin turning into a more sombre expression. 'But I didn't come out here to talk about winkling.' It was a subtle reminder they hadn't much time. 'How are you, Dasha? There hasn't been a moment to see you, to touch you.' The naked hunger of his blue eyes stole her breath, confirmation she had not been the only one to burn. It was almost her undoing. She would have flung herself into his arms if she hadn't been so acutely aware that anyone might come down the trail at any moment.

'I am fine, as good as can be expected. And yourself?' Dasha studied his face, taking in the tiredness that lurked behind the smile and the tell-tale shadows beneath his eyes.

He shrugged, dismissing her concern. 'You are remembering, more and more every day. I can see it in your face.' She heard the quiet joy in his voice, saw it in his eyes, the way they lit like blue flames. He was happy for her. She had not forgotten how to read him. Even apart, they remained in tune to one another's moods.

'I am remembering. Your London doctor was right. All the familiarity has brought so much back.' She could hear the excitement and relief rising in her own voice as she told him. 'I remember rooms, decorations, little things I had like a hair brush, or a favourite dress, where I went to celebrate holidays.' It felt good to share that news—she had not realised how hungry she was to unburden herself, to share her news, her secret.

These long two weeks, there'd been no one she could tell, no one who could be privy to that part of her struggle. And yet, she would disappoint Ruslan. She had to tell him the good and the bad. 'I still don't know who I am, Ruslan.'

She shook her head and gave voice to her frustration. 'Every day I wake with the hope that this will be the day I remember I am the Princess. But every night I go to bed without the answer.' Of all the things she remembered, she couldn't remember the most important item of all.

Ruslan reached for her hand, squeezing in sympathy. 'It will come, give it time.' *And us?* she wanted to ask. *Will that come, too?* She was not sure there was an answer. If there was, she was not sure she wanted to hear it. What if this was all they could have, stolen moments beneath the autumn leaves, always on alert for an intruder? For now, it would have to be enough to hold his hand, to walk beside the river, to feel his body move alongside hers, his long strides shortening to match her own.

'Do you like being home?' Dasha redirected the conversation away from herself. She watched his face come alive as she knew it would. She'd caught him in a few unguarded moments since their arrival, a certain contentment on his face as he took in the scenes around him.

'Kuban is very beautiful, very wild. I don't think there's any place quite like it in the world.' Ruslan smiled at her and she could see the genuine pleasure he took in his country. 'I've been remembering, too, Dasha. I had forgotten just how lovely it was.' A trill of pleasure rippled through her at the veiled compliment. Just for a moment, they weren't talking of nature any more. His gaze lingered for an instant and then the moment was gone. 'When I walk along the river, when I look up at the trees, or into the hills, or hear a wolf howl at night, I remember why I love this place, but I am also remembering why I left it. There is great joy for me here, Dasha. But there is also great sorrow.'

They'd reached a bend in the river where a slender birch grew beside the water. They stopped beside it in silence, taking in the raw beauty of the landscape. 'Does it have something to do with Ryabkin?' Dasha ventured quietly.

Ruslan gave a wry smirk. 'Has Ryabkin been talking?'

'Yes.' She would not lie. 'He maligns you at every council meeting.' She paused, hesitant to continue.

'And what else?' Ruslan's eyes narrowed.

'In private, he has insinuated you seek power for yourself through me.'

'In private? When have you been alone with him?' Anger flashed in Ruslan's eyes. She'd not anticipated such a reaction. She'd simply meant to assure Ruslan that the accusation had not been made publicly. Public would mean a duel. Rus-

lan would not be able to let such remarks pass
uncontested.

'Just once, in Ekaterinodar. It was not by
choice.' Good heavens, Ruslan was jealous.
'Your animosity is unlikely. The two of you
should be on the same side, both of you want
reform. The only difference is that you want it
through my restoration and he does not.'

'It is because of my father,' Ruslan said slowly
and she could see what the confession cost him,
the hurt the memory brought him. She reached
out her other hand and covered his. This time,
she would be the one to offer comfort.

'Will you tell me?' she asked softly.

Ruslan leaned a shoulder against the birch
trunk, his thumb running idly over the knuckles of her hand. 'My father spoke out against the
Tsar, politely of course. My family was a great
favourite of your father's. My father felt because
of that favour he was well placed to bring an un-
popular opinion to the Tsar's attention. He also
believed that those who encouraged him to be
the messenger of that news would stand with
him once the message was delivered. He went to
the Tsar, telling him how unhappy noble families were with certain laws regarding marriage
and service to the country. But the news dis-
pleased the Tsar. A few families were dispos-

sessed of their lands in retaliation and Ryabkin began to fear he would be next. So, he went to the Tsar and turned the Tsar's ear with tales of treason, suggesting my father conspired against him. My father was imprisoned, and he chose to die there instead of facing trial so that no definitive claim of dishonour could be attached to the family name.' He paused and cleared his throat against the emotion summoned by those words, the wound still fresh after all this time. 'It was a vain gesture. My mother died shortly afterwards from grief.'

'Thank you for telling me,' she said softly. He was giving her the sanitised version. She noted the omission of words like betrayal and suicide. He was omitting the hurt, too, how much it had pained him to experience the loss. She risked a more intimate touch, the sweep of her hand against his cheek. She understood better now how much this homecoming meant to him, how much he was counting on her. She understood what drove him. How strange. All this time, she'd felt she was the one relying on him, when, in truth, he had been relying on her. They were not dissimilar in that regard, both of them bound by duty and honour to see this task through.

'I will not fail you, Ruslan.' She could not bring back his family any more than she could bring back her own memories, but she would restore his pride.

Ruslan gripped her hand before she could take it away. 'Do not be alone with him again, Dasha. The Count is dangerous. He will not hesitate to kill if there is no other way to clear his path. If we are successful in winning the throne, there may shortly be no other option left to him.'

She nodded, understanding the gravity of that circumstance. 'But I will have you beside me.'

'Yes. I will be beside you, as I have been from the start,' Ruslan vowed, letting her hand go. He stepped away, loosening the reins and preparing to mount, preparing to leave her; his words were a poignant reminder that the two of them existed in a half-world where their very closeness to one another fed the chasm that kept them apart. Dasha watched him ride away with an ache in her heart. If they had not loved one another so well, that chasm would not exist. This was what came of loving someone more than oneself and it was a most exquisite pain indeed.

Chapter Twenty-One

Work could not overcome the pain, but it could dull it, Dasha discovered. She threw herself into efforts to reconcile the opposing Loyalists and Rebels and to assert her claim to ruling the country. The 'Return', as she had privately branded it, was going as expected, in good ways and in bad. But Dasha liked to think anticipated resistance was a better form of resistance than encountering the unexpected. The Rebels, whipped to a paranoid frenzy by Ryabkin, still worried they couldn't afford a Tukhachevsken on the throne and, as long as the Count led them, her acceptance would remain in question. In fact, it was that very issue that brought the council to a stalemate: the Rebels, on the Count's advice, were unwilling to accept her claim to the throne on the grounds that she was an imposter.

'I say we exhume the bodies.' Ryabkin unleashed his latest salvo in the council room of the capital late one afternoon. The announcement brought discussion to an abrupt halt.

Dasha felt herself pale at the vulgar audacity of his request. The man was an ass. Did he say things simply to get a rise out of people? It unfortunately worked. A murmur went up around the table. 'Why not?' Ryabkin spoke over the rumble. 'It's only been five months since they were buried. We can still identify the bodies and count them. We can end speculation from the Loyalists that Rebels did not really kill the royal family.' He shot a malevolent glare at Dasha. 'We can do away with this pretence and get back to the business of governing.'

He enjoyed painting her as a traitor. She couldn't help but shoot a rare glance in Ruslan's direction where he sat at the middle of the table. He was well dressed in a suit of brown wool that brought out the russet hues of his hair, but these weeks had taken a toll on him. Exhaustion edged his eyes and lined his mouth.

'Do you call this governing?' Ruslan interrupted, deflecting the man's attention from her and directly challenging the Count himself. 'In the weeks I've been here, I've seen nothing but factious squabbling over petty spoils instead of any real attempt at governance.' He waved a dismissive hand. 'Rebels, Loyalists, you're nothing. You've been given a taste of power and you're drunk on it, looking for ways to better your own personal positions. The Princess has a real plan. You should start listening to her.'

'The Princess!' Ryabkin scoffed. 'Care to join her on the block, Pisarev? I'll keep the axe sharp enough for two.' He twisted his mouth into a sneer. 'Although I doubt you'll need it. You'll probably do yourself in beforehand, a coward like your father.'

Ruslan half-rose in a posture of aggression. 'How dare you!'

Ryabkin gave a cold laugh. 'How dare *I*? How dare you? You, who accuses me of being power hungry when you're the one who acts as the supposed Princess's lackey, you, who claims a seat at this table only because of her. I am not blind, Pisarev. I know what you want and I know what you're willing to do to get it, because I've known *you*. I know how you wooed for the Tsar, seducing diplomats' wives on command. You were the Tsar's lapdog and now you're hers, still hoping for the same thing: power and control.'

'I should call you out for that,' Ruslan snarled. Dasha had never seen him so fierce, not even the night he'd killed the assassin in Lord Hampton's hall. She was acutely aware that if not for her bid for the throne, if not for the state of the country, Ruslan would not have hesitated. But now, he could hardly risk killing the Rebel leader without shattering the tenuous truce. The Count had insulted Ruslan beyond the pale. Ruslan's face was drawn tight, exhaustion prominent in the starkness of his cheekbones. Whatever leash Ruslan had himself on wasn't going to last much longer.

'Call off your dog, Princess. Show us he is under your control and not the other way around,' Ryabkin growled, sitting back in his chair, secure in the blasted knowledge that she could do no less. 'He is using you, whoever you are, for his own gain. It's what he's been trained for.' He gave an evil stare. 'But maybe that's all right with you.'

Dasha glanced around the table. Was no one else going to stop Ryabkin? No one met her eyes. Of course not. Ryabkin had them all cowed, all of them afraid they'd be the next victims of his threats. Dasha cleared her throat. She would not give him the complete satisfaction. She chose her words with care, keeping them neutral, and focused on him instead of Ruslan. 'Count, I would like to return to the work at hand before it grows much later.' Servants had set out the lamps. People were tired and tempers were high after another day of getting little accomplished but soothing ruffled feathers. But perhaps the more rational among them would sleep on the ideas discussed and wake up inspired. A girl could hope.

Ryabkin turned his sneer her way. 'No. No, I will not return to work. I am done taking orders from a woman who claims to be a princess, and an exiled prince.' He rose, bracing his hands on the polished table, eyeing each member of the table in turn. 'I will listen to her when we exhume the grave and prove beyond a shadow of a doubt who she is.' His gaze swept the rest of the council. 'I suggest the rest of you do the same. When I wake up, I expect a message telling me the time and the place. Until then, I will not sit down and negotiate.' The Count was holding the council hostage until he got his way. He knew full well nothing could be decided without him.

What did she do now? Ryabkin had trussed up the council like a Christmas goose. She fought the urge to turn to Ruslan, to seek direction in his gaze, knowing to do so would be a grave error. To glance at him now, while the council was looking to her to calm the uncertainty Ryabkin left behind, was to add credence to Ryabkin's slanderous claims about her virtue and Ruslan's ambition. She turned instead to her father's old ally. 'Serebrov, please conclude the session and make whatever arrangements are required.' And she departed the room with all the dignity left to her, hoping no one guessed just how much turmoil her thoughts were in.

Dasha staggered in the hall, putting out a hand to the wall to keep herself from falling. Ryabkin's tirade had been overwhelming. Exhumation! Not just of the bodies but of nasty 'truths' as well. Dasha stumbled over the thought. Ruslan! Part of her hoped he'd come after her, even as the more logical part of her brain knew he wouldn't, *couldn't*. He was aware of the risks of such a choice as she was. If he had, she could have confronted him, could have laid Ryabkin's charges to rest. Was he right? Was Ruslan using her? She shouldn't even think it and yet how could she ignore the accusations when they so neatly provided the answers she'd been seeking?

The accusations made sense. Hadn't she been looking for an explanation for Ruslan's kindness, an explanation for his level of investment and risk in her? Ryabkin's revelations certainly offered that explanation. It was the second time he'd introduced them. But she didn't want to accept them. Accepting such conclusions made a lie of all she and Ruslan had shared. It called into question her good judgement, it questioned all she knew to be true. How could she rule a nation if she'd so badly misjudged a single man? She tamped down on the doubts. She was *not* wrong. Ruslan cared for her. She was wrong to let the insinuations of a man who wanted her removed or dead destroy what she and Ruslan had so carefully built.

But tamping down those doubts was easier said than done. Alone in her room, haunted by doubts over Ruslan and over what the grave might reveal, it was no surprise sleep did not come. After hours of tossing, Dasha threw off the covers and lit a lamp, her mind full of what ifs. What if Ryabkin was right? What if she wasn't the Princess? What if he was wrong? What if his outlandish request was more than a ploy to torture her? What if it was a sign of desperation? It would be a dangerous victory for her.

Finding there weren't enough bodies would prove her infallibility, but such a defining act would force the Rebels to either accept her or eliminate her permanently. She feared the latter. Deep in her gut, she knew Ryabkin had no intentions of accepting her leadership even if the Rebels would. She calmed herself with reminders. She had faced assassination before. But then, Ruslan had been beside her. Then, she'd trusted him implicitly. Today, whether she willed it or not, Ryabkin had cracked the armour of that implicit trust a little further.

You chose this, came the punishing mantra.

Yes. She had and she didn't want it any more. She wanted to un-choose it. How many times had she wished for the impossible? To go back in time to those early days in London when the choice was still hers? She didn't want to be Queen, not if it meant being alone, not if it meant being without Ruslan, not if it meant questioning the motives of the man she loved.

There was nothing for it. She could not sit here and stew. She had to confront him before things went further, consequences be damned. Dasha got up and searched for a cloak. Ruslan would not come to her. But she could go to him. And tonight she would. Whatever happened tomorrow, she was done being alone. Politics and plots could be damned.

Dammit, not now. A soft knock on his chamber door shortly after midnight had Ruslan gritting his teeth. He set aside his reading, a copy of Locke's *Concerning Human Understanding*, and tightened the sash on his banyan. He'd been looking for enlightenment and a way forward. His mind needed a break from meetings and managing people, from thinking about Dasha and the horror on her face when Ryabkin had uttered his remarks, exhuming more than bodies, exhuming doubt, which was just as dangerous. Ryabkin thought to divide them. Every bone in Ruslan's body cried out to go to her, to comfort her, to protect her. He pushed a hand through his hair. Oh, God, what she must be feeling, knowing what Ryabkin demanded of her. He wanted to hold her, to tell her it would be all right, that she need not be scared. Would she believe him or did she believe Ryabkin's cruel hypotheses? That he'd orchestrated all this for his own gain? That he'd seduced her for his own purposes?

The knock came again, more persistent this time. It would not be ignored. Ruslan gave a resigned sigh. Apparently, there was one more item that needed his attention. He uttered a single, terse word, 'Come.'

He regretted the harshness of his command immediately. It was not a politician who slipped inside his rooms, but Dasha, swathed in a cloak, the white of a nightdress peeping beneath its folds, a midnight vision in wool and white silk. She'd come for answers, of course.

She simply stood in the room and spoke one choked word. 'Ruslan.'

Only then did he realise she'd been crying. 'I

can't…' Her voice broke. Her face told the rest of the story.

I can't do this any more. Not alone. Not without you. I need you. I want you.

Desire and desperation were naked in her eyes. She had not sought him out for answers alone.

Ruslan crossed the room towards her, he would reach her in two strides but Dasha was unwilling to wait. She met him halfway. Then, she was in his arms, her mouth taking the hungry, needy onslaught of his. Weeks of denial had led to this. 'God, Dasha.' His voice was husky against her throat. If he did not devour every inch of her, his body would explode. He was the starving man and she the feast. 'I cannot be gentle about this.'

'Then, for heaven's sake, don't be.' Her response trembled with the weight of her own desire, her hands digging into the depths of his hair for anchorage, for leverage, holding him to her as much as he held her.

Ruslan lifted her legs, taking them about his waist, and bore her back against the sitting-room wall with a primal growl of promise. 'As you wish, my lady.'

Chapter Twenty-Two

She wished for his hands on her aching breasts, for his mouth on her pulsing mons, for his tongue at her seam, for his cock inside her, hard and strong, anything that would push her thoughts towards oblivion. She framed his face with her hands as he pushed back the silky folds of her nightdress, baring her thighs, as he balanced her between his body and the wall. 'Ruslan, I want you inside me, *now*. I can't wait. Don't make me wait.' After months of wanting to remember, all she wanted to do tonight was forget, to obliterate Ryabkin's potent cynicism with Ruslan's lovemaking. A man who could bring her such pleasure, who could look at her with such a gaze, surely would not betray her. Surely the very intensity of his lovemaking was powerful evidence against Ryabkin's claims.

His banyan fell to the floor and he answered

with a deep, hard thrust that had her arching against the wall and moaning inanities of relief. She had needed this, needed *him*—oh, how she'd needed him! She locked her legs about his lean hips, her body joining him in the heated rhythm of his thrust and pull, his mouth on hers, swallowing her cries in rough kisses that devoured and delighted. She wanted to be used, wanted to be marked by this man, owned by this man who understood her so well, who'd respected her decision to return to Kuban, even at the expense of their own happiness.

And still, he had proven stalwart beyond measure these past weeks, tireless and protective on her behalf. The image of his knife slicing through the Count's sleeve when he'd grabbed for her wrist remained imprinted in her mind even weeks later. The Count hadn't stood a chance against the speed of Ruslan's blade, or the speed of Ruslan's mind. Ruslan was two steps ahead of the man, ahead of all of them, all the time. He had countermoves for moves that hadn't yet been made.

Ruslan's hips ground into hers, hard and relentless in the pursuit of their passion. Climax wasn't far off now and her body revelled in it, in being set free if only for a few moments. His final thrust came and they fell into oblivion, his body taking hers with it in a powerful, explosive release she'd been craving. Her breath came in ragged gasps. Her hands gripped his shoulders, feeling his body slicked with the sweat of his exertions. His mouth was buried against her shoulder, his breathing laboured. She put a soft hand to his head, stroking lightly. 'There now, everything is better now.' A beautiful truth if only for a while. The darkness would be back. Ryabkin with his barbaric remarks would return. But for now there was bliss. For now there was obliteration.

Ruslan carried her to the bed, his phallus still deep inside her, where she knew it would rouse again. She didn't care. Let him take her over and over tonight without respite. She wanted to give him everything they'd denied themselves these long weeks. Already he was growing hard again. His lovemaking would be gentler this time, now that the initial thirst of desire had been slaked. He worked her nightgown up over her head and made a trail of slow kisses down her neck, her breast bone, taking one nipple at a time in his wicked mouth.

'I miss you and to what end? I hoped our separation would keep you safe.' She was drowsy now. What a delightful way to fall asleep: Ruslan's mouth at her breast, his phallus deep inside her where she could feel him coming to life, her mind free of doubt. A man who could love like this could be guilty of nothing, 'But people accused you anyway. Ryabkin has all but called me a whore and you my throne-hugging paramour,' she said with drowsy distaste, but in the wake of Ruslan's kisses, the words lacked any real invective. There was no room for hate in this bed. She hadn't wanted Ruslan to throw himself away on her, but he'd done it anyway. She hadn't been able to stop him. He'd waded into the fray, knife drawn, his wit razor-sharp. 'I couldn't protect you, it was all for nothing.' Her doubts seemed silly now. Too silly to bring up.

'Never, Dasha.' Ruslan kissed her mouth. 'I have never considered anything I've done with you as thrown away.' He began to move inside her and she sighed, her body relaxing around him. This was pleasure at its finest. She twined her arms about his neck and smiled up at her lover. Yes, *her lover*. She would acknowledge the terms now. The tempo of his thrusts quickened and she matched him with her hips. Ruslan had never failed her. He'd saved her life, he'd stood as her objective, worthy counsel, encouraged her to explore choices. But beneath it all, he'd wanted her for herself, memory or not, princess or not. It had taken these weeks in Kuban to realise that and the rareness of it. She felt her pleasure build in response. There would be release once more, sanctuary once more. In his arms, she didn't have to be a princess.

They lay quiet after that, bodies happily replete. She rested her head on his shoulder, her finger making idle circles around the flats of his nipples. 'Will the Count actually dig up the bodies?' Dasha asked. Now, perhaps they could talk a bit, safely, softly, secure in the privacy of Ruslan's bed, the heavy damask cover pulled up over them for warmth against the cold early winter nights, the bed curtains drawn about them. They might be the only people in the world in this cocoon.

'Yes, he won't be satisfied. I am sorry, Dasha.' His hand moved up her arm, warm and firm, raising delicious goose bumps in its wake.

'I can't bear it,' she whispered. 'I know I should be brave. But I don't know how I will stand there and look at the bodies. I can't imagine…' Her voice broke and she had to stop speaking. She feared the things she'd remember at the sight of those bodies. All the grief she'd held back for lack of remembering would flood her. It would no longer be a general grief but a personal one. It was *her* family in the ground.

'You will bear it because I will be beside

you. You will bear it because you will call the Count's bluff. Not only will you show up tomorrow, you will be there when he is proven wrong. The Moderates will side with you out of empathy if nothing else. You are not the only one who finds Ryabkin's request barbarous in the extreme. His latest gambit will serve you far better than it will serve him. He has handed you victory and he doesn't realise it yet.'

'Tomorrow?' Dasha murmured. 'So soon?' She'd hoped for a day or two's reprieve, hoped that someone would talk Ryabkin out of it in the interval. But Ryabkin had got what he wanted.

'Yes. We need him back at the table. We need progress. The Rebels grow restless with all the talking and nothing to show for it.'

Dasha sighed. 'Where are Grigoriev and Varvakis? I thought they'd be here by now.' Every day she looked for them like a general waiting for reinforcements.

She felt Ruslan shrug in the dark. 'Any day, I think. Don't worry, Dasha. I have men out looking for them. Messengers will come with news of their arrival the moment they are in sight.'

Dasha was not fooled by the assurance. 'You're worried, too.' She levered up on an elbow, trying to see him better. Ruslan was so seldom worried that it was worth noting.

'Yes,' he admitted. 'I had expected them last week and if not that, at least sight of them.'

'You don't think anyone rode out to do them deliberate harm?' Dasha tried to piece together the rationale for such violence and couldn't make it work. Such action seemed too rash.

'No. The Count and the Rebels can only stand to gain from British assistance. The Loyalists can't touch them because it would be too obvious and they would immediately be blamed if something happened. For the Moderates, it's simply not worth the risk,' Ruslan reasoned. 'But power-hungry Kubanian politicians aren't the only danger.' There were highway brigands, swollen rivers, snowy mountains, storms at sea. Any one of those occurrences would put a large entourage behind schedule.

Ruslan snuggled her close and she welcome the warmth of him. 'Sleep now, Dasha. The morning will come too soon.'

She would sleep, soundly, for the first time in weeks. 'I have one request. Wake me at dawn. I would see the sunrise with you.' There would be time for lovemaking, for a final memory to fortify her against the horrors that awaited. Tomorrow would be best when it was over.

Ruslan woke her at dawn, as promised, with warm kisses on the back of her neck, her body spooned into the curve of his. Oh, to wake like this every morning.

She reached up a hand to stroke the stubble of his beard, liking the masculine rub of it against her hand. 'Mmm.' His phallus prodded against her bottom in welcome.

'Don't move, don't do a thing. I want to take you like this.' Ruslan's whisper was hoarse at her ear. 'From behind, your body tucked against mine.' He came into her as he spoke, a gentle easing that took her breath away with its tenderness. 'My mouth at your neck, your breasts in my hands.' He sheathed himself in a long, slow motion, creating a delicious anticipation that started low in her belly. 'Sweet heavens, Dasha, how you fit me so well.' His thumbs ran over her breasts and she moaned, loving his wicked words as much as the press of his body. She could climax on his words alone.

'Like this, you're all mine.' Ruslan thrust again, holding her tight against him, his hands anchored on her breasts, reminding her that she was entirely in his thrall. Her pleasure was at his mercy and her body wept for it. But Ruslan did not disappoint, did not seek to play a game of torture, but to satisfy them both. They would both have their moment, that place in time where the line between falling apart and coming together became very grey indeed.

* * *

The sun was long past rising when Dasha woke the next time. Ruslan was up, her body knew it immediately the way a body could sense when another beloved has entered the same room. The low murmur of voices in the other room confirmed it. She was thankful for the bed draperies that hid her, although she knew Ruslan would not allow anyone to discover her here. There was a brisk command from Ruslan followed by the shutting of the door. Then nothing, only silence. Not the rustling of the movement or the clinking of breakfast china. Not the sound of Ruslan's bare feet padding across the floor towards her. Ruslan was a busy man, always in motion. The silence, the lack of movement seemed ominous.

Dasha sat up and dared to call out. 'Ruslan?' That set the sound of feet in motion. The bed curtains drew back, daylight revealing Ruslan's face, clean-shaven now, but far more grim. Something had happened. 'Another evil pronouncement from Ryabkin?' Dasha smiled, although the Count's announcements were no laughing matter.

Ruslan shook his head. 'I've just received word.' Instinctively, she reached for his hand, clutching it tight. 'Grigoriev has turned back.

There was trouble in Germany and they were waylaid after difficulty with a band of brigands. They could not resupply quickly enough to beat the snows. Grigoriev feared if they didn't turn back, they wouldn't beat the winter storms on the Channel either.'

'Difficulty with brigands?' It was hard to imagine General Vasiliev and his men overcome by common highwaymen, few as they were— Vasiliev wasn't bringing an army with him, just a small group of military observers—they were still trained professionals, and there were Grigoriev's men as well.

She watched Ruslan's throat work as he swallowed. 'It was an ambush at night. The men were disoriented, according to Grigoriev's report.' He hesitated and her pulse leapt in fear of more bad news. 'Dasha, Captain Varvakis was killed.'

A cry of dismay escaped her. 'No!' Not Varvakis, her last link to the night she should have died. He was the one person the British delegation couldn't afford to lose. He could collaborate her story. He could remember for her what she didn't remember herself. Now he was gone.

Ruslan knelt before her, taking her hands, his eyes steady. 'Dasha, I need you to be strong. You've done well without Varvakis this long, you will be fine without him. Serebrov believes you. He will not publicly denounce you and the Moderates want you on the throne, they will not scrutinise you too closely for fear of losing their own chances.'

It took her a moment to focus on his words. In hindsight, she wished she hadn't. He was not giving her reassurance. He was bracing her for more. Ruslan took a note from his jacket pocket. 'This came with Grigoriev's report. It's meant for you, I think. If I had known, I would not have broken the seal.'

Dasha scanned the note and then re-read it in disbelief. 'Varvakis's last testimony?'

'Grigoriev was with him at the end. We can trust Grigoriev wrote down the truth.'

She gave her attention to the note again, reading each word carefully. She raised her head slowly to meet Ruslan's patient gaze. 'Dear God, there *was* a second woman on the landing.' Just as there had been in her dream. But it was the worst news possible on the worst day possible when her very vindication hung in the balance. She breathed the damning verdict in surreal disbelief. 'Varvakis lied.'

All the doubt she'd held at bay for months came flooding back. Dasha wanted to weep, wanted to scream. Would the nightmare never end? If only she could remember. If only Varvakis were alive. If only Varvakis hadn't lied. So much now hung on his tiny omission. Had he rescued the wrong woman? Was she the Princess? Was the other woman the Princess? Had Dasha even been on the landing? 'Why did he do it? Why did he lie?' She was angry now. The final bulwark of her foundations had been kicked out from under her. She had counted on that singular piece of information for so much. Now her world was upside down. Now, nothing was as she'd believed it to be just hours ago.

Ruslan's answer was quiet. 'I think you know.'

She did know. Varvakis had done it for the Moderates, for their grab at power. She was a vital key in achieving their agenda, a convenient link to both the past and the future. She simply didn't want to accept it. She let numbness take her as she made the next necessary leap of logic. If Varvakis had used her, then who was to say Ruslan had not done the same, only he'd done it so much more convincingly. All the peace she'd fallen asleep to, all the security she'd felt in Ruslan's bed, evaporated. She'd been a fool.

'What Ryabkin said about you, it's true, isn't it? You seduced women to change their husband's minds. You used sex for leverage.'

'You can't be thinking that's what I've done here. Dasha, be reasonable. I was the one who warned us against any intimacy,' Ruslan argued in disbelief. 'I gave up my home, my friends, my comforts. I *killed* a man in Lord Hampton's hall. I fled across a continent for you. Are those the actions of a man who isn't in love?'

'Varvakis did the same,' she refuted. She was breaking. She could feel it inside, pieces of her shattering, her very soul fracturing at the betrayal. The bastard, Ryabkin, was right. She'd been used and she'd been oblivious to it, distracted by passion and pleasure. 'Varvakis rescued me from fire and took me into hiding at great risk to himself, for a cause. Not for love.'

'Dasha, *golubushka*.' Ruslan reached for her, but she stepped away. If he touched her, he would steal the last of her strength, he would find a way to persuade her. She needed anger now. Anger would make her strong. Every moment of their time together played through her mind in a painful kaleidoscope, each event taking on a different cast when seen through the lens of betrayal: he'd fled London because he needed her alive; he'd argued against her doubts in Marseilles because he needed a princess to take to Kuban. His agenda could not be advanced if he arrived empty-handed. He'd worked tirelessly in Kuban to advance his own power and prestige. Even now, he argued Varvakis's confession changed nothing because he needed a princess. Not because he loved her, but because she was his tool.

Of all the people she should have questioned, she should have questioned him the most and she hadn't. She'd simply accepted his gifts, his hospitality, his affections. She should have asked why long before this. 'Do you want to be King?' As the words left her lips, she felt the fabric of their relationship rip a little further. Soon there would be nothing left but shreds.

Did he want to be King? The words fell on Ruslan like a hammer and just as stunning. Did she truly imagine he was capable of such a duplicity? That he was a man who would bed a woman for the purpose of stealing her crown? 'No.' The word was choked, his emotions churning. 'You know that, Dasha.' They'd never talked of it. But she knew, didn't she? Dasha would never have come to his bed if she'd feared he'd angle for what some men would consider the biggest prize of all. Sex would have given him too much leverage and she was too smart for that. But who could say any more? This entire conversation had become surreal. Just hours ago, they'd been engaged in rather more intimate activity.

'You *are* a Prince of Kuban. You have rendered me enormous services, you have risked yourself, left your comforts. I owe you far more than money. Perhaps you think I owe you the throne. If not you, then perhaps I owe your son?' Her eyes were knife-sharp. 'Greater men than you have sought kingships through any means possible: armies, marriage, children.'

The last word lingered between them. 'Dasha, you know I've been careful. I do not aspire to put a son of mine on the throne through you.' He said the words in slow, measured tones, but his temper flared. To think that she doubted him! That Ryabkin had managed to take her from him with the sowing of distrust. 'I risked my life for *you*, Dasha, not for a kingdom.'

'You don't even know *who* I am!' she hissed. 'But that's all right, isn't it? You don't *need* to know, you just need a body. You and Ryabkin aren't so different after all. You both need bodies, only you need yours alive.' She stormed towards the door, picking up her cloak where it had fallen last night. Had it only been last night they'd been locked in an embrace against that wall? And now their world had come apart. He did not know how to fix this.

Ruslan gripped her arm, not wanting her to run heedlessly out into the corridor. 'Dasha, stop! You're overwrought.'

Her eyes locked with his. 'Or maybe I'm seeing the truth for the very first time.'

'I know you, Dasha. I know your heart, I know your goodness, your intelligence, your compassion,' Ruslan said solemnly. 'Kuban could not wish for a better queen.'

'No.' Her voice softened. '*You* could not wish for a better queen.' She tugged at her arm and he let her go, not willing to hurt her in order to make her stay. 'I can't do this any more, Ruslan. I can't be wondering who to trust, so I will trust no one. We're done.'

Chapter Twenty-Three

They were *not* done. He'd sworn to protect her and he would. He'd promised he'd be beside her today. Ruslan fingered the dagger at his belt as he stood at the grave site, surrounded by others. There was a knife in his jacket sleeve and another in his boot. He'd come discreetly, but well armed, expecting trouble. Dasha stood a short distance from him, a veil over her face for privacy and respect for the occasion. The Count would not take her, no matter what was found in that grave, no matter what doubt Ryabkin had sown in her mind. He had lost his father to the Count's scheming. He would not lose the woman he loved no matter how determined she was to the contrary, no matter how bleak the prospect seemed.

Exhumation was the most distasteful event Ruslan had ever been part of, made worse by the fact that Ryabkin had turned it into a spectacle. The council members were not the only ones in attendance. Noble families had driven out from the city as well, looking to make entertainment of this horrific event. They sat in their parked carriages, chatting with each other. Some had even brought picnics. Apparently, they hadn't taken the possibility of unpleasant odours into account.

'Good day, Pisarev.' The Count passed by, looking smug. Ruslan detained him with a firm grip. Regardless of what Dasha thought of his ambition, he would serve her still and in that service there was hope he could convince her his motives were pure.

'This is not what was agreed upon,' Ruslan said in low tones. 'You have turned this into a circus. It was supposed to be private.'

Ryabkin smirked. 'In the new Kuban, there will be transparency. There will be no more hiding of secrets. Why should only the council be entitled to the truth? Why shouldn't everyone know what we know? See what we see?' He narrowed his gaze. 'I'm surprised you don't agree with me, Prince Pisarev. I recall you were quite the liberal. Has that changed?' The slur was intentional. 'Do you no longer seek democracy?'

'I never sought democracy,' Ruslan answered.

'A republic will serve just as well. If I were you, I'd fear the mob.'

'If I were me, which I am, I would control the mob and I do. You'd best remember that.' Ryabkin eyed Dasha. 'I hope she was worth it, Pisarev. She must be one hell of a woman in bed. When she goes down, you go with her. I'll personally see to it.' Ruslan's hand curled about the hilt of his dagger.

Serebrov hurried over to them, interrupting. 'Count, your diggers are here. You'd best get them started.' His tone was cold and it was obvious he would lend Ryabkin no hand. If the Count wanted the grave exhumed, he'd have to see to it himself even though the council agreed to it.

Digging took a while. The ground was already chilled with winter and the dirt was hard. The bodies had been buried deeply if unceremoniously. This had not been a state funeral with coffins and embalming. Nearer to the site, Ryabkin swore and covered his mouth with a handkerchief. It was all the signal Ruslan needed. Dasha would not tolerate his touch, but he could stand in front of her, a bodily shield against the grotesquerie of the grave. He would bear this for her. He would not give Ryabkin the satisfaction of watching her break.

Serebrov had loud words for Ryabkin as the

doctors came forward to verify the grave's contents. Ruslan drew Dasha to the back of the crowd. There was no need for her to look, only to wait. Serebrov made the announcement shortly. 'There are five bodies. Not six. It is the opinion of the doctors that a female, aged twenty, is not among them. The official conclusion is that Princess Dasha was not executed with the rest of the royal family.'

Behind him, Dasha's relief was a palpable thing. Around him, excited conversations sprang up. Serebrov's announcement was met with talk and speculation. Would the Princess be crowned now? What did that mean for the revolt? Would it be a return of old-fashion policies, had their revolution been in vain? Throughout it all, Dasha remained silent. Now, she spoke, ostensibly to him, Ruslan thought. 'I am going to the palace.'

He moved closer to her, his voice low. 'Dasha, the palace was looted, it was partially burnt,' Ruslan tried to dissuade her. There had already been so much tragedy today. Revisiting the site of even more tragedy seemed a poor choice, but she would not be put off.

'I want to see it now, Prince Pisarev. I've been delaying it, like a coward. I should have come here straight away, but I didn't. Please tell Serebrov that I've gone up.'

'I'll go with you.'

Dasha shook her head. 'No. I want to go alone. I need time to think.'

Every instinct in him argued hard against acceding to her wishes. In the end, he let her go. He couldn't protect her from this and maybe he shouldn't. Some things needed to be faced alone. This had to be her pilgrimage to the one place that might solve her last mystery. She would never find her way back to him until she found the way back to herself.

She could not be his until she knew. She could not live her life in doubt of her very identity and by extension in doubt of Ruslan's motives, although she was already regretting her harsh words this morning. She had been angry and overwrought. Her words had destroyed him. She'd seen it in his eyes. Yet he'd served her, stood by her at the grave, protecting her still even though she'd rejected him. More than that, she'd questioned his honour. Beneath her clothing, she could feel the weight of his ring against her skin, a reminder of his pledge. Why was it so hard to accept that one man had acted out of good simply because so many other men had acted out of self-interest? If she asked him to, would he forgive her? Would it matter?

Dasha began the long walk up the drive, summoning her courage in every step, wishing for Ruslan in every step. If he were here, he would walk beside her and recreate the palace with his words so that it would look as it once had, not this ruin that lay before her. She couldn't say he hadn't warned her. Not much had been done to clean it up in the aftermath of the storming. The beautiful gates hung by torn hinges, listing awkwardly. The grass had been churned into mud by hooves and boots and hordes of people carrying off treasure. She understood an angry populace and their grievances, but she did not condone needless destruction and this was what that was. The palace hardly resembled the elegant home of the midsummer ball.

Dasha smiled as the memory took her. She'd not been old enough to attend, but she remembered sneaking peeks of the guests from the balcony. Dasha looked up automatically to the broken remnants of the balcony railing. Her smile broadened and in her mind's eye the palace was beautiful once more. Carriages would arrive up the drive. Three vehicles could travel abreast easily without coachmen worrying over colliding wheels. Others who chose to arrive by barge sailed up the river to where the gardens met the dock. The backside of the palace was arranged much like Peterhof, with its gardens leading down to the water. The ball took place everywhere, not just in the ballroom. There were always three orchestras engaged: one for the front lawns, one for the back gardens and the one for the ballroom. People could dance under the stars. She knew. She'd watched them. Dasha twirled in celebration, letting elation take her. She was home! Really, truly home.

At the top of the front steps, she cleared a path through the rubble of what had been the exquisite wood-carved front doors and her elation dimmed as she stepped inside. What would she learn here? Would it change anything? Inside the grand hall splintered wood lay on the ground, remnants of furniture that had once been. Even the marble tiles of the hall had been chipped and dug up in places, the wallpaper wantonly ripped. Walls charred and black from the smoke. Her gaze moved past the destruction to the famed staircase with its wide, elegant, curve. The place where it happened.

Dasha looked up the staircase, reliving Varvakis's account. Her eyes went to the landing where the carved balustrade was shattered and the fire had burnt away the floor. She put a foot on the stairs, her hand gripping the remaining balustrade as the memories surged in a jumbled haze. Her mind struggled for order. Every step up the stairs was a step back in time. She could practically smell the smoke. The stairs weakened, the balustrade crumbled beneath her hand, falling away in places where she touched it. She should stop, go back. But she couldn't. She had to know. For herself, for Ruslan, for what they might have together. She had to be brave.

Her heart raced, it was hard to breathe. At the top of the stairs, her vision started to fade, the edges of her periphery going black, images of the past blending with the present. Someone was behind her. Of course. That was how it had happened. There was a man on the landing. Dasha turned, knowing full well a man, an enemy, would be there when she did. But she couldn't stop the dream. The dream had merged with reality. The enemy had become Ryabkin. A real man, or a phantom of her imagination? It was hard to tell.

'You've picked a perfect place to die.'

His knife was out. Ryabkin had come for her, or was this the soldier in the dream? Did it matter? Both were lethal. Both would see her dead. She should be fighting. Where was her sword?

Dasha stumbled backwards, dangerously near the gaping floor. There was no weapon. Panic seized her, the dream blending with the now.

She had to fight, she couldn't faint. Dasha was counting on her. She had to protect Dasha, the others were dead. Shot on the lawn. She wouldn't let them get Dasha, she'd promised she'd see her safe—Dasha, not just her Princess, but her best friend, the sister of her heart.

The realisation swamped her.

She was not the Princess... Oh, God, oh, God... She had to tell Ruslan.

She felt her legs buckle. She was down on one knee. Ryabkin had his hand in her hair, hurting her, pulling her head back, his knife to her neck, reality overpowering her at the last. This wasn't part of the dream. She was going to die here. There would be no waking up. There was so much Ruslan would never know. Perhaps it was better this way. He would be safe. The secret would never be exposed.

'You should have died a long time ago,' Ryabkin's voice rasped at her ear. The world spun. Her last thought was that she'd been meant to die that night in June. She'd come back so that now she could. Perhaps it was true, one couldn't escape their destiny. She would never be Queen. She'd never been meant to be Queen. She would regret not seeing Ruslan again, not being able to tell him, to claim what might have been. The blade was cold at her throat. It would all be over soon. Very soon. She just had to be brave one last time. A lone tear slid down her cheek. Most of all she regretted she wouldn't get to tell Ruslan she was sorry.

Ruslan paced at the burial site, checking his watch while the gravediggers buried the bodies once and for all. Dasha should have been back by now. He was beginning to worry. The crowd was starting to thin, the excitement having settled. Serebrov was talking with a man in a dark coat. Ryabkin was... Where was Ryabkin? Ruslan quartered the area with his gaze, studying each remaining group for sight of the Count. His blood started to chill. Ryabkin wasn't there. Dasha hadn't come back. One didn't need to be a genius to connect the possibilities. Ruslan turned towards the palace drive and began to run.

Each step closer validated his fears. There were boot prints in the muddied drive, the debris at the entrance had been roughly shoved aside, some of it too heavy for Dasha to have lifted on her own. She'd been followed. Ruslan reached for his knife and stepped into the hall, his eyes going up the staircase.

Horror met him. Ryabkin held a knife to Dasha's throat, her head drawn back and exposed, her eyes shut tight, a single tear on her cheek.

Oh, his dear girl, brave to the last! He fought back a wave of impotence. What could he do from here? A knife-throw of his own would never reach Ryabkin at this distance. Ruslan threw his voice instead, a loud, booming demand as he kept moving towards the stairs. 'Let her go, Ryabkin! You do not want royal blood on your hands.'

Ruslan was rewarded. Dasha's eyes flew open and it was enough to distract the Count, to force him to give his attention elsewhere. 'Stay where you are, Pisarev! She'll be gone long before you reach her.'

Ruslan ignored him, taking the steps two at a time, wanting to get as close as he could before Ryabkin found his wits. Ruslan assessed his options. He could peg a target at fifty feet. He only needed twenty here. However, conditions were not optimal. There was only a small space at the Count's right shoulder that remained exposed. It would be a risky throw. He could easily hit Dasha instead. Words might be a better weapon of choice.

'What is it that you want, Ryabkin? Dasha wants what you want. She's not your enemy. She wants to abolish the marriage laws, wants to move Kuban into the nineteenth century.' He had no real expectation of reasoning with Ryabkin. A man who would kill an innocent woman was beyond logic. But he could keep the man talking, keep the man distracted.

'I have worked hard for this country. I will not stand by and let her take it from me. Kuban is mine to rule.'

Ruslan shifted imperceptibly, flexing his hand around the hilt of his knife, his eyes concentrating on that damnably small spot on Ryabkin's shoulder. It was the only target he had. He would have to throw soon. Dasha was gasping now, the blade against her throat starting to draw blood where Ryabkin had broken skin. Ryabkin would pay for that. No man laid hands on his woman. But Ruslan knew better than to throw mad.

'After I kill her, I am coming for you, Pisarev. I can't leave any witnesses, especially when they're angry lovers.'

'Why don't you come for me now?' Ruslan prompted. He was not surprised by Ryabkin's response. All Ryabkin really wanted was power. The Rebels had needed a leader and Ryabkin had given them one: charismatic, handsome, outspoken, willing to advocate for change. Ryabkin had sold his soul to the revolution, seeing himself as the next King. He cared nothing for the concepts of democracy and republic. The mob was nothing to him but a tool to be used. Then Dasha had come back and stood in his way.

'Ruslan!' Dasha cried out in panicked anguish. The knife pricked her skin, deeper this time. While they argued, she was bleeding, hurting.

Ryabkin's hand flexed, readjusting his position. The small gesture was the signal that galvanised Ruslan. It had to be now or it would be too late. He had failed his father once, he would not fail Dasha. He took a long look at Dasha, signalling her with his eyes. Then, he stopped thinking, stopped analysing, drew a deep breath and threw. 'Dasha, duck!'

She seized the moment without question. The loudness of Ruslan's command distracted Ryabkin. His hold loosened for an infinitesimal moment. Dasha took advantage, wrestling away Ryabkin as Ruslan's knife struck the Count's shoulder. The Count went down, falling to his knees against the pain of the blade. Mad with agony, he grabbed for Dasha as she scrambled, her skirts tangling her feet. He had her beneath him, the gaping landing nearing as they struggled, the floor creaking dangerously beneath them. Ryabkin had his hands at her throat, choking her, blood oozing from his shoulder.

Then Ruslan was there, pulling Ryabkin from

her, but not in time. The floor gave way, the weight of three bodies too much for its ruined state. She screamed as she fell, a body falling past her. A hand reached for her, catching her wrist at the last. 'Dasha, hold on!'

Ruslan! She looked up. 'I can't!' She hadn't anything strength left. Even now, so close to rescue, she felt her hand slip in his grip. But Ruslan had strength for both of them.

'I have you. Give me your other hand, Dasha.' His voice was tight but steady. 'You can do it.' From somewhere she found the strength. Then Ruslan was pulling her up, dragging her close against him, carrying her down the stairs, away from the tragedy. He set her down at the foot the stairs, cradling her against him. She'd never felt so loved, so cherished, as she did in those moments. 'I thought I'd lost you, I thought I was too late, Dasha,' Ruslan murmured, giving way to his own emotions now at the last when it was safe.

'Don't call me that.' She looked up at Ruslan, her saviour, her anchor. The man who loved her. She had to tell him. It was what she'd come here to find out and he deserved to know. She drew a deep breath, touching his face, wanting to remember him like this. Then the memories began to overwhelm her and she began to shake. All of it was real: the loss, the love. There would be more loss. Amid the flood of memory, that one thought emerged. She was about to lose him now for good, in a way far different than she'd contrived to lose him this morning or even in Marseilles when they'd chosen separation. He was in love with someone she wasn't, someone she could never be. She was an imposter. 'Ruslan, I am not the Princess. I'm not Dasha.'

All she now knew to be true rushed out in halting sentences.

'Dasha is dead, consumed by the fire. She was the second woman on the landing. I tried to protect her.' She swallowed hard. 'I couldn't save her. I couldn't save my Princess.'

She waited for him to despise her. He'd risked everything for a fraud and lost. This time it would be over for good.

Chapter Twenty-Four

'How could you?'

This was where the hate would start. *How could she?* How could she fail in the most important task she ever had? How could she leave the Princess to die while she lived? How could she forget all that? She'd expected the words, but not the tone. There should have been angry disbelief. He should have dumped her from his lap in disgust, should have risen and separated himself from her. There should have been a look of horror, of disgust on his face.

There was none. Ruslan's tone was gentle. 'How could you? How could you be expected to face down armed men, to hold back a fire, all on your own? And you nearly did it anyhow.' His touch was unyielding. His voice was quiet as he spoke. 'We can't always save the ones we love. When my father was arrested on charges of slander against the Tsar, I tried everything to save him, used every influence I had. When he took his own life, I thought it was my fault. I'd failed him. I should have been able to save him.' His hand stroked her hair. 'I know what it feels like to fail someone you love. But he made his choices and I have to accept them. You did everything you could, you have to believe that, and you have to forgive yourself or it eats at you,' he sighed and she felt his breath against her hair. She knew without doubt this was not something he spoke of lightly or often.

'Ruslan, I am sorry about this morning. I was wrong to accuse you. You've been nothing but good. I let fear get the better of me.'

'I must confess, Ryabkin was not entirely wrong. When I first considered coming back to Kuban and helping you, I saw a chance for myself, a chance to come back and redeem my family. But those were poor motives. The night at Lord Hampton's, when the assassin came for you, it all became too real.' His arms tightened about her. 'I think that's when I recognised I loved you and that you were far more to me than a chess piece on a board.'

'You loved the Princess, Ruslan.'

'No, I loved *you* with your grand heart that chose the runt of the litter at Nikolay's stable, that gave herself tirelessly to an unappreciative country because it was the right thing to do. It doesn't matter to me what your name is. I *know* who you are. You are the woman I love. If you need a name, I will give you my own, if you'll have me.'

He was not giving her up. The revelation was so stunning it took her breath away. Instead of dumping her to the ground, he was kissing her, his hands smoothing back her hair from her face, his lips taking hers in something akin to joy. 'Oh, my dear, brave girl, you've been through hell,' he whispered against her mouth. 'You are safe now, I will see to it. You are mine, who-ever you are.'

'I am Elizaveta Semenova,' she said softly, letting the awe of having a name take her. For the first time in months she knew who she was.

Ruslan smiled. 'Elizaveta. A queen's name. It suits you.'

'Ruslan, I am not a queen. I was never meant to be Queen.' She searched his face, looking for direction. She knew what she wanted him to say. That they would run away and put all this behind them.

'Elizaveta, you have declared yourself the Princess and you have been validated by the con-tents of that awful grave. Your claim has been accepted and proven true most publicly. Serebrov is already planning your coronation while the political climate is positive.' Ruslan spelled it out for her. 'For all intents and purposes, you *are* the Princess.'

'I am… I *was*,' she corrected, 'a lady-in-waiting to the Princess.' The reality of Ruslan's words was beginning to dawn on her in full. Even with the truth, would she never escape this responsibility?

'I think you were more than that, if you were willing to die for Dasha,' Ruslan prompted with gentle insight.

'She was my best friend,' Elizaveta said, squeezing back tears. Perhaps some day it wouldn't hurt so badly to remember. 'I came to court when I was fifteen. It had been arranged by my aunt, my guardian, before she died. I was to be a ward of the Tsar's. He thought I'd suit his daughter as a companion. We were of the same age and we became fast friends, almost immediately.' She looked up at Ruslan and smiled. She held up her wrist, showing off her scar. 'We did these the first summer I came, as a sign of our friendship. That explains, too, the candles in Marseilles. My parents were already dead, you see. That's why I wanted to light a candle for them.'

'And Dasha was like a sister to you?' he prompted, perhaps sensing she needed to talk and now was the time to do it, not later. A little of her sadness dissipated in the memories— there were so many of them, of happier times. Maybe later, she would take those memories out, one by one, and walk through them. For now, she wanted to tell Ruslan the truth about that last night. 'That night, we were lucky. We'd hidden and we'd been overlooked, but the fire was driving us out of our refuge. Dasha wanted to go out the window, but I wanted to try for the servants' stairs. The window was too high from the ground—even if we'd been undetected we wouldn't have escaped sprained ankles, or worse. We nearly made it, but...' Her voice trailed off. 'You know the rest. Dasha was behind me, but she turned back when the soldier attacked, only she couldn't go back, the flames had made returning to the room impossible. She panicked, she lost her bearings. She fled into the flames anyway and I couldn't stop her.' She didn't want to remember Dasha like that, her beautiful hair on fire, her screams.

'People said we looked alike.' Elizaveta turned to a happier topic. 'It's often said that when two people spend a lot of time together, they come to mirror the other's gestures, their way of speaking, their way of thinking.' She was grateful for Ruslan's steady grip on her hand. 'But I'm not the Princess, even if I do look like her and act like her. I'm not her. I'm not the woman the Loyalists want to put on the throne. I am not a Tukhachevsken. I don't want to be Queen.' But Ruslan was right. How did she stop being what people thought she was? Panic threatened again.

'Are you sure?' Ruslan seemed startled by the sentiment. 'Elizaveta, this is not to be undertaken lightly. To not accept the crown is to turn down the chance to do great good. You will be a young queen. God willing, you will sit on the throne for many years. You will affect two generations of governing with your decisions. That is no small thing to weigh in the balance.'

'I want a life with you.' But she had no idea how to get it. She gripped the lapels of his coat. 'What do we do now, Ruslan?' she whispered against his chest. It couldn't be hopeless, not after she'd come this far, not after she'd found the man she loved. 'Find me, find *us* a way out.'

There was always a way out. One simply had to be brave enough to take it. This was supposed to be his speciality and yet he had no answer for her. Not yet. Ruslan was silent for a long while, holding Elizaveta against him, letting his mind quiet after the events of the morning. He closed his eyes and focused his formidable brain, remembering his John Locke. A plan began to form. This would be his greatest escape yet and it would be accomplished in plain sight with an entire nation watching.

'Can you be strong just a while longer?' he asked. So much had been asked of this brave woman and yet the asking was not over.

She smiled. 'Yes, what do you have in mind?'

'A coronation.' They needed that. Serebrov would not rest until there was a crown on a Tukhachevsken head. He and Elizaveta would not rest until the country had peace. They wouldn't be able to live with themselves otherwise, knowing they could have prevented a civil war.

But Elizaveta doubted. 'I don't want to be Queen. I want a way out. I want a life with you, away from all of this.'

Those words made his blood sing. 'Be patient and trust me,' Ruslan murmured. Trusting was somewhat new ground for them. They had not trusted one another completely until now and it had nearly broken them. This time it had to be different if their love stood a chance of making it out of Kuban.

She nodded. 'I trust you, Ruslan Pisarev, with my heart, my life, my for ever.'

He stood and raised her to her feet. With words like that ringing in his ears, it was hard to be patient. He would marry her today and leave Kuban behind if they could get away with it. But their consciences wouldn't allow it. 'Then come with me. It's time for step one. I walk out of here with you in my arms.'

He lifted her into his arms and carried her from the palace. To those who remained at the travesty of a grave at the end of the drive he looked like Sir Ruslan of legend, a folk hero come to life, his fair Ludmila in his arms. It was a potent image and the story of the Princess's rescue from the hands of Ryabkin spread with the speed of wildfire throughout the capital, a fairy tale come to life, just as Ruslan intended.

It was too bad happy-ever-after couldn't simply follow as it did in the stories. Behind the scenes of the fairy tale Ruslan had created, there was work to do. He'd had a week to set his plan in motion. Serebrov wanted a coronation and Ruslan would give him one. He worked tirelessly, sending letter after letter, answering response after response, working with the council to assure a smooth succession.

The sooner it could happen the better. It would put paid to any more questioning and it would give the country the stability it was looking for—a stability the council had not been able to provide on their own. With a princess on the throne, stability would have a face. The Loyalists would have their Tukhachevsken, their link to the past. The Rebels and Moderates would have their new political agenda of modernisation, although, Ruslan smiled to himself as he worked, it might not be as they imagined. But it would work and in the end they would be far happier. But first, the kingdom had a queen to crown and tradition to preserve.

Chapter Twenty-Five

Elizaveta entered the council chambers to the pop of champagne corks and the polite applause of the council members, her velvet and white fox–fur ceremonial robes draped on her shoulders, the crown of Kuban atop her head, the silver and sapphire cross that signified her right to divine rule about her neck. She was the Queen in truth, for the moment at least.

On a good day, this was what it would feel like to be Queen: adored, applauded. She felt regal in the coronation robes and the crown on her head was a temptation indeed. The ceremony had been official but small, conducted by the Archbishop of Kuban in a chapel on the grounds of the Tsar's city palace, with only her council in attendance. Serebrov was planning a formal public coronation at Christmas to coincide with her father's for the sake of historic symbolism.

Serebrov's ceremony would never come to pass, not if today went well.

She gave a nod to the council, acknowledging their applause. Serebrov made the customary toast which was followed by others. She let them have their pomp. She caught Ruslan's eye as he raised his glass, a private look passing between them. Only the two of them knew what today would entail. This morning, Kuban had crowned its Queen. By evening, Kuban would usher in a new era of governance, and she—well, she would have her heart's desire. But that was hours away yet and much still stood between her and that most private victory.

The formalities appeased, Elizaveta motioned for the council to take their seats. Dossiers had been placed in front of each member's seat. Elizaveta sat up straight, summoning all the regal demeanour she possessed. She had to carry out one final act for the people she loved—for Dasha, for Ruslan—and for the life she might have as her true self, a life lived outside of a lie.

'Gentlemen, I thank you for your attendance and for your willingness to begin the work of nation-building so immediately. Our country cannot wait any longer for the issues raised by the revolution to be addressed. If you will open your dossiers, you will see that I have compiled a collection of royal decrees regarding the revoking of certain laws.' Elizaveta was well aware that today she played the part of benevolent tyrant. Today, in these hours, she alone had the power to decide law. It was what a monarch did. As things stood, the council might make suggestions to her, but ultimately, her will decided the law. It was too much power for any one person to have, even when advised by a group of supposedly diverse councillors. The margin for error in ignoring the true needs of the people was great. Too great. A single monarch would always, inherently, be too insulated to decide for those he or she ruled. The system could not last. It bolstered her confidence that her decision was not only in her best interests but in her country's as well. The time had come for something different.

'We'll start with the marriage laws.' She smiled at the council, directing them to the first sheet in the dossier. It was the one likely to meet with the least resistance and the most acceptance. 'As of today, the laws binding noble families to matches sanctioned and arranged solely by the ruling Tsar will be repealed. Families are welcome to arrange their own children's marriages, as are individuals over the age of twenty-one, as they see fit.' The repeal was not perfect. A woman who married at eighteen would still be under her family's rule. She would not be able to decide for herself until she came of age, but it was a start, and starts were made on compromises.

'The next law regards the terms and conditions of a noble male's service to the crown...' Ruslan had arranged the dossiers strategically, presenting the easiest issues to resolve first and moving towards the more difficult. The idea was to build a culture of success before hitting the hard issues. A group that saw themselves making progress would deal with difficulty better than a group who viewed a situation as a logjam.

The morning became afternoon. Lunch was served. Jackets came off. Progress was made, alliances established that she hoped would last. Elizaveta felt the stack in her dossier thinning as they reached the last of the business. Afternoon gave way to Kubanian twilight. The end was nearly here. She glanced at Ruslan, something she'd refrained from doing throughout the long day, afraid she'd give away too much. He gave her a nod.

Elizaveta rose. 'Gentlemen, we have accomplished much and I commend everyone on their work today. This has been a true beginning.' The laws might have been her laws, in truth no one could have gainsaid her, but she hadn't wanted acceptance through force. 'We have one last issue before us today and that is the future governance of Kuban.' She was met with inquisitive looks from some, confused looks from others like Serebrov, who'd crowned a new queen today and felt the issue decided.

'There is a new world beyond our mountains, one that is not ruled solely by kings and queens, but by parliaments and prime ministers. It is time for Kuban to join that world. In your dossiers you will find a new structure for ruling.'

'Your Highness, will St Petersburg allow this? We are but an independent province. We still answer to the Russian Tsar,' Serebrov put in as he scanned the radical document.

She was ready for this. Ruslan had briefed her. 'We are not breaking away from Mother Russia. We simply feel answering to one Tsar is enough. On a local level, we feel we can better serve the Tsar in St Petersburg through self-governance.'

'Respectfully, Your Highness, Ekaterinodar, indeed most of Kuban, is land gifted to us by the Tsar,' Serebrov said, voicing the most logical of fears that the land would be taken away.

'A gift the Tsar needs defended,' Ruslan put in from his seat further down the table. 'To be blunt, the Tsar needs us to defend the port and the mountain passes from the Ottomans. It was the whole reason Russia settled Kuban in the first place. We are an outpost, the first line of defence against invasion. We are too important to the Tsar for him to squabble about what we do a thousand miles from St Petersburg. He has enough to defend.'

The questions came and Elizaveta fielded each one tirelessly. Every question resolved was one step closer to freedom. Darkness fell outside, snow had begun. It would be a beautiful night for a drive in a troika, with stars overhead, lap robes warm, the man she loved beside her. Elizaveta answered the last question and reached to her head, taking off the crown. The time had come at last. The diamonds in the diadem sparkled in the candlelight as she set the crown on the table. 'Gentlemen, as the last act of your Queen, I commend you for your service today, and in the months preceding. I commend you for your vision and I exhort you to finish the work begun here. You have been given the tools from which to start our new republic. I expect you to do so.'

She nodded to Ruslan. 'Prince Pisarev, will you take things from here?' She bowed to the council. 'Gentlemen, your Queen bids you fare-well. When and if we meet again, I will be a citizen of this grand republic you will build. Prince Pisarev, the future is in your hands.' Ruslan moved to the head of the table before anyone could protest or question and she quietly slipped into the hall.

She could hear Ruslan's voice as she shut the door. 'Gentlemen, I have here the recommendations for the various posts you will want to fill...'

At the entrance of the building, a footman met her at the door. 'Your Highness.'

'I need you to take these for me. Put them away safely.' She exchanged the heavy robes for her own dark cloak, feeling lighter already as the last ruler of Kuban stepped out into the snow.

An hour later, boots crunched behind her in the snow. Ruslan. 'Is it done, then?' she sighed, leaning back into the arms that encircled her.

'It is done. Kuban, by royal decree, is now officially a republican principality, probably the first of its kind.' Ruslan's arms were strong and warm, the snow on her face, cold. It was a perfect moment. She could live in it for ever. 'You are free, Elizaveta.' Free to go anywhere she liked, free to love as she pleased.

She turned in his arms, brushing the snow off his shoulders as she kissed him. 'Thank you.'

The sound of bells on harness broke the quiet night. The troika arrived, the blades fast and light on the snow. 'I believe we have business of our own?' Ruslan helped her into the sleigh and dismissed the driver, taking the reins himself. He called to the horses and they set off, bells jingling. Elizaveta had thought she might feel sad leaving the city palace behind, that she might have some remorse over leaving the crown. She had done good for her people today, but how much more could she have done if she'd stayed Queen? But she felt none of it—no second thoughts, no remorse. This was the right choice for both her and Kuban. She tucked her arm through Ruslan's and smiled.

'Where are we going?' she asked. He'd been very secretive about these arrangements.

'I am taking you to a little chapel I know at a very fine estate in the country.' He grinned. 'I am taking you home.'

'Does that chapel happen to have a priest?' Elation was starting to take her now, the euphoria of a plan complete. Happiness was within reach. There would be no more daggers in the dark, no more wondering where she belonged. She knew. She belonged with this man whether it be in Kuban, or in London, or in the French countryside growing grapes.

Ruslan winked. 'It just might.'

He'd planned everything carefully, right down to the hour and the setting. It was fitting to him that the most important event of his life to date happen at a place that meant the most to him— his home, the one trapping that remained from his past life in Kuban. When they arrived at his beloved estate, all was ready. Lanterns lit the way to the stone chapel, his servants lined the drive with candles set amid small evergreen wreaths. Inside, the home was decked with evergreens and satin ribbon, candles instead of flowers.

He and Elizaveta might have a quiet wedding, attended by none but Ruslan's housekeeper and his butler, but that didn't mean his bride would have a ceremony devoid of decoration.

'The candles are lovely!' Elizaveta's eyes sparkled. 'You always move me to tears with the simplest of gestures.'

Ruslan leaned close. 'The candles remind us even in a season of darkness, there is light.' This woman had experienced darkness enough. From now on, he vowed silently, she would have nothing but light. His voice was low at her ear. 'Are you ready, Elizaveta? To be my wife?'

'More than ready...' she breathed.

They walked down the short aisle together. The priest and the two witnesses were waiting. But for all the planning Ruslan had done, the next surprise was his. Instead of his servants,

Illarion and his wife, Dove, stood there, wrapped in furs and beaming. Their cheeks were flushed with the cold night air as if they'd just arrived.

'How?' Ruslan was at a loss for words.

Illarion came forward and embraced him, reading his mind. 'Some things can't be planned. We were in the area visiting a family friend,' he said obliquely. That would be an interesting story to hear. *Later.* Illarion stepped back with a knowing smile. 'All my news will keep. There is more important work at hand.' He nodded in Elizaveta's direction and the priest began.

The rings were blessed and Elizaveta made a blushing bride as a birch crown was settled upon her head, a very different sort of crown than the one she began the day with, Ruslan thought. As magnificent as she'd been today, this one suited her far better.

'Are you happy?' Elizaveta murmured as the priest intoned the final blessing.

'Yes.' Happy didn't begin to describe the way he felt. It was as if he'd never been happy before, that all other previous joy was merely a shadow of the emotion that now consumed him. He'd always thought he needed a place to serve, a place to be needed. But he was wrong. He'd not needed a place. He'd needed a person. He'd needed her.

'You may kiss the bride, my son.' The priest smiled at him.

'The first kiss of our married life,' Ruslan whispered to Elizaveta, tipping up her chin.

'The first kiss of for ever,' she answered, tears sparkling on her cheeks like diamonds. He kissed her then, long and full and satisfying, a wish for all their life would be together.

'I love you, Elizaveta Semenova.' He pressed his forehead to hers. 'You are *my* Princess, now.'

Epilogue

London

Ruslan had done it! Stepan Shevchenko laughed out loud at the letter in his hand, the sound echoing in the empty town house. Around him, furniture was covered in sheets against the dust in anticipation of a long absence and his travelling valise stood ready at his feet. Had the letter arrived five minutes later, it would have missed him entirely. He meant to be on the road to Little Westbury before the afternoon grew too dark. This time of year, darkness fell early.

He re-read it again, just to savour the news. Kuban had abolished the monarchy that had oppressed it for years. Their fight had not been in vain, their protests, even their exile had mattered. And of course, Ruslan was just the man to orchestrate such a feat. But the best news was that Ruslan had married, that his heart was whole. They would winter in Kuban, honeymooning in his family home on the river. Stepan smiled fondly at the thought. There would be ice skating and bonfires on the frozen river bank and snuggling beneath furs. In the spring, though, when they could travel, they would leave Kuban and make their way to France. Ruslan had it in his mind to become a vintner in Burgundy. He suspected there was a story behind Ruslan's decision, but had no doubt Ruslan would be a success at whatever he chose.

He folded the letter up and put it carefully away in his pocket. Dimitri would want to read it. Stepan was already anticipating sitting by the fire in Dimitri's study, their feet propped on the fender, the house quiet after everyone else had gone to bed, and watching Dimitri's face as he read Ruslan's news. More than that, Stepan was looking forward to going home to Little Westbury. After all, home was where the heart was, and his heart was there, such as it was.

* * * * *

COMING SOON!

We really hope you enjoyed reading this book. If you're looking for more romance, be sure to head to the shops when new books are available on

Thursday
23rd August

To see which titles are coming soon, please visit
millsandboon.co.uk

MILLS & BOON

MILLS & BOON

Coming next month

THE MYSTERIOUS LORD MILLCROFT
Virginia Heath

'My purpose here genuinely is a matter of national importance, a mission I was entrusted with and I am single-handedly about to ruin it with my woeful social skills. Months of hard work, the lives of many good men, all wasted while I fail abysmally at being a lord. I have never felt so out of my depth before.' Seb's stupid heart was racing again and a cold trickle of sweat was making its way down his spine. Less than one hour in, his plan was shot to pieces and for the first time in his long and successful career with the King's Elite, failure seemed inevitable.

Clarissa's face softened and she touched his arm. Seb felt the affectionate gesture all the way down to his toes. 'Don't worry. You didn't seem out of your depth in the slightest. Truth be told, had I not known you were the shy Mr Leatham from Norfolk, I would have been none the wiser. You seemed supremely confident and added just the right splash of aloofness to give the intriguing Millcroft exciting gravitas. You also look the part. Very debonair and handsome. Dashing even. For a fraud, you play a lord very well.'

Dashing? Handsome? Him? 'Hardly. Have you not seen the scar?'

'I have.' He stiffened as she reached out her hand

and traced one finger down its ugly length. 'It gives you an air of the dangerous. The ladies love a dangerous fellow. Didn't you see them all watching you? Wondering in what exciting and adventurous circumstances you acquired it?' Her hand dropped and she smiled. 'How did you get it, by the way? Seeing as we both know you've never set foot in the Antipodes.'

'An accident.' Seb had accidentally assumed his half-brother had a heart and a conscience, but like his father before him and all persons of his ilk he considered the low-born disposable. 'Caused by my own stupidity. Nothing exciting or adventurous in the slightest.'

'Well, I like it. You wouldn't be half as handsome without it.'

Continue reading
THE MYSTERIOUS LORD MILLCROFT
Virginia Heath

Available next month
www.millsandboon.co.uk

LET'S TALK

Romance

For exclusive extracts, competitions
and special offers, find us online:

f facebook.com/millsandboon

⊙ @millsandboonuk

𝕏 @millsandboon

Or get in touch on 0844 844 1351*

For all the latest titles coming soon, visit
millsandboon.co.uk/nextmonth